D1250171

A HERO'S CHANCE

BAYTOWN HEROES

MARYANN JORDAN

Cover design by Graphics by Stacy

ISBN ebook: 978-1-956558-05-7

ISBN print: 978-1-956588-06-4

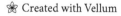 Created with Vellum

1

"Trevor! Are you out of the shower?" Ryan Coates lifted his hand and banged on the door.

"Yeah, Dad!" The shout came just as the water turned off.

"Downstairs in five."

"I'll be there. I'll be there. I can just grab a muffin!"

Ryan sighed and shook his head. "Not good enough. Five minutes, Trevor." Turning, he walked past Trevor's open bedroom door and glanced inside despite telling himself not to. The room was clean, but multiple shirts lay on the bed, a few on the floor, and at a glance, he could see at least two pairs of jeans tossed about, as well. *When did he start worrying about what he looked like in the morning?* Heading down the stairs, he was able to hear his almost-fifteen-year-old son still grumbling behind the bathroom door.

At the bottom of the stairs, he curved to the left and walked down the hall to the open kitchen. Whoever owned the house before him had knocked down a few walls to create a combined kitchen and dining room, divided only by a kitchen island.

At the time he'd been looking for a house, he was more concerned with the number of bedrooms and bathrooms, the size of the yard, and ultimately, the price tag. For the most part, he'd lucked out. It was a small house with only three bedrooms, two full bathrooms, a powder room, and a comfortable family room. There was no formal living room, which was fine with him. *One less room to furnish and clean.* It did have a small extra room downstairs that he'd turned into an office with a foldout bed. With family close by, he'd never needed to use it as a guest room, but considering he hadn't got rid of the old sofa-bed when he'd moved into the house, it was shoved into the corner.

Of course, none of the furniture in the house was very new. He made sure the kids' rooms were furnished the way they wanted, the family room was comfortable, and the dining room table large enough for any friends the kids wanted to have over. As far as his bedroom, the furniture was cheap, but he'd splurged on his mattress. After eight years in the military and eleven years working in law enforcement, his back needed a good mattress.

The kitchen door led to a deck and generous backyard that was fully fenced. There was even a two-car garage. Not that he had two cars. But it wouldn't be long before Trevor would need something. *Christ... more money, and the insurance will take a dent out of our finances!*

Entering the kitchen, his gaze landed on Cindy, already dressed, hair pulled back in a ponytail, backpack sitting next to the back door, and a bowl of cereal and glass of orange juice on the counter in front of her. Another bowl of cereal and a glass of juice was on the counter next to hers.

Her gaze lifted from the book her nose was buried in, landed on him, then shot over to the clock hanging on the wall. "He's going to be late."

Walking over to the coffee pot, he poured his first cup of the day, smiling at the sweetener and low-fat creamer sitting next to his mug. Twisting his head, he lifted a brow. "Taking care of your old man?"

"You're not old, Dad," Cindy said, her lips curving upward softly. "But you're old enough you should take care of yourself." Glancing at the clock again, she repeated, "And he's still going to be late."

The sound of heavy footsteps clomping down the stairs met their ears, and it only took a couple of seconds for Trevor to appear. "I'm here! I'm here!" he called out as he skidded to a stop right next to Cindy, in front of the extra bowl of cereal and juice she'd set out. "Thanks, Cin!" Pouring the milk, he began wolfing it down. In between bites, he said, "And I agree, Dad. You're not old. One of the senior cheerleaders called you a silver fox. She said her mom said you were a real hottie in high school and that you only get better with age."

Nearly spitting out his coffee, Ryan sputtered, "What the… you've gotta be kidding me!"

"It's true, Dad," Cindy nodded, her face blushing bright red.

Barely taking a break to swallow, Trevor continued,

"I figure that works for me. I've already got junior cheerleaders looking at me, and I'm only a freshman. Everyone says I look like you, so if I've got your genes, then I'll keep being a hottie, too."

"If you've got Dad's genes, then you'll go gray early, also," Cindy said matter-of-factly.

Trevor set his bowl down, looked at his dad, cocked his head to the side, then shrugged. "It works for Dad. It'll work for me. I can keep being a hottie, and the girls will love it."

Cindy rolled her eyes, a long-suffering expression on her face. Shifting her gaze over to her dad, she said, "You need to eat, too."

"I'll be fine with coffee for now—"

She opened her mouth to speak, but Trevor and Ryan said in unison, "Breakfast is the most important meal of the day."

She lowered her brow and pursed her lips. "Well, it is!"

Seeing his daughter blink her eyes rapidly as though ready to cry, Ryan moved to the counter, bent deeply, and reached his arms out, placing them on hers. Her gaze lifted, and he stared deeply into the beautiful face of his thirteen-year-old daughter. She had always been pretty but now had definitely moved out of the awkward child stage and entered the already-beautiful-and-going-to-get-more-beautiful stage. Swallowing deeply, he wasn't sure how he was going to be handling her getting prettier. "Thanks, baby. Believe me, I appreciate you making sure Trevor and I eat breakfast." Her lips curved upward again, her smile warming his heart and starting his day the right way.

Trevor finished his cereal, lifted his bowl, and slurped loudly, draining the last of the milk. "Yeah, thanks, Cin!" Walking over, he rinsed out his bowl before putting it into the dishwasher.

Cindy and Ryan shared a look, his daughter obviously surprised that her brother remembered to take care of his dishes. She smiled and glanced at the clock again, jumping up to take care of hers, as well.

"Bus will be here in a couple of minutes. I just have to brush my teeth," she called out as she hurried out of the room.

Trevor's brow lowered, his expression blaring that he'd forgotten about brushing his teeth. "Shit—shoot!"

Watching him rush after his sister, Ryan called out, "Language, Trev!"

"Sorry, Dad!"

He leaned his hip against the counter, glad for the momentary reprieve before the sound of shoes on the stairs met his ears again. "Make sure you get everything. I'll be on patrol this morning and won't be able to get back to the house to get something if you forget it."

"My backpack is ready," Cindy replied, not surprisingly. Looking over her shoulder, she called out, "Trevor, your algebra book was on the sofa." As usual, her voice was gentle as she looked out for her brother.

"Oh, right! Thanks!" Trevor raced out of the room and back again, shoving the well-worn book into his backpack. Pulling out a sheaf of papers, he tossed them onto the counter. "Forms for baseball, Dad. One of them is a sports physical."

"No problem," he replied automatically, glancing at the calendar on the refrigerator, wondering when they'd have a chance to add that to the list of activities. He walked around the counter and accepted a hug from Cindy, kissing the top of her head. "Have a good day, sweetheart. Don't forget that your mom is picking you up from school, and she'll bring you back after taking you out to eat."

Cindy offered a quick nod, her eyes downcast, not meeting his. He opened his mouth to say something, then changed his mind. Pressing his lips to her hair once again, he muttered, "Love you." He felt her nod against his lips, and he straightened, allowing her to slide off the stool.

Trevor remained quiet, but they fist-bumped, their new thing since his son declared he was too old for hugs unless they came from the cheerleaders. He held open the door and watched as the school bus picked them both up. He trusted Trevor to keep an eye on his sister, knowing the bus would drop her off at the middle school first and then take him to the high school close by.

Just like when Ryan had gone to those schools, Baytown Middle and Baytown High were on opposite sides of the football stadium, close enough to be convenient but separate enough that the two groups didn't mingle except on the bus. And considering how pretty his eighth-grade daughter was, having Trevor around would keep the punks away. Working in law enforcement and with the youth leagues of the American Legion, he knew there were lots of good kids, but he also knew there were a few that weren't. And the last thing he wanted sniffing around his daughter were the punks.

Finishing his cup, he poured fresh coffee into his travel mug and made his way around the house, assuring the doors were locked. As he walked to his SUV, his phone vibrated in his pocket. Pulling it out, he glanced at the caller ID. With a heavy sigh, he climbed into his vehicle, hitting the connect button. "Leslie, if you're calling for any other reason other than to confirm that you're picking the kids up after school to take them to dinner, I don't want to hear it." The silence on the other end of the phone confirmed his suspicions. "Goddammit, Leslie, did you forget? Again? Why the hell should I even be surprised?"

"I'm sorry, Ryan," Leslie said with neither rancor nor contrition in her voice. He sometimes wondered if she ever felt either emotion. "It's not that I forgot... I just didn't realize it was Thursday."

He closed his eyes, focused on taking a deep breath slowly, and tried counting to ten. He'd only made it to six when his lost patience spilled out. "How the fuck did you forget that this is your day with your kids?"

"I have a lot on my mind—"

"Yeah, I'm sure you do. And first and foremost should be your kids."

"I'll get them. I'll get them. I'll take them to the diner, and we'll have dinner before I bring them home."

He knew she would but had no idea what mood the

kids would be in by the time they got back. He'd long since given up trying to convince them they'd have a good time with their mom or convince her to be a better mom. Sighing, he started his SUV and backed out of his driveway, the call now connected through his vehicle. "So, what was it you called about so early this morning?"

"I wanted to let you know that I'm getting a new job."

He was surprised but not overly optimistic. She'd had several jobs since their divorce, the last one being the best with good pay and benefits, working as a records clerk for one of the medical groups near the hospital. But when she'd been caught gossiping about patients, they'd let her go. Before that, she'd worked filing for an accountant, but asking for too many days off cost her that job, as well. And before that, she'd worked in a jewelry store, losing that job when she got into an argument with a customer over a piece of jewelry that she'd wanted to purchase herself even though she had no money to do so. Before that, he'd taken care of her.

"Really? What makes you think this one will be any better?"

She huffed loudly. "The least you could do is be supportive, Ryan."

It was on the tip of his tongue to say that he'd been supportive of her since they were in high school, certainly since they'd got married after he joined the Navy and discovered she was pregnant. If he wasn't driving, he'd have closed his eyes again. Instead, he decided the easiest way to get the conversation over with was to play along. "Okay, Leslie. What do you want to tell me about the new job?"

"I'm going to be working for Sophie Ward at her interior design business—"

"Oh, hell no! There's no way you're going to work for Sophie!"

"Ryan, what is your problem? You know things are hard on me. Since you have full custody, I don't get a lot—"

Losing his hold on his temper, he growled, "Don't go there, Leslie. Don't even fucking go there. Me having full custody of the kids because that's what's best for them should bother you for a lot of reasons about what kind of mom you weren't, not about what money you don't get to squeeze out of me. We sold the home, and you got half that money even though I'd always paid the mortgage. You got your car even though I'd paid for that, too. You got half of the furniture, enough to get set up in your condo—"

"I know, and I'm sorry. You were more than generous with the divorce, and I didn't mean what I said to come out the way it did. I just don't understand why you're not happy that I'm getting a new job. I thought you'd be glad because that'll make me more independent."

By that time, he was in Baytown proper, passing by the small downtown area, heading toward the harbor. Parking outside the Virginia Marine Police building close to the small Baytown Coast Guard station, he cut off his engine but made no move to climb from his vehicle. "Because Sophie is a sweet woman, and I don't want your bullshit to manipulate her. She's also married to one of my officers and friend, and I don't want your bullshit to interfere with my workplace relationships, either."

Silence filled the air space before she finally spoke. "I know my track record isn't good, Ryan. Believe me, I'm well aware of my faults. But I'm trying to learn from my past mistakes. Sophie was very clear, especially since I was upfront with her about my other employment efforts. I know that I can't talk about our clients to anyone else. I know that I'm handling records only. And you're right, she's very sweet for offering me this chance. Plus, Ryan, I think this is something I could be really interested in."

"Leslie, I hope like hell you find a job that works for you. But Sophie runs a high-end interior decorating business. With your track record, you'll fall in love with every expensive piece of furniture and decide that's what you want in your house. You will spend money that you don't have, and then come to me wanting more than we agreed upon or telling me you can't afford to get the kids anything for their birthdays because you don't have any money."

This time, instead of silence, he heard a long sigh. "I know, and you're right. I really want to make this work."

"I do, too. Well, if that's all, I've got to get into work. Don't forget to pick the kids up after school."

"Thanks, Ryan. I won't forget."

Disconnecting, he looked out over the harbor while still sitting in his SUV, drawing upon the calming, familiar view. Some of his first memories growing up on the Eastern Shore of Virginia just outside of Baytown were going fishing on his grandfather's boat. He'd loved the water. When his dad had taken over the fishing business, Ryan had spent many weekends out on the Chesapeake Bay.

A lot of years had passed since those days. The Navy, marriage, fatherhood, working for the VMP. Now, throwing in divorce, single parenthood, being the captain of this station, plus coaching for the American Legion, life had become filled with no time left over to worry about what his ex-wife was doing—or forgetting to do.

Sucking in a deep breath, he let it out slowly before heading into the building. Time to go to work.

2

Ryan finished the morning briefing, then lifted his head to look over to his officers. "Any questions?" Everyone shook their heads, so he jerked his to the side and said, "Next week's assignments are on the board."

As everyone stood, he caught Callan's eye and waved him over. Waiting until everyone else had left the room, he said, "I want you to know I didn't have anything to do with this, but I feel like I need to apologize anyway."

Callan's chin jerked back slightly, his head cocked to the side. "What are you talking about?"

"I got a call this morning from Leslie. It seems she's going to start working for Sophie."

Callan nodded slowly, understanding dawning, his lips curving in a sympathetic smile. "I know what you're going to say, but it's okay. Sophie talked to me about it before she hired Leslie. She and I were too young to remember Leslie from high school but just knew her as your ex-wife since Sophie wasn't around Baytown during your earlier married years."

"She doesn't have a good employment record, so her working for a friend makes me nervous."

"I know this isn't my business, but won't it be better for you if she's working? Moneywise, I mean?"

Ryan had always been careful what he said about Leslie to anyone, but as in most small towns where everyone knows everyone else's business, he found that most people already knew a lot of their dirty laundry anyway. Shaking his head, he said, "When we got divorced, I hated to do it but had no choice. I gave the judge years of her credit card bills that I'd tried to cover, all of them with her not working. I'd close out an account, and she'd open another. As soon as he looked through that, he agreed that my offer was more than generous. We sold the house, and I gave her half. She'd never lifted a finger to do yard work, so I advised her to buy a condo so that she wouldn't have to because I wasn't going to pay for someone else to mow her grass. We also split the furniture. And she wasn't contesting my getting full custody, either, which I think surprised the judge."

Callan's dark brows lifted to his forehead. "Seriously?"

"I know she loves her kids, but she was never very maternal. The older they got, the harder she struggled to figure out how to be the kind of mom they needed. Since I have the kids, she was able to buy a smaller condo, and I had to turn around and buy another house that would fit me and the growing kids. Other than giving her a small amount which comes from me and wasn't part of the judgment, I don't pay her anything."

Callan lifted his hand and squeezed the back of his neck. "I hate to ask this, but what do you think about her working for Sophie?"

"As I said, she doesn't have a good employment record, so I don't have high hopes that she's going to work out well for Sophie. But she's honest and has never stolen anything, so there shouldn't be a problem with that. I just don't want it to interfere with either our working relationship or our friendship."

Callan laughed, shook his head, and clapped him on the shoulder. "No worries. It's all part of living and working in a small town."

"I just want Sophie to make sure that while I'd love for this job to work out for Leslie so that she'd stop coming to me with her hand out, I don't expect Sophie to keep her employed one second longer than she would anyone else who screws up."

"I hear you, Ryan. Sophie will keep an eye on her, and I assure you, she cares too much about her business to let someone mess it up. Who knows, this might just finally be the job that Leslie succeeds at."

"It'd be nice to think so." The two men walked out of the briefing room, stopping by the equipment room to check out what they'd need for the day.

An hour later, they were on the water. Ryan peered over the Bay, his eyes protected with sunglasses and the bill of his cap. His body armor vest was worn over his navy blue uniform, a life jacket over that. Breathing the briny air deeply, he smiled. He, Callan, and Joseph Newman were on the boat. Joseph was new to the VMP, having just finished his law enforcement training.

Joseph's brother was Wyatt, the chief of police of one of the neighboring towns, and he'd completed all the requisite coursework in training, not-so-patiently waiting for a position to finally open up.

The dispatcher over the radio alerted them to suspicious activity near one of the local fishermen's crab pots, and with a nod from Ryan, Joseph steered the boat in a different direction. It didn't take long to come upon the fishing area in question, but the situation before them had escalated, with one man in a boat holding a rifle pointed toward another boat with two people seated, their hands in the air.

Recognizing Arnold Bushman as one of the longtime crab fishermen from the shore, Ryan called out, "Arnold! Put your weapon down!"

The older man glanced over his shoulder, his tanned, leathery skin indicating years in the sun, and his deep-set wrinkles from years working on the water increased even further. "Captain," he called out. "I got me some poachers to turn over to you."

"Okay, Arnold, we can talk about this and figure out what's going on. But we're not going to do that with your weapon raised."

"I don't trust them to not skedaddle!" Arnold called out.

Glancing toward Callan, the two men read each other without words. Callan moved toward the side of their boat. "Arnold, we're going to latch to your boat, and then we're going to tie them, as well. No one's going to skedaddle. But we sure as heck don't want anyone to get hurt accidentally. So, take your finger off

16

the trigger, lay your rifle down on the bottom of the boat, and keep your hands where I can see them while I board."

Arnold obeyed but grumbled the entire time Callan latched the boats. "Don't see why I have to put down my weapon when all I'm doing is protecting what's mine. You know these are my crab pots. I shouldn't gotta prove anything to y'all."

"I know these are your pots," Ryan acknowledged as he stepped over into Arnold's boat. Callan had already handed Arnold's weapon over to Joseph, who'd emptied the ammunition before returning to his place at the wheel. Callan now latched the smaller boat to the other side of Arnold's.

"We're going to need to see your identification and fishing licenses," Ryan ordered the two men.

They looked at each other, then stood carefully and pulled out their wallets. "We don't have any fishing license, officer," one of them said, handing over his driver's license. "We're out here to take pictures." The man inclined his head toward the bottom of the boat where several camera cases lay, filled with what appeared to be expensive camera equipment.

"Then why were you stealing my crabs?" Arnold shouted, waving his fist now that he no longer had his rifle to point at them.

"We weren't stealing! We were photographing."

"You had two of my pots pulled up onto your boat and your gosh-darn hands on them!" Arnold argued.

"We weren't stealing anything," one of the men said, aiming his beleaguered, pleading expression toward

Ryan. "We didn't think there'd be a problem with pulling up a pot to see if there were any crabs and then taking pictures."

"We can show you the pictures we took," the other man insisted, reaching for his camera.

"Just wait. We'll need to inspect your bags," Ryan said, glad when the two men's heads bobbed up and down emphatically.

Callan squatted on the bottom of their boat, moving the camera equipment around before standing and jerking his head up. "All clear." Turning to the man, he said, "You said you had photographs?"

"Yes, officer." The photographer squatted and carefully picked up his camera, turning it around so Callan and Ryan could view the screen. Picture after picture of herons, gulls, terns, and then the blue crabs filled each screen. There were several where one of the pots was balanced on the edge of the boat, all just showing photographs of the crabs behind the mesh of the traps.

Nodding toward the two men, Ryan said, "You're free to go. Officer Ward will release your boat. My advice in the future would be to ask the owner of any property you're disturbing before you take a picture. These pots represent this man's livelihood. You would be responsible for any damage to the pot or the marine life inside."

"Yes, sir," both men said, their heads bobbing up and down again.

Turning back to the older man, Ryan said, "Looks like they were just doing what they said they were doing, Arnold."

Arnold continued to mutter to himself, grumbling about people not respecting other people's property. Looking over at his weapon, he asked, "You going to give me my gun back?"

"Yes, but we're keeping the ammunition." Gasping, Arnold started to argue, but Ryan threw his hand up in front of him. "Arnold, I've known you since I was a kid. You're a good fisherman, but you're hotheaded and are known to drink while you're out here. Those men could've pressed charges for you threatening them with a firearm. Hell, I can run you in for doing the same. I'm not going to—this time. But I'm also not going to make it easy for you to discharge this weapon. You did good by calling this in. So, my advice is get back to fishing and leave the law enforcement to us."

Still grumbling as Callan unlatched the boats, Arnold still managed to toss his hand up in a wave as Joseph steered them away. They continued their patrol, checking a few fishing licenses from those they were unfamiliar with, pulling alongside and chatting with several of the fishermen from the area that they knew, and then making their way back into the Baytown harbor.

By the time they'd cleaned and readied the boat for its next trip out, checked in their equipment, and logged the day's activities, it was already mid-afternoon. Grateful that the Seafood Shack was close by, they decided to grab a quick late lunch. Ryan often brought a sandwich from home to keep down the expenses of eating out too often. When he did go out, he'd divide his business between the Seafood Shack and Finn's Pub, having become close to the McFarlane brothers, Aiden and Brogan, that owned the pub. But the Seafood Shack was so close to the VMP station, it was always a good choice, also.

As he and Callan took a seat, a pretty server came over and greeted them, her shy smile only making her appear younger. *Damn, when did I get so old?* She took their drink orders and had just turned when Joseph came bounding in, his arms snapping out to catch her as their bodies collided. He grinned widely and winked, holding onto her arms longer than was necessary while she blushed a deep red, ducked her head, and rushed toward the kitchen.

Callan chuckled. "Smooth move, Joseph."

"I've been trying to get her to smile at me for weeks," Joseph laughed.

Ryan shook his head. "Looks like she's immune to your charm."

Joseph puffed out his chest. "No woman can be immune to my charm for long."

She came back to the table with Ryan and Callan's drinks, obviously looking everywhere except at Joseph. As soon as he gave her his drink order, she turned and rushed away. As Joseph plotted and planned his attempts to get the pretty server to go out with him, Ryan once again felt his age.

It wasn't that he was old in years, but in life experiences, he was way beyond most of the men and women who worked for him. He'd joined the Navy right out of high school, and a few years later, while stationed nearby in Norfolk and still dating Leslie, she'd gotten pregnant with Trevor. They'd married, and he was a dad by the time he was twenty-one. Cindy came along eighteen months later. While neither of his kids were planned, he'd never regretted one second of being their dad. He'd stayed in the Navy for eight years and was currently completing his eleventh year with the VMP. And now, having just turned thirty-six, he felt a lot older than many others his age.

Listening to Joseph talk about his single life and the rewards of dating as many women as he could before settling down, Ryan sighed. He wasn't opposed to female companionship or to the idea of marriage, but except for his children—the best things in his life—his marriage had not been a good one. And between his kids, being divorced while still keeping track of Leslie's shenanigans that affected his kids, being the captain, and coaching the area youth, the idea of dating only made him feel exhausted. The idea of dating, starting over, having no history with someone... *Not enough hours in the day to make me want to go down that road now.*

3

_____

By the time they finished their meal, a couple of teenage servers had arrived for their evening shift after school. Pulling his phone from his pocket, Ryan checked his messages, glad to see that neither of his kids had tried to call, so he could assume their mom had picked them up. With a silent prayer, he hoped Cindy and Trevor were having a good time. With Leslie, that was always a crapshoot and he never knew what he might face when they came home. If Leslie was in a good mood, that carried over to the kids. If she wasn't, then she made everything about her and the kids internalized that, also.

Even with an end-of-day meeting followed by more paperwork, he managed to pull into his driveway with time to spare before Leslie brought the kids home. Stepping into the kitchen, he was greeted by Zuzu, whose enthusiasm at finally having a human had her twirling in circles. "Let's go, girl," he said, letting her into the backyard before she happy-danced-peed all over the floor. He stepped onto the back deck, grinning as she raced to her favorite bushes, sniffed around, and squatted. After she took care of her business, he spent a few minutes tossing a ball while she chased it with glee.

Glancing down at the stumpy mutt, he laughed. He'd never intended to add one more thing to their plate, but after the divorce, both Trevor and Cindy had expressed a desire to have a pet. Leslie hadn't wanted to take care of one, and while he thought families should have a pet, he'd capitulated like he had on so many things. But as soon as they'd broached the subject again, he'd agreed easily. They'd gone to the animal shelter, and he was sure his son would want a big dog. Somehow, both kids fell in love with her, and Zuzu came home that evening.

Back inside, he fed her and then grabbed a beer for himself, not hungry since he'd eaten so late. Standing at the kitchen counter, he flipped through the mail and, as usual, most ended in the recycle bin. Looking at the sheaf of papers that Trevor had left that morning, he flipped through the permissions and sports physical form. Taking another swig of beer, Ryan's mind traveled down past roads to a time when he was Trevor's age and playing baseball for the Baytown Boys.

He and his friends had often complained that the rural Eastern Shore of Virginia had to be the most boring place in the world to grow up, and yet they'd all managed to have fun. And playing baseball for his high school filled him with some of his best memories. It was hard to think of high school without thinking of Leslie and who they were back then. *Young. Idealistic. Dreamers.* Taking another swig of beer, he chuckled. *And horny.*

He'd been the athlete, and she'd been the cheerleader. *Christ, how cliché.*

But he'd dreamed of joining the Navy, and she'd said at the time that she couldn't wait to see him in his uniform. She hadn't handled the separation well, and while he didn't blame her for that, he'd already seen the handwriting on the wall. Leslie liked things to be easy. Her way and easy. He'd finally decided it was time to break up, especially considering he was shipping out... *not to mention he'd liked his freedom to pursue someone else if the time was right.* Then the bombshell. She'd been so excited to tell him she was pregnant, already planning their wedding. He'd agreed, knowing it was the right thing to do, getting excited about the baby, as well, and planning the future. But when she'd worried more over the way the pregnancy made her look than talking about becoming a mom, worry had begun sneaking through him. When Trevor came, she'd been so sure Ryan would get out of the Navy, and when he hadn't, she'd gotten pregnant very quickly again. The suspicion that she had children as a way to control him had been concerning, but as the kids had gotten older and her interactions with them were more distracted, he'd become angry.

His trip down memory lane was gratefully interrupted at the sound of car doors closing. Walking to the front, he threw open the door and stepped onto the porch. He smiled, the reaction he always had when he saw Trevor and Cindy. Laying eyes on them at the end of the day, knowing they were safe and healthy and soon to be tucked under his roof, his heart warmed, and he always breathed a little easier. But coming back from spending time with their mom was always dicey, and his eagle-eyed gaze was pinned on his driveway.

Leslie sometimes just dropped the kids off, but tonight, she stepped out of the car. Trevor, who'd been in the front seat, slung his backpack over his shoulder and walked to his mom. They didn't hug, but she patted his shoulder. The gesture appeared awkward as though she wasn't sure how to say goodbye even though this was a scenario that had been played over and over for years. Trevor grinned, thanked her for dinner, and said goodbye.

But instead of heading toward the house, Trevor stayed next to the car, angling his body toward Cindy as she climbed from the back seat. Ryan's senses were on alert considering Trevor was a good albeit sometimes annoying older brother, he was still protective of his sister. Cindy's head was down as she tucked her hair behind her ears, her arms around her backpack as she held it in front of her like a shield. She nodded ever so slightly at something Trevor must've said. Lifting her head, she offered a smile to her mom that even Ryan standing far away on the porch could tell was forced. Leslie also nodded, reaching out to pat Cindy on the shoulder as well. Cindy didn't flinch, but Ryan had no doubt she was ready for the visit to end.

His jaw tightened as he watched Trevor walk with Cindy up the path toward him, knowing something must have happened that upset Cindy enough for her brother to both notice and feel like he needed to protect her.

Trevor's eyes met his and, as usual with his easy-going son, he smiled. "Hey, Dad."

Cindy's gaze jumped up to his, and he could swear her shoulders relaxed. "Hey, Dad," her soft voice greeted.

His smile was genuine as he reached out and held the screen door open, allowing Cindy to walk under his arm. Just as she moved by him, he leaned down and kissed the top of her head. "Welcome home, sweetheart." Her smile widened as she headed into the house.

Trevor followed, and it didn't pass Ryan's notice that he had to lift his arm a little higher for his son to go under. He wanted to stop Trevor and ask about how their dinner went, but Leslie was following the kids toward the front door, and he wasn't about to invite her inside. "Go ahead and start your homework, guys. I'll be there in a couple of minutes." Lowering his voice, he whispered, "Close the door behind you, son."

Trevor offered a chin lift, a motion he'd been doing more of lately, reminding Ryan of himself. Turning toward Leslie, he stared at the woman that he'd known since her family had moved to the Shore when she was in middle school. Taller than the other girls at the time, she'd caught his eye at the age of thirteen with her long, blonde hair. *Hell, that was the same age as Cindy is now.* They'd fallen in love in high school... *probably more lust than love.* For years, he couldn't imagine living his life without her. Now, if it wasn't for their children, he'd be fine not having her in his life at all.

As she approached, she tucked a strand of her shoulder-length hair behind her ear. The color and cut were expensive as were her manicures and pedicures. Her height was accentuated by the heels she wore, and she was dressed for lunch at the club instead of out with her teenage kids. "Hello, Ryan."

"Leslie." He debated for a moment what to say, torn between wanting Cindy to confide in him whatever was upsetting her and wanting to know from Leslie what he faced when he got inside his house. Giving in to the latter urge, he asked, "How was dinner?"

"It was fine. I took them to the Italian place in Easton."

He knew that restaurant wasn't expensive but neither was it cheap. He half-expected her to ask for reimbursement for taking the kids out, but instead, she simply said, "I think the kids had a good time."

"And you? Did you have a good time with your kids?"

She blinked as though she didn't quite understand his question. "Um, yes. I mean, they talked about what they were doing in school."

He opened his mouth to ask why their kids didn't feel like they could talk to her about feelings or emotions or their friends but snapped his lips shut. She'd never expressed a true interest in what made them tick, so there was no reason to expect her to do that now. Instead, he crossed his arms over his chest and leveled her with his gaze. "Then can you tell me why Cindy had such a hound-dog expression on her face if you had such a lovely dinner?"

Leslie's gaze left his, shooting to the side, her fingers tightening as they clasped together in front of her. If they weren't talking about their daughter, he would've laughed at her tell-tale sign that she knew he wasn't going to like her answer.

"I've got two teenage kids who need to get their homework done, have time to relax, and get to bed so they can get a good night's sleep for school tomorrow. What I don't have is time for you to come up with an excuse for why our daughter didn't have a good time."

She narrowed her eyes and shook her head. "You always take their side. You always did."

"Jesus, Leslie. This isn't about sides. This isn't about you. This is about her."

She huffed loudly, throwing her hands up to the side. "I know it's about her, Ryan. I care about my daughter. I care about how she's doing and how she is. That's why I told her she shouldn't have the breadsticks if she was going to have the pasta! The last thing she wants is to start putting on pounds at this stage. God knows it only gets harder to take it off the older she gets."

Ice water ran through Ryan's veins, and he had to fight to keep from physically staggering back at her words. Then, with a flip of a switch, the cold turned to a scorching heat as he thundered, "You what?"

Once more, she blinked, her wide-eyed expression showing more surprise at his reaction. But he did give her a chance to speak. "Our daughter is thirteen years old. She's beautiful. She's healthy—"

"Yes," she rushed. "And I want her to stay that way."

"She's going to have a lifetime trying to fit into society's expectations. What she needs now is learning how beautiful she is, just the way she is."

"It's never too early to learn how to take care of yourself."

"Hell, I don't even think she has an ounce of body fat on her—" His words halted as a thought slammed into him, once more threatening to stagger him backward. "Oh, fucking hell, Leslie. Have you been saying these things to her before?"

He watched as Leslie pinched her lips together, seeing the familiar expression of frustration on her face that she always got when he didn't agree with her.

"I've never told her to diet! I have occasionally mentioned to her that young women need to learn to eat healthy because it's harder to take the weight off down the road." She lifted her chin in the defiant way she used when she wanted him to back off, but this time it didn't work.

"If I ever hear of you trying to body-shame Cindy again, you'll find yourself back in front of the judge explaining why you should keep having visitation rights." Just as he was ready to turn, he noticed her chin quivering, and she blinked back tears.

"I'm sorry, Ryan. I wasn't trying to upset her. I'm just trying to be the best mom I can be. It's not easy for me. I've never really understood what I should do."

A heavy sigh left his lips. *No truer words were ever spoken.* "Leslie, just spend time with them. Ask them how their day went. Ask them about their friends. Ask them what's important to them. What they want to be when they leave high school. Don't try to fix something that's not broken. Don't try to change them because they're fuckin' perfect as they are. If you can't figure out how to be a mom, then at least just be someone they don't dread being around."

"You make that sound so easy," she said, her face still tight.

"Hell, nothing about parenting is easy. But it is good. And you've only got a few more years to do this before they leave home, and you'll have lost your chance. Now, I need to go inside and see to them."

She nodded and walked back to her car. He waited to make sure that she'd driven off before he sucked in a deep breath, letting it out slowly. Glancing down at the empty beer bottle in his hand, he was startled when the door opened and Trevor was there with a fresh beer, holding it out for him.

"Thought you might need this, Dad."

His heart expanded in his chest, and he hoped his son could tell how much he loved him. Not taking a chance that he didn't, he grabbed the back of Trevor's neck and squeezed. "Thanks for this. But mostly, thanks for taking care of your sister."

Trevor offered another chin lift, then glanced over his shoulder.

Ryan pushed, "Was it bad?"

A wince passed over Trevor's face, but he shrugged. "Not bad. Just... I don't know." He sighed, "It's just that Mom's kind of clueless when it comes to saying things."

Ryan bit back the words he wanted to say.

"Mom told Cindy that she looked good and was turning into a pretty young woman. You could tell

Cindy really liked that, but then Mom went on to remind her how if she didn't watch what she ate, it could be bad later on. After that, Cindy just shut down. I started talking about shit at school just to move things along."

"You're a good man, Trev." He dropped his hand from the back of Trevor's neck, and the two of them walked inside. Not seeing Cindy, he headed back to the kitchen where she sat at the dining room table, her school books spread out in front of her. He opened his mouth to speak, but she didn't look up, and he took that as a signal she didn't want to talk right then. Sighing, he hesitated even more, unsure how to handle her. When she was younger, she'd always wanted him to read her a bedtime story, talking easily in her soft way, telling him all about her school day, her friends, and even her hopes and dreams. That continued even after he and Leslie divorced three years ago and their lives were turned upside down. But lately, this new adolescent Cindy, complete with hormonal changes that could have her smiling one minute and frowning the next, gave him pause.

Knowing she was on edge from what her mom had said, he was torn between wanting to tell her to ignore anything Leslie said and pretending everything was fine. Finally making up his mind, he walked over, bent, and kissed the top of her head, whispering, "Glad you're home, sweetheart." With that, he headed back to the family room where Trevor was pulling out his books, deciding to give Cindy the privacy it appeared she craved.

An hour later, after catching part of a ball game, he moseyed back into the kitchen and rummaged inside the refrigerator, pulling out the leftover apple pie that his mom had made for them. Cutting three generous slices, he topped them off with ice cream. Trevor, always available when he heard the refrigerator door open, wandered into the kitchen, his eyes alight as he saw the pie. Ryan grinned, inclining his head toward one plate while he picked up the other two and set one on the table in front of Cindy, then took a seat next to her.

Her gaze landed on the pie before shooting up toward him. He saw the hesitation and held his breath for a second until her lips curved upward, and she slid the plate closer.

"Thanks, Dad," she said, and he could swear he heard a lot more gratitude in those words than just for the pie.

"Any time, beautiful," he replied before digging in, pleased when their conversations eased into the comfortable evenings they usually had.

"Dad, did you look at my forms for baseball?"

Nodding, he swallowed his bite before replying, "Yeah. I went ahead and signed the release, filled out the insurance information, but we'll need to get you in for a sports physical."

"The coach says we have to have the physical in before we can start practice next week," Trevor said. "How soon can you get me to the doctor's office?"

His chin jerked back. "We? How long have you been carrying those forms around in your backpack?"

"Not long," Trevor defended, his voice giving away his guilt.

A slight giggle came from Cindy, and Ryan glanced over to see her face relaxed in a smile. Turning back to Trevor, he sighed. "I'll call tomorrow, but you'd better hope they have an opening on Monday after school."

"I heard Baytown Family Medicine has a new doctor. A couple of guys have gone in for their physicals and got her. They say she's hot."

"Trev. Respect," Ryan said firmly, his voice low as he pinned his son with a hard stare.

Trevor lifted his hands in supplication, cutting his eyes toward Cindy. "Sorry. What she looks like has nothing to do with what kind of doctor she is. But, just saying, if they got another doctor on board, they might be able to fit me in."

"I'll see what I can do."

The evening quickly passed, and the kids headed upstairs to get ready for bed. Checking on them was a habit he'd had since they were little. Trevor offered a grin when he popped his head in to say good night.

Knocking on Cindy's door, he entered and smiled, seeing her reading. Standing at the foot of her bed, he said, "Sweetheart, I know what your mom said at dinner. It's important for you to know that you're a beautiful young woman, but more importantly, you're a really good person. And you're sweet in ways that, unfortunately, your mom never has been. But you know she loves you."

Cindy held his gaze, and he was struck with how she managed to look like his little girl and a young woman all at the same time. Her hair was light brown, natural streaks of blonde highlights that she got from her mom framing her face. But she had his eyes and, thank God, his practicality.

"I know Mom loves me, Dad. And I know that sometimes, she just has a hard time expressing herself. And I don't want you to worry that I'm going to start having an eating disorder because my mom talks about eating and weight." Shrugging, she added, "I guess I was just embarrassed,"

"The embarrassment is on your mom's shoulders, not yours. You have enough to worry about without taking on her issues. You just focus on yourself, sweetheart. Right?" Her smile shot a sweet arrow straight through his heart, and he grinned in return. Walking toward her, he kissed the top of her head again and muttered, "Love you, Cin."

"Love you too, Dad. Good night."

Letting Zuzu out again, Ryan stood on the back deck. Inhaling deeply, he was once again struck with the beauty of the way the few lights on the Eastern Shore allowed the stars to shine brightly. It was only ninethirty, but he was exhausted. His job, his kids, his life. He wouldn't trade any of it for anything, but as he locked up the house and climbed the stairs, he wondered if there was ever going to be time for anything else. *And if there was time, would I even have the energy to notice?*

4

"I sure hate to take up too much of your time, Dr. Foster," the elderly man said.

Judith smiled and shook her head. "Mr. Dundee, don't worry about my time. I'm here for you." She stood behind him and held her hand on the diaphragm of the stethoscope, hoping to warm it before placing it on his skin. Placing the earpieces in her ears, she listened to his lungs and heart, pleased at the sound of both. "I see on your records that you've never smoked."

Shaking his head, he said, "Oh, no. My parents never allowed any tobacco at all in our house when I was growing up. Even when I was in the military, I never took up smoking. Got married when I got back, and our oldest boy had asthma, so I wasn't about to do anything to make it worse."

"Well, for someone in their eighties, not smoking has gone a long way to keeping you this healthy. Your heart and your lungs sound good."

He grinned, bobbing his bald head up and down. "I

knew I was in good shape, but my Myrtle worries. She always wants me to come in and have my yearly physical, so here I am. I thought I'd be seeing Dr. Preston. Been seeing him for a few years after old Doc Benning retired. But don't get me wrong, it does me good to see a pretty doctor, too." As soon as the words left his mouth, he scrunched his face, shaking his head again. "I shouldn't have said that. My daughter is always telling me that I need to make sure I don't say anything sexy... sexty... um... sex-tist... oh, something like that."

Judith laughed and patted his back. "Don't worry, Mr. Dundee. I'm not offended at all. Now, the nurse is going to come in and take some blood for routine labs. Our office will give you a call in a couple of days when we get the results back. Would you like me to ask your wife to come to sit with you?"

"Since the news is all good, absolutely."

Just then, one of the nurses in the clinic knocked on the door, and she looked over her shoulder as Sam, one of their nurses, walked in. He greeted Mr. Dundee like an old friend while she typed the lab order into the computer. "I'm going to go get his wife and have her come back."

Walking down the hall, she attempted to smooth her wayward, honey-brown curls that had escaped the neat ponytail she'd subdued them with early this morning. The gesture was more habit than a successful maneuver. She and her hair had had a love-hate-love relationship her entire life. As a little child, she'd loved the curls that everyone commented on although she hated the way the brush pulled the tangles when her mom tried to tame her hair into less of a riot before going to school. As a teenager, she'd hated the curls when other kids joked that it looked as though she'd stuck her finger in an electric socket. And as an adult, she'd learned to accept her natural curls with the help of the stylist who introduced her to products that worked for her.

And now, as a doctor in a busy clinic, she barely gave her hair any thought other than to keep it out of her face.

Popping her head through the door into the waiting room, she spied an older woman sitting by herself. "Mrs. Dundee?" The woman looked up, worry lines deepening. Walking over to her, Judith held out her hand. "It's nice to meet you. I'm Dr. Foster. I'm the one your husband had an appointment with today. Everything's great, and he's just finishing up some blood work. He'd like you to come back and sit with him if that's okay."

The woman beamed, shaking her hand. "Oh, Dr. Foster. How nice to meet you. This clinic has needed another doctor in here for so long." She bent and gathered her purse and placed her e-reader inside. Judith walked her back, and as they entered the exam room, she watched as Myrtle hurried over to the examining table, her hand landing on her husband's leg as he bent toward her and kissed her lightly.

Sam looked over his shoulder toward her and winked. "These two lovebirds have been married for sixty-three years and still act like honeymooners. Don't tell me that romance is dead!"

Mr. Dundee cackled, and his wife blushed. Judith

waved goodbye as she walked out of the examination room. "I'll see you next year for your annual physical." Jotting the last note in his chart, she stretched her back, hearing it pop. *Oh, thank goodness he was my last appointment for the day.* She loved what she was doing and her patients, but she was ready for the day to end.

"Dr. Foster, you have a patient in room three."

Judith looked up as she came out of another examination room to see Natalie standing nearby. The pretty nurse was holding back a smile. Stepping closer, she cocked her head to the side and whispered, "What is it?"

"Finn Harrison. Three years old. And he shoved a bean up his nose."

"Oh, Lordy. He must've been at the Daytime Playtime Center today."

Natalie nodded, losing the battle to chuckle. "Third one today. It seems they had a playtime activity with dried beans and cups, and as soon as one child decided to shove a bean up their nose, several others did, as well. Who knows how many more followed suit but were able to pull or sneeze out the beans, leaving us with the three we've had to deal with?"

Seeing Natalie giggle, Judith pressed her lips together tightly, refusing to give in to the urge. It was late in the day, and her appointments were finished, leaving little Finn and his nose-bean issue as the last walk-in.

Walking into the exam room, she saw the cherubic, dark-haired, tear-streaked face as he was held by his beautiful mom, an exasperated expression on her face.

"Hey, sweetie," she cooed toward the preschooler. "My name is Judith. What's yours?"

"Finn," the little boy replied, eyes wide as Judith neared.

Turning her gaze toward the mother, she said, "The nurse has already determined that the foreign object isn't very far up the nasal passageway. That's good news." Looking back at Finn with a big smile, she said, "Can I look into your mom's nose?"

Clearly not expecting that to happen, the little boy nodded with enthusiasm.

Turning to the mother, she said, "I'm going to have you sit on the examining table, and you can have Finn sit next to you. I'm going to use the same type of scope that Nurse Natalie used and just look up your nose to give him another chance to feel at ease." After accomplishing that with Finn staring wide-eyed at his mom, she turned to the little boy. "Now, I'm going to do the same with you." Moving slowly but not giving Finn a chance to object, she bent low and, using the otoscope, easily discovered the bean not far up his nostril. "Thank you!" she smiled. "You are such a good boy!"

Turning back to the mother, she said, "I can remove it easily. We just want to be sure not to push it further. In order to do that, I'm going to use suction."

Natalie stepped back into the room, her smile beaming toward the preschooler. "Everything okay in here?"

Judith nodded. "I think Finn is doing fine sitting next to his mom, but I'll have you nearby." Taking the small suction tube, she held it against his hand, eliciting a giggle from him. "This is like a tiny little vacuum cleaner. You see, it doesn't hurt at all." Nodding toward Finn's mom and Natalie, she said, "Here goes. Let's find a bean!" It only took a few seconds for the suction to pull the bean out. "There it is!"

"Oh, thank God!" gushed his mom, hugging Finn tightly.

Judith held the bean in the palm of her hand and let him look at it, wide-eyed. "Now, remember that we don't stick things in our ears and noses, okay?"

Finn nodded, his eyes wide as he peered at the bean in Judith's hand. He reached out but bypassed the bean and patted Judith's long curls. "You pretty."

"Well, I think you're pretty handsome, too!"

Finn finally smiled widely, and his mom rolled her eyes. "You're a flirt just like your Uncle Aiden used to be!"

"I thought you looked familiar," Judith said. "Are you Katelyn McFarlane? Brogan and Aiden's sister."

Katelyn nodded and laughed. "I thought the same thing about you. I think you were in the class ahead of me. I should have recognized your name."

Inclining her head toward Finn, now happily playing with his stickers, she grinned in return. "Well, you had more important things on your mind when you came in."

"Have you been here long?"

"No, I just moved back and started here."

"Do you remember Jillian Evans? She's Jillian Wilder now, but she owns Jillian's Coffee Shop. You must come in, and when you do, let me know. I'll get a group together to welcome you back to town. And of course, Aiden and Brogan own the pub. You'll have to stop by there for lunch sometime."

"Sounds perfect. I really haven't had a chance to get out and see what all is new."

Natalie popped back in, and with goodbyes said, the nurse escorted Katelyn and Finn out. After they left, Judith headed back toward her office. Her day had begun when she'd arrived at seven this morning. Reviewing cases, making notes, and preparing for the day's appointments, she'd seen her first patient at eight. Back-to-back appointments kept her busy until she finally managed to hit the break room where she inhaled a peanut butter and jelly sandwich, some chips, and a protein drink. Having just enough time to run to the ladies' room, it was time for her afternoon appointments. Those had run late considering teenagers were already coming in for their sports physicals, and that didn't include her last-minute walk-in of Finn.

Now, it was after five o'clock, and she had an hour's worth of records and notes to take care of concerning today's patients. Passing by the medical director's office, she heard her name called out and stepped inside. Dr. Harry Preston had been at the practice for many years. Beloved by their patients, the practice had grown and now included Dr. Roberta Martinez and herself. Along with a nurse practitioner, three nurses, an office manager, a receptionist, and a records manager, they were a full family medicine practice.

Smiling at Harry and Roberta, she sat in the chair he

indicated. Roberta looked over and grinned. "Successful bean extraction?"

Laughing, she nodded. "I understand we had three of those today. Did you get the other two?"

Roberta inclined her head toward Harry. "I got one, and he got the other. I talked to one parent who says she's going to complain to the preschool about having beans in the classroom for an activity. I told her if it wasn't beans, it would've been something else!"

The three doctors chatted for another few minutes, then Harry glanced at his watch and said, "I promised my wife I'd be home on time today since it's our anniversary. But I wanted to let you know that we're going to have an influx of sports physicals coming in next week."

"I know we had several today, but why so many next week?" Judith asked.

Harry chuckled. "It seems the Baytown High School baseball coach was late getting the information and forms out to the parents. Practice starts toward the end of next week, so phone calls have been coming in today like crazy. I've asked Arlene to shift around some patients next week so that each of us has a day we can come in later and stay later. I have a church meeting on Monday evening. Would either of you be able to take Monday?"

"Monday is fine with me." Judith shrugged as she laughed. "You guys know I have no life anyway!"

"Don't let this office be the only thing in your life," Roberta said, wagging her finger toward Judith.

Harry nodded, his wisdom lines deepening. "It's

hard with the calling to be a healer like ours to not let it take over everything. But Roberta is right. You've got to have some balance, Judith."

She smiled her thanks. "Intellectually and emotionally, I know you're right. But finding the time to get it all done? That's the part I can't quite figure out."

"You will," Roberta said, patting her leg before standing. "Or you'll burn out, and the medical profession would hate to lose someone as good as you."

Standing as well, she followed Roberta out of Dr. Preston's office after saying goodbye to him. "I've got to get some notes written up, but I'm going to do those as quickly as I can. I confess I'm really looking forward to having the weekend to rest up considering next week we're going to get slammed with the physicals."

An hour later, she walked out with Sam. He waited to make sure her car started, then waved as she headed down the road toward her house. She'd grown up outside of Baytown in a large brick house with a huge yard and white picket fence. Smiling at the memory as she always did, she wished her parents still owned the house or at least had waited to sell to her. But when they'd decided to downsize, she was still finishing her residency in Alexandria, and they didn't think she'd come back to the area to practice.

She still remembered their excited phone call to tell her they'd sold the home and were going to buy a condo. As heartbroken as she'd been over the sale of her family home, the reality was she couldn't begrudge her parents having that money to rely on in their older years. They'd moved to a two-bedroom condo near the beach, which suited them perfectly.

Of course, when she'd accepted the position at the Baytown Clinic, she'd had to find a place to live, and the idea of her family's large home ran through her mind. But the house had sold for way more than she would've been able to afford at that time.

She drove down a long lane outside of town, coming to the very end where a small cottage sat next to a grove of trees. The rent was affordable considering she had loans to pay off, and as soon as she'd laid eyes on the little house, it had felt like home. *At least, home for now.*

She climbed out of her car, glad she'd left on the front porch light considering it was already dusk. Once inside, she flipped on more lights, chasing the shadows away. The front of the house consisted of the small living room to the left and the L-shaped, eat-in kitchen to the right. A short hall bisected the house, with the single bedroom to the left and the large bathroom to the right. The bathroom contained a clawfoot tub as well as a stackable washer and dryer. A door from the back led to the small yard, complete with two Adirondack chairs. So far, she'd had no visitors other than her parents, but her older brother was supposed to visit again soon, so she hoped she might have more company.

She opened the refrigerator door and stared, now grateful that some of the clients had brought in casseroles for her. Of course, they were usually accompanied with comments like, "It's so nice to have a new doctor in town. My nephew is going to be home from college soon. He's twenty-two and needs to settle down, so perhaps you'd like his number." Or, "My son is a dentist, and you'd have a lot in common with him." Or even the occasional, "My brother is getting divorced and looking to date."

She chuckled as she pulled out the closest chicken and pasta casserole, tossing it into the microwave. She'd forgotten how small-town life made it easy for everyone to be in everyone else's business compared to her residency in the Washington D.C. area where the clinic was huge, her apartment building had hundreds of residents, and she could be completely alone in a crowd.

But here, most of the people she graduated with from Baytown High School she'd known since kinder-garten. It was hard to keep a secret even then. Some-how, though, she'd managed. Memories from the past sifted through her mind as she waited for her dinner to heat. Memories of her fun childhood, her awkward middle school years, and then the agony of her adoles-cence. *Stop being melodramatic!* In truth, the only true agony she'd experienced was a secret, unrequited love. The stuff of teenagers everywhere who long for what won't be until they decide to put those feelings away as they enter adulthood.

The microwave timer dinged, jolting her from her musings of the distant past. With her meal now plated, she sat at the two-seater table with a glass of wine and reveled in the quiet peace. Her life was full and complete—and usually so busy that she came home and crashed every day. The idea of dating someone now only made her more exhausted. Sipping her wine, she leaned back in the chair, her gaze drifting over her tiny cottage. *Maybe someday... but only when the right person comes along.* "Until then," she said aloud, holding her glass in the air in a one-person toast, "I'll celebrate alone."

5

"Dad, let's go!"

Ryan looked at his son, unsure what the hurry was but very sure Trevor had never been this anxious to get into the doctor's office. "We're here and have five minutes to spare," he grumbled. To be honest, he was surprised they'd made it at all. This had been Ryan's day for administrative duties, but Joseph was spending the day in Norfolk for training and one of his new recruits was out sick with food poisoning, which he hoped was not the code word for a hangover. His crew was short today, and he'd gone out on patrol with Jared that morning, planning to cover his administrative tasks in the afternoon only.

But strong gusts of wind had caused several small boats to have difficulty, most of which had launched from one of the area campgrounds and were not staying within the close-to-shore boundaries they were supposed to. The rescues were easy, but then there was a rash of citations that followed, leading to angry campers dealing with the campground officials.

He'd skipped lunch, determined to get everything that had piled up on his desk out of the way, but in the time it took to deal with running the station, more requests for state reports had come in. The Virginia Marine police were not part of the Virginia State Police but instead were the law enforcement division of the Virginia Marine Resources Commission, another state agency. But the cooperation between the local police, state police, and VMP was not only vital but something he enjoyed. With few law enforcement leaders on the Eastern Shore, they had bonded by working together, and the group now included him in their monthly meeting which he was hosting the next day and needed to prepare for.

Trevor, obviously afraid his dad was going to forget about the sports physical, had been blowing up his phone for the past two hours. Having made sure that Cindy was at a friend's house after school, he'd swung by the high school and picked up his anxious son. Now, having barely parked before Trevor hopped out, he followed his son to the door of the clinic.

"See, Dad, it says they're only open until four!"

"Trev, chill. I told you that they had extended hours today. You've got an appointment, and we're here on time." Stepping inside the clinic, he was not surprised to see the waiting room crowded considering the parking lot had been, too. Making their way to the reception desk, he smiled at Arlene, who'd worked at the doctor's office for more years than he could remember.

Surprised she hadn't retired yet, he wasn't surprised that, amid organized chaos, she appeared calm and collected.

"Ryan," she greeted. Her eyes cut over to Trevor. "There's no way your son is already in high school! Lord, have mercy! He looks just like you did back in the day! And I bet he breaks hearts the way you did, too!"

Shaking his head as Trevor looked at him, brows lifted, he said, "Good to see you, Ms. Watkins. And yes, this is Trevor. He's here for the—"

"Sports physical. You and everybody else here. I tell you what. I could give that forgetful coach a piece of my mind. We've been filled up with kids and parents since before school got out today. The next couple of days are going to be the same! Now, have you got your forms?"

"Yes, ma'am," Trevor piped up, nodding. "They're all filled out and signed."

"Good for you. If you weren't so old, I'd give you one of the stickers that we give to the kids. Half of these teens come in here and don't have their paperwork, and if they do, they don't have them filled out!"

Once checked in, he and Trevor moved to the side to wait. He knew quite a few of the parents and kids in the room, nodding politely but not looking to make conversation. He closed his eyes for a few seconds, looking forward to when the appointment was over and he could relax at home with the kids. *This would be a good pizza night. Hell, this would be a fuckin' perfect pizza night.*

With the number of students in the waiting room, he sighed, assuming they were going to have to wait, but it didn't take long to figure out that many came as walk-ins. Since he'd made an appointment, he was thrilled when the door opened and one of the nurses called Trevor's name.

Falling in behind Trevor, he caught his son's lifted brow and shook his head. "You got anything you want to talk to the doctor about, I'll step out of the room." Trevor nodded, and they followed behind the nurse, entering one of the examination rooms.

"I'm Rosa, and I'm going to go over the basic information, get your stats, and then the doctor will come in."

"Sure, that'd be great," Trevor agreed while nodding again, and Ryan hid his smile at Trevor's attempts to stifle his nervous enthusiasm and be suave at the same time.

Once Rosa was finished, she stepped outside after saying, "Doctor Foster will be here in just a moment."

As soon as the door closed, Trevor let out a breath, looking down at the forms in his hands.

Ryan carefully watched his son. Trevor was blessed with athleticism and had played sports since he was little. Ryan couldn't imagine that he was worried but didn't want to ignore what his son might be feeling. "You worried, Trev? Worried about making the team?"

Trevor shrugged. "Kind of. A little, I guess."

"You've been playing ball since you could hold a bat. I don't think making the team is going to be a problem."

"Yeah, the freshman team. That'll be easy. But the coach mentioned that they'd consider freshmen playing varsity if they were good enough."

Brows raised, he asked, "Are they that short of upperclassmen?"

Nodding, he said, "Yeah. It seems like most of their starting players were seniors last year. With them now gone, the coach said the varsity team was a little slim in numbers."

"Are you more worried about not being considered for varsity or actually making varsity?"

Trevor chuckled and admitted, "Both. I'd hate to not be chosen if others make it. But then, if I do get on, there'd be a lot more pressure."

"I think you're smart for considering everything, but let's not get ahead of ourselves. We'll take it one day at a time. Let's get the physical over with today, start practice, have tryouts, and we'll see how it goes."

Trevor was nodding when the door opened, but before Ryan had a chance to greet the doctor, his phone vibrated, and he looked down at the text. *The station.* BobbieJean was the daytime dispatcher, and her sister, BettsAnne, was the station's administrative assistant. Getting a message from either of them after hours didn't indicate an emergency but generally wasn't good news.

Eyes down, he read her text. Jared's training had been extended for another day. Joseph had reported difficulty with one of their boats and had put in a request for maintenance. And Chuck's daughter had gone into labor, and he was going to be out the next day. *The scheduling shit never ends.* He began composing the text back, focusing on what he needed to do, barely hearing the doctor and Trevor in the background.

"... known allergies? Ever passed out after exercise? ... dizziness? Good, good."

He and Trevor had already filled out the form answering all these questions, so he knew Trevor could handle himself. Continuing to text BettsAnne what the updated schedule for tomorrow would be, he glanced at another text coming in, this time from Cindy. Worried, he quickly read it, smiling when he realized she was suggesting pizza for dinner, as well.

He looked up just in time to see the doctor as she turned and headed out the door. A riot of honey-colored curls was held back from her face by a pink headband, but he only caught her profile. *Dammit!* While he didn't have concerns about Trevor's health or suitability to play baseball, he'd hated that his attention had been on his phone during the rather quick exam. He prided himself on giving his attention to whoever he was speaking with, didn't allow cell phones at the table, and made sure the kids practiced cell phone etiquette. Heaving a sigh, he shook his head, cutting himself some slack, seeing Trevor's wide grin.

"Sorry about that, Trev. First, I had work I needed to deal with, and then your sister texted. Everything okay here?"

"Yeah!" Trevor enthused, the sports forms carefully folded in his hand. "She was really nice! She'd already reviewed my forms before she came in. We went through all the questions, and she said everything looked good. I got her signature on the forms, and she even said that because she had a chance to meet so many of the players, she was going to come to some of the games. I thought that was really cool. And, you have to admit, I was right about her being hot."

"I'm afraid my attention was somewhere else, son, but I'm sorry that I didn't get a chance to greet her properly."

"That's okay. Although, I gotta admit when she walked in and looked at me, her eyes got big. Like she was trying to figure out who I was. It was kind of weird, and then she looked over at you, and her eyes got even wider. I guess you are the silver fox that some of the moms say you are."

Grabbing his son by the back of the neck and giving a little shake, he said, "Come on, let's get outta here before you get us thrown out. We're going to swing by and get pizza before we pick up your sister."

"Yes!" Trevor enthused again, this time with a fist pump in the air.

Laughing and making sure the forms went into Trevor's backpack, Ryan steered his son out of the doctor's office, his mind already on what needed to be done for the rest of the day and lining up his duties for tomorrow. Glad that the trip had been successful, he regretted not having had the opportunity to meet the doctor that had made his son's day.

⸻

Judith stepped out of the examination room, her face flushed, and placed her hand over her chest, feeling the fast beat of her heart. *Heart palpitations from a blast from the past?* Hearing sounds from inside the room, she bolted down the hall, mumbling to Rosa, "Need a quick trip to ladies' room."

Once inside, she stood with her hands clutched onto the edge of the sink counter, her head down as she dragged oxygen into her lungs. When she'd walked into the patient's room and looked at the teen sitting on the exam table, she'd been struck dumb. She knew that face. She knew that cute smirk. But how could that be him? Looking down quickly to scan the forms in her hand, she read: Student - Trevor Coates. Father - Ryan Coates.

Her gaze shot from the student to the man standing to the side of the room, his salt-and-pepper-hair all she could see of his head as he focused all his attention on the phone in his hands. Dark blue uniform with a badge of some sort on his breast pocket. His arms were muscular, evident as they strained against the material of his short sleeves. *He'd always had great arms. He'd always had great everything.*

Forcing her attention back to completing the sports physical with Trevor, she'd found the young man to be every bit as delightful as she remembered his father was at that age. Funny, witty, confident without being cocky. She couldn't help but continually shoot gazes to the side, wondering when Ryan was going to look over and whether or not he'd recognize her. But he kept his attention on his phone, and she soon became irritated. *Can he not even be bothered to pay attention to his son's physical?* Granted, the sports physical was very general, but Ryan's lack of interest grated on her nerves. She and Trevor had finished the quick exam, and she signed the forms, handed them back to him, and turned to leave. And now, she was hiding in the ladies' room.

Ryan Coates. Mrs. Ryan Coates. Mrs. Judith Coates. She couldn't begin to count the number of times she'd written those words in her middle and high school notebooks. Probably thousands. Many with accompanying hearts and flowers swirling amongst the letters.

Until the day she'd finally grown up and buried her broken, adolescent heart.

Leaving Baytown shortly after, she'd returned for visits with her family but never for long. Since moving back to the area, she'd had the opportunity to meet with some people she'd grown up with, but seeing him was a surprise. *He'd joined the Navy and left the shore. With Leslie.*

Wincing at how teenage memories could make an adult feel as though they were sixteen years old again, she shut down those thoughts. Quickly washing and drying her hands, she lifted her gaze to the mirror and smoothed her hair back with her headband. Leaving the restroom, she reentered the fray, smiling at Rosa as they moved into the next examination room. "Hi, I'm Dr. Foster. You must be here for the sports physical…"

Several hours later, arriving home, she was thrilled that tomorrow was her assigned late-arrival day. Kicking off her shoes at the door, she wiggled her toes. She occasionally wore dressier shoes to work but knew that she'd be on her feet all day and was glad she'd worn comfortable flats with arch support. *Shoes with arch support… now there's a fashion statement!* Ruefully snorting as she walked into the kitchen, she nuked another plate of casserole, fixed a salad, and poured a glass of wine.

As she sat at her small table, she finally gave up her attempts to keep her mind off Ryan. *Ryan Coates. The boy I loved. The boy I was sure would one day notice me as more than Brad's sister. The boy I thought I was going to marry.*

Looking down at her plate, she realized she'd eaten without tasting a bite. Frustrated, she rinsed the dishes and poured another glass of wine before plopping down on the sofa, her feet propped on the coffee table. Leaning her head back against the cushion, she allowed her mind to wander down past roads.

For a frizzy-haired, book nerd, short, flat-chested twelve-year-old, middle school was not a place of fun memories. She'd had a few friends, but once the ties from early childhood fell behind, the preteen years were marred with cliques and wannabes. Always a good student, the teachers had loved her, but school was a bit lonely. Her brother, Brad, was two years older, athletic, and already popular as a freshman. And one day after school, she'd walked into the kitchen, looking for a snack, discovering Brad and his new friend sitting at the kitchen counter, shoveling in cookies and milk that her mom was placing down for them.

As they turned her way, she could still remember the way her feet stumbled to a halt, her breath catching in her throat and words flying from her mind as she stared at the most gorgeous fourteen-year-old boy she could ever have imagined. And he was sitting in her kitchen. Brown hair flattened a bit on top where the ends curled up around his ears and the bottom, obvious he'd just taken off his ball cap. Dark brown eyes that were staring straight at her. Just when she wondered if he were a figment of her overactive imagination, his lips curved upward, and he mumbled, "Hey."

As though the heavens had opened up, the angels had begun singing, the clouds had parted, and the fates had shone down around her, she'd believed to her very core that he was her one true, forever love.

Falling for Ryan Coates had not been hard. Getting him to notice her was a different story. For the next two years, whenever he was at their house, she'd desperately wanted to capture his attention but always found herself tongue-tied. When he'd stay for dinner after he and Brad had a late practice, she managed to sit next to him, convincing herself that just being near him was enough. After all, they were going to have a lifetime of talking just to each other. Whenever he scored a run, she'd cheered just as loudly for him as she did for Brad. She'd always managed to be around when he was over.

But she never told anyone how she felt, making sure to keep her scribbled-in notebooks carefully hidden. Not even her mom although she wondered if her mother knew from the glances sent her way when Judith sat near Ryan at their table. Her secret was hers, afraid that it would become jinxed if she shared it with someone else.

By the time she entered high school, he was a junior, and it hurt to realize how out of reach he seemed, but she was convinced they were destined to be together. *I clung to that fantasy with all my heart, but looking back now, it seems ridiculous.* He and Leslie were connected at the hip. And probably every other place, as well. But he'd always smiled at her whenever he happened to notice her standing in the hall staring, cheering loudly from the stands, or when she'd be lucky enough to find him in her kitchen.

It had been so obvious to her that Leslie wasn't right for him, and not just because Judith loved him. "Leslie's so pretty," everyone said. *Yeah, because at sixteen, her parents already let her go to the salon for expensive high-lights, manicures, and pedicures.* "Leslie's so nice," was another oft-heard phrase. *Maybe she's not a bitch, but she acts so entitled, hardly what Ryan deserves.* "They make the perfect homecoming king and queen." *That one made her gag. He'd look so much better with a natural beauty... or maybe a short girl with curly hair!*

Her first two years in high school had turned into agony as she was forced to watch the Ryan and Leslie show play out every day. It was almost easier when he and Brad graduated, Ryan joining the Navy as her brother headed to college. Gossip might let her know that Ryan and Leslie still dated, but it wasn't shoved in her face all the time, giving her notebook scribblings more credence.

She'd finally started coming into her own during her junior and senior years. Her curly hair was long and lush, drawing admiring glances from others. Still short, she was no longer flat-chested, pleased to fill out her bikini in the summer. By older adolescence, it was cool to be a smart girl, and she'd embraced her academics, already deciding that medical school was in her future.

She'd even dated but never anyone long term because, quite simply, they weren't Ryan.

And then, the night of her senior prom. She'd already accepted a date when she heard from her mom that Brad and Ryan were going to be back in town during the same weekend.

Excited to see her brother, she was even more excited to see Ryan on leave from the Navy. She toyed with the idea of breaking her date and asking Ryan to take her to the prom but couldn't bring herself to do it.

But it was Ryan she called when her date became too handsy and she walked away, leaving her without a ride home. Technically, she called Brad, but it was Ryan who answered the phone, telling her that Brad was drinking and he was the designated driver. Ryan rushed to the high school to pick her up, and with Brad snoring in the backseat, he drove her home.

He was angry, threatening to beat the crap out of her date. Standing in her driveway with just the moonlight casting shadows over his beautiful face, her heart swelled at her hero who'd swooped in to save her. It was their time. She was sure of it. She'd just turned eighteen, a few weeks away from graduating from high school. After six years, ready to finally declare her love for him. After all, Brad had told her weeks ago that Ryan was ready to break up with Leslie.

And after assuring him that she was fine, they stood, staring at each other for a long moment. She watched a flash and some other emotion she couldn't define move through his dark eyes, and she held her breath, waiting for his lips to descend upon hers. Her tongue darted out, moistening her lips, preparing.

The sound of retching caused them both to swing their gazes to the side, seeing Brad hanging out of the car, throwing up. "Shit, man," Ryan laughed, walking over to the other side of the car.

Their magical moment halted, and she raced over, as well. "Brad, are you okay?" she asked stupidly, unsure what she should do to assist.

"Yeah," Brad said, his grin sloppy as he climbed from the car. With Ryan's help, he stumbled over to where she stood in her prom dress, her curls tamed into a lovely chignon.

"Damn, Sis, you look great. Doesn't she look great, Ryan?" Brad slurred.

Ryan met her gaze and grinned. "Yeah, man. She's gorgeous."

Her heart threatened to beat out of her chest. While declaring her love for him with Brad drunkenly standing almost between them wasn't her choice of the most romantic settings of all time, she wasn't willing to let the moment pass.

"Ryan..." she began, her palms sweating and chest heaving with each breath.

"But you shouldn't call my sister gorgeous, man," Brad interrupted as he weaved unsteadily on his feet. "Not since you're getting married next month."

Cold ice water filled her veins as her chest depressed when all the air left her lungs. Barely able to catch her breath, she stared, open-mouthed, stupidly numb. For a second, just a brief second, it seemed as though Ryan was going to say something as he stared back at her. And whatever she'd seen in his eyes a moment ago flashed through them again.

"And gonna become a dad," Brad kept going, completely

unaware of the path of destruction he'd cast down with his words. "Can't believe you and Leslie are gonna have a baby."

Turning, she'd raced into the house, dreams dashed, hopes crushed, plans decimated.

The clock on the wall chimed, and Judith looked up, surprised to see that she'd been sitting on the sofa reminiscing for over an hour. Sighing, she downed the rest of her wine, planted her feet onto the floor, and pushed herself to a stand. Climbing into bed after her long, hot shower, she closed her eyes, willing sleep to come, but the face of the teen in the exam room and the still-handsome man standing nearby stayed in her dreams.

6

"Trev, are you sure we got everything signed for you to start practice?" Ryan asked as he poured a cup of coffee. He'd already had a bowl of oatmeal and glanced over to make sure the kids were eating, as well.

Trevor rummaged around in his backpack and pulled out the papers, pushing them across the counter. "I looked at them, Dad, but maybe you should double-check."

He leaned over the counter and scanned the forms, making sure everything had been filled in and signed. As he glanced through the sports physical, he again regretted that his attention had been called away, normally completely focused on his kids, especially when it came to their health or education. *Hell, anytime it came to the kids.*

Looking at the bottom of the form, the signature was hard to read but the stamp stated, "Doctor Foster." The image of the petite doctor with the long, dark-blonde curly hair ran through his mind. *Foster.*

"Is everything okay, Dad?" Trevor asked, leaning over the counter to glance at the forms. "Did we miss something?"

"No, no. Everything looks fine. I was just looking at the doctor's name. I feel bad that I was so involved with what was happening at work that I was focused on the phone and not your appointment."

"It's fine. She was cool, and it was just for sports, not like I was sick or anything."

"You have a weird look on your face, Dad," Cindy said. "Are you okay?"

"Yeah. It's just her last name reminded me of someone."

Trevor wiggled his eyebrows. "I don't know, Dad. She looks way too young for her to be an old flame of yours."

"Gross!" Cindy said, rolling her eyes.

Ryan chuckled and shook his head. "My best friend in high school was Brad Foster. He had a younger sister with curly hair."

"Foster is a common name," Cindy replied, moving to the sink to rinse out her cereal bowl. Looking over her shoulder, she added, "You never mentioned a friend named Brad."

"He was a friend from long ago. We kept up with each other for a while, but our lives went different directions when I joined the Navy and he went off to college. When we could, we'd hang together when we were both home at the same time, but then, I got married. and the last I heard, he'd settled in North Carolina."

"And his sister?" she pressed.

He wasn't surprised by Cindy's curiosity, his daughter often asking probing questions. What was surprising was the image that came to mind since thinking of the Fosters wasn't Brad but Judith. "Oh, she was a couple of years younger. I just remember her being around all the time. I don't guess I've seen her since... well, since she graduated." Lost in thought, he jumped as Trevor grabbed the papers from the counter and shoved them into his backpack.

"Bus is almost here!" Trevor shouted, and he and Cindy hurried to finish getting ready.

As always, Ryan stood and waved goodbye, watching the bus go down the road. But strangely, this morning, his mind went back to years before when he and Brad rode the school bus, Brad keeping an eye on his younger sister to make sure no one bothered her much like Trevor did for Cindy. Judith was quiet, very smart, and usually had her nose in a book or was doodling in a notebook. *Now that I think about it, she was a lot like Cindy.*

Walking back into the house, it was another memory that moved through him, one that wasn't as pleasant: starting to notice Judith as a young woman and not as just Brad's sister. But he'd had little time off in the Navy, even stationed in Norfolk, and Leslie was determined that they should be together. He'd convinced himself that what he and Leslie had felt for so long was love but wasn't sure she was the person for him. He had already decided that he was ready to break up with her and explore his freedom, especially since he would soon be going to sea. But before he had a chance, she'd told him she was pregnant. Trevor and Cindy were the light of his life, but there was no denying that becoming a father at twenty-one was not what he'd expected to have happened.

That last weekend of freedom, when he and Brad had met up and then rescued Judith from a prom date from hell, he'd stared into her eyes, realizing she was the whole package... beautiful, smart, sweet. She'd always looked at him as though he hung the stars, but now that she was eighteen, she was no longer off-limits. And for a moment, even with everything going on, he stood in the moonlight with her and stared, a flash of what life might be if things were different moving through him.

And then Brad threw up, staggered around, and announced in a blundering way that he and Leslie were not only getting married but having a baby. For a brief second, Ryan imagined hurt and regret passed through Judith's eyes. But she hurried inside their house, and he never saw her again. He and Brad had stayed in contact for a couple of years, and then, like so many friends from childhood, they went their separate ways. He thought he remembered his mom saying that Brad and Judith's parents had left the area and moved to North Carolina, as well.

Rinsing out his coffee mug, he poured a fresh cup into a travel mug, secured the house, and climbed into his SUV. He knew the new doctor in town wasn't Judith, but the memories brought to mind caused him to heave a sigh. The greatest gift he had in life was his kids, and therefore, he had no regrets, but it was only human to think of the different twists and turns life might have taken if he'd made different choices. Another sigh escaped. Pushing past those thoughts, he drove to work.

His morning was routine, but before he had a chance to get lunch, things kicked into high gear. He and his team had to coordinate with the Coast Guard to rescue a Bay tour boat that had first stalled and then began taking on water. There were ten passengers, all senior citizens. The boat's captain had ensured they were all wearing life vests, and he'd thankfully radioed for assistance as soon as his boat's engine stopped.

Ryan, Callan, and Beth were in one boat, and he directed his other team's boat nearby. The Coast Guard station out of Baytown had sent three boats, as well. With one of the Coast Guard boats providing stabilization, they managed to transfer all the passengers to the various rescue crafts. Moving away, Ryan and his crew left the Coast Guard to deal effectively with the captain while they quickly brought the passengers back to Baytown.

The passengers were all grateful, some even laughing about their adventure while others were quite anxious to get off the water. There had been no injuries, but he'd radioed for Zac Hamilton, the Captain of the Baytown Rescue Squad, to check them over. He'd known Zac for several years, both serving in the American Legion. Zac's smiles and jokes had the passengers at ease as he checked blood pressures and heart rates, asking questions to ascertain that none of them felt the need to be seen by a physician and certainly not to go to the hospital.

The tour boat had originated from another town farther north on the Shore, so Ryan had BettsAnne arrange transportation for the passengers to be taken back to where their cars were parked.

After they'd all left, he and Zac stood in the parking lot and talked about the AL baseball teams they were coaching. "Is Trevor playing for Baytown High School?"

Nodding, Ryan smiled. "Yeah. Hard to believe he's in high school."

"Tell me about it," Zac agreed. "It was only a couple of years ago that I remember him running about the AL ball field. Damn, the years are passing."

"Yeah, and you're a dad now. How old is the baby?"

Zac laughed and pulled out his phone, scrolling through pictures of him, his wife Maddie, and his baby. "He's almost a year."

"No shit. Man, we are getting old." His stomach growled, and he shook his head. "Sorry about that."

"Sounds like you missed lunch," Zac laughed.

"Par for the course around here." Shaking hands, he watched as Zac climbed back into the ambulance and drove off before he headed inside. He was hungry but knew he needed to get his report written up and wanted to call the Coast Guard station to see what had happened with the captain and his boat.

He glanced at the time and realized Trevor and

Cindy would soon be getting home from school, but suddenly, the radio blared. Two small yachts had just collided on their way into the harbor. He bolted from his desk, another emergency to race to.

7

"Dr. Foster, you're needed immediately in examination room four," Rosa called out.

Responding quickly, she hurried down the hall and followed Rosa into the room. A girl sat on the table, tears streaming down her face. She held her left hand tightly with her right, blood seeping through her fingers, leaving a bloody trail smeared on her blouse.

"Hey, sweetie, I'm Dr. Foster. What happened?"

"Cut it... with a knife," she said, her words shaky. "I was cutting potatoes for dinner and the knife slipped."

"Okay, let's take a look." She gently lifted the injured finger, seeing a long slice that thankfully did not appear overly deep. "What's your name, honey?"

"Cindy."

"Well, Cindy, we're going to get this taken care of, okay?" Glancing at Rosa, she said, "Let's get this cleaned up, and then I'll get this sutured."

As soon as the word 'sutured' left her lips, the girl

whimpered. Since there was no adult in the room, she asked, "Are your parents with you?"

She shook her head. "My brother."

Just then, the door opened, and she heard footsteps entering the room. She turned and spied the young man, blinking in surprise. *Jesus, it's him again.*

"Hey, Dr. Foster. I don't know if you remember me, but we met yesterday for my physical."

Recovering, she nodded and smiled. "Yes, I do remember you. Coates... Trevor Coates. I assume you're the brother?"

"Yeah, I brought her straight here. I didn't know what else to do." He walked directly to his sister, putting his arm around her, pulling her in for a hug as she sat on the exam table.

His face held worry, and as she watched the interaction, she was struck with the reminder of how Brad had been with her when they were about the same age. She remembered Trevor was only fourteen, but he was showing such maturity.

"Did either of your parents come with you?" she asked.

"No, Dad's at work."

Knowing Trevor was too young to drive, she cocked her head to the side and asked, "How did you get here?"

"Our next-door neighbor. He's kind of old, but he can still drive." He looked down at Cindy, a wide grin on his face. "I know you're hurting, Sis, but it was kind of funny."

Despite her obvious pain, Cindy managed a little

smile as she looked up at Trevor, and Judith felt the squeeze in her chest at their affection.

"I don't think he sees very good, Trevor. He almost drove in the median!"

Glad that Trevor had managed to distract Cindy, she still needed to get parental permission. "If your dad's at work, can he get here so that we can have permission to put several small stitches in Cindy's finger?"

"I've been trying to call in, but I can't get ahold of him," Trevor replied. "He's out on the water."

"Okay, then how about your mom?"

"Well, I didn't try her," he admitted, his brow furrowed, and Cindy just shrugged.

Judith looked between Trevor and Cindy, surprised at their reaction. "I'm sure if you call your mom, she'll come in."

"No, she won't," Cindy said. "She doesn't like to be bothered—"

"That's not true, Cin," Trevor jumped in. "It's just that she doesn't really know what to do."

Judith opened her mouth, then snapped it closed for a few seconds, trying to filter the information coming in and read between the lines. But finally, still not having an idea of the true situation, she insisted, "I at least need to have verbal permission from a parent or guardian. So, why don't we try to call your mom, and if she'll at least let me talk to her over the phone, we'll be okay."

Trevor nodded and shrugged, bending over his phone again. "Mom, I've got Cindy at the doctor's office because she cut her finger, and the doctor needs to talk to a parent." He paused, listening. "I know, but I can't get hold of Dad. Here, at least talk to the doctor." He huffed as he handed the phone to Judith.

Taking it, she nodded her thanks to him and placed it to her ear. "Hello, this is Dr. Foster at the Baytown Family Medical Clinic. Who am I speaking to, please?"

"Leslie... Leslie Coates."

The hesitant, almost distracted voice wasn't what Judith expected, but pushing all personal thoughts to the side, she plowed ahead. "Cindy needs a few stitches in her finger, and I want parental acknowledgment of the treatment plan. Even over the phone will do."

"Their father usually handles all of that," Leslie replied.

Judith's chin jerked back slightly. "That may be, but your son is unable to get hold of him right now due to work."

"How is she?" Leslie asked.

Wondering why that wasn't the first question Cindy's mother asked, Judith began losing patience. "She will be fine, but I need to get her finger treated. Are you giving me verbal permission?"

"I suppose, I don't know what else I can do."

She glanced down at Trevor's phone and hit speakerphone now that Rosa had reentered the room. "Mrs. Coates, I have a witness with me. Please give me verbal permission to treat your daughter's finger."

"Yes, please do everything you can for her. Thank you, Doctor."

Judith handed the phone back to Trevor and turned to face Cindy with a smile. "Okay, I say we can get going now, and I promise we're going to get this taken care of where you'll barely feel a thing."

A tear slid down Cindy's cheek, but she nodded, pressing her lips together. Drawing upon all of her professionalism, Judith tried to push thoughts of both Ryan and Leslie's disinterested attitudes when it came to their children's doctor visits. *What the hell is wrong with them?*

"Hey, Cin, don't worry," Trevor said. "I'll be right here." He once again stepped closer and placed his arm around her shoulders, helping to hold her steady. Cindy closed her eyes and leaned her head against her brother's chest, and Judith's heart melted at the sight.

She kept a running dialog going as she numbed Cindy's finger, quickly sutured it with three stitches, and then wrapped it in a bandage. Complimenting her, she took a moment to study Cindy. She tried to see Leslie in her but mostly came up with a beautiful female version of Ryan. Leslie had almost-white blonde hair and blue eyes, but Cindy's hair was light brown, and her eyes were dark brown. She was a pretty thirteen-year-old with the promise of only becoming more beautiful as she got older.

"I'm going to go out and see if I can get hold of Dad," Trevor said.

After he left and she was alone with Cindy, she said, "I'm sorry your mom couldn't be here."

Crinkling her nose, Cindy said, "I'm not. I love my mom, but she's not very… um… good with things like this. I know she loves me and Trevor, but I'm not sure that being a mom is all that easy for her." Shrugging, she added, "I see her one evening a week for dinner, and sometimes, we'll try to have a whole weekend together, but that's a bit much."

Not expecting that information, Judith's eyes bugged. "Oh, I'm sorry I didn't understand. So, are your parents not together?"

"No, they got divorced about three years ago. Trevor and I live with our dad full-time since he has custody and that's the way we want it. Mom gets involved in her own world, and it's hard for her to get out of her head."

"That's a rather adult way of looking at things for someone who's only thirteen," Judith said softly, admiration filling her. Sitting on the stool that she'd rolled close to the table, she held Cindy's gaze. "But then, you strike me as very mature."

As though she'd given her the greatest compliment, Cindy smiled.

A new thought popped into Judith's head. "You said you were cutting potatoes. Were you doing the cooking?"

"Sometimes, I do. Trevor and I take turns along with Dad. Since he wasn't home, I thought I'd go ahead and start dinner."

So many thoughts were flying through Judith's mind, it was hard to separate them all. She saw the mature thirteen-year-old in front of her who was trying to fix dinner for her absent father and older brother. A mom who couldn't be bothered to be concerned that her daughter was injured. And a dad who sticks his nose in his phone instead of paying attention to his kids.

"Um... Doctor Foster?"

Cindy's soft voice jerked Judith out of her thoughts. "Yes, sweetie?"

"Can I ask you something?"

Cindy's cheeks were red with blush, and it struck Judith that living with two men and an absent mother, Cindy might not have another woman to talk to. "You can ask me anything."

"I'm thirteen years old. But I wondered about when I start my period… um, that hasn't happened yet. I mean, I know what they teach us in school," Cindy said, her cheeks flaming even redder.

"Cindy, periods are something every woman has to deal with. I'd much rather you get your information from me than your friends or even what you might learn in school. So, if you've got questions, honey, sock it to me."

A giggle slipped out, and the tension seemed to ease from Cindy's shoulders. "It's just that I haven't started yet, but sometimes, I have cramps. And then I keep running to the bathroom to see if anything happens. Some of my friends say that they just started gushing, and that terrifies me. What if that happens at school?"

"Well, rarely will someone bleed heavily right at the beginning. But, since you already have cramps, it sounds like your body is getting ready. Do you have any sanitary products?"

"Like tampons? To be honest, they kind of scare me," Cindy admitted, her nose scrunching again.

"I'd suggest you have some pads that can adhere to your panties. You can keep them discreetly in your purse and, of course, the school nurse will have some. I take it your mom isn't someone you feel like you can ask?"

"No way." She shook her head vehemently. "We don't really talk about anything personal at all. And my dad usually does the grocery shopping. I don't want to ask him—"

"I've got some here, honey. I'll give you some before you leave."

"Really?"

"Yeah. And I'll give you my card. You can call if you ever have questions, okay?"

Cindy's eyes held such relief, Judith wanted to throw her arms around her and hug her tightly.

A thunderous voice sounded in the hall. "Where's my daughter?"

Suddenly, the door slammed open, and like a tornado whipping through, a large presence rushed in. Jerking around, she watched as Ryan stalked in, not stopping until he scooped Cindy into his arms. His eyes were squeezed shut as he held her in his arms. They whispered a few words to each other, his embrace tight.

Trevor followed quickly, his gaze on his dad and sister before glancing toward Judith, his smile wide. "I guess you can tell I finally got hold of him, Dr. Foster."

Standing, her cold gaze stayed on Ryan, noting the instant he opened his eyes and looked over at her. He blinked several times before his eyes widened and he turned slightly so that he was facing her while still holding Cindy.

Lifting a brow, she crossed her arms over her chest. "Hello, Ryan. Glad you could finally join us."

8

Ryan had raced to the Baytown Family Medical Center as soon as Trevor's call and message came through. Hearing the words, "Cindy cut herself with a knife and she's getting stitches," had sent chills straight through him, fear threatening to choke his breathing as he drove the short distance it took to get to the clinic. Cursing the stupid yacht owners who'd gotten into a fight, he hated that he'd been late and wasn't with his phone.

Charging into the clinic, he'd run into Trevor who'd told him Cindy was fine, but until he had her in his arms and saw for himself, he wasn't to be stopped.

"Daddy, I'm fine," Cindy whispered.

He couldn't remember the last time she'd called him Daddy, knowing it meant she'd been hurt and scared, and he tightened his grip. Her soft voice sounded again in his ear.

"You're squishing me."

"You gotta give this to your old man, honey. I need to make sure you're okay."

Trevor spoke, calling Dr. Foster by name. He turned and stared at the honey-colored curls surrounding the face of someone he remembered fondly from long ago. Judith Foster, all grown up and wearing a doctor's coat as she stood nearby. Realizing she'd been the one to treat Cindy, the air rushed from his lungs. He opened his mouth to greet her but instead blurted, "Why didn't the clinic call the station? Didn't you need parental permission to treat her?"

"Dad!" Trevor and Cindy shouted in unison.

Fuck. Why the hell those words came out he couldn't imagine but chalked it up to fear and frustration. Opening his mouth to thank her instead, he realized his error when Judith's eyes narrowed.

"Considering your son had attempted to reach you numerous times, each time unsuccessfully, I might add, I spoke to the children's mother. I understand that you have physical custody, but as a parent, she was able to give permission. Now, if you'll excuse me, I'll send the nurse in with your discharge papers."

She whirled and charged through the door before he had a chance to call her back. Setting Cindy carefully on her feet, he rubbed the back of his neck as both kids stared at him.

"Dad, you shouldn't have said that to her! She was really nice to me. She talked to me, and I wasn't afraid, and it didn't hurt. At least, not too bad."

"Yeah, Dad!" Trevor jumped in. "I know you're all concerned about Cindy, but you came blowing in here and then blasted the doctor instead of thanking her? Jeez, you'd be pissed at me if I'd done that."

Sighing heavily, he nodded. "You're right. I goofed." Looking over at Cindy, he lifted his hand and cupped her cheek. "I was scared, sweetheart. I promise I'll talk to Judith... um... Doctor Foster and thank her."

There were a few seconds of silence before both kids grinned, once again speaking in unison. "Judith?"

Cindy said, "That's why she called you Ryan. She remembers you!"

Trevor clapped him on the shoulder. "Way to go, Dad. You haven't seen her in years, you didn't pay attention to her yesterday when she was in here with me, and she obviously remembers you. Man, you gotta up your game!"

Leveling a hard glare toward his son, he shook his head. "My *game* is not your business." Snorting, he continued to shake his head. "Not that I have game."

Laughing, Trevor added, "Yeah, and you won't if you keep that up."

Rosa entered with the discharge paperwork, saving Ryan from the conversation his kids seemed to want to have. Hearing about the injury in detail, how Trevor acted so quickly, and how brave Cindy was, the tension that had filled every cell eased. Walking out of the examination room, he hoped he would be able to see Judith. He needed to apologize and thank her but refused to give headspace as to any other reason why he swung his head from side to side, hoping she'd appear.

They'd almost made it to his SUV when the front door of the clinic opened and she ran toward them. He smiled, but she ran past without looking at him, her focus solely on Cindy.

She placed one hand on Cindy's shoulder and smiled, leaning closer. Handing a small bag to Cindy, she said, "These are for you. There are several different kinds, and you can see what you like best." She reached into her white coat pocket and pulled out a business card, handing it to Cindy, as well. "And here's my card along with my cell phone number. If you need anything or just want to talk, you can call."

She shot a glare toward Ryan, almost daring him to object. Since he had no idea what they were talking about, he wisely kept his mouth shut.

She squeezed Cindy's shoulders, smiled toward Trevor, and called out, "Goodbye, kids." With that, she jogged back into the clinic.

Trevor opened the back door and helped Cindy fasten her buckle so that she didn't have to use both hands. Knowing everyone was exhausted, Ryan pulled into a locally owned fast-food drive-through and grabbed burgers and fries.

It only took a few minutes to arrive at their home. "Trev, take the bag while I get your sister."

Cindy's face was pale with dark circles under her eyes from the stress. As he wrapped his arm around her shoulders and ushered her inside, his gaze landed on the blood drips on the floor and kitchen counter. "Shit," he muttered, walking her to a chair. Looking over his shoulder, he said, "Set the food out for you all, and I'll get this cleaned up."

It only took a few minutes to wipe up the blood droplets, and with bleach, he sanitized the counter. When that task was complete, he sat at the table and they greedily dived in. Once finished, he pushed the plates to the side and stared at his kids, experiencing an ache in his chest that he'd felt the first time he'd ever held them in his arms—and every day since then.

"I know everybody's exhausted, but now that we're home, fed, and we know Cindy's going to be okay, I need to hear about how everything went down."

He listened as Cindy explained how the knife slipped, going into great detail about Trevor immediately jumping in to help stop the bleeding. Trevor told how he got Mr. Garver to drive them to the clinic once he realized he couldn't get the bleeding under control.

"I'm proud of you. Both of you. Cindy, I know it was an accident, and honey, accidents happen. One thing to learn from this is how to use knives in the kitchen while staying safe. We'll talk about that once you've healed. And Trevor, you thought fast on your feet, took care of your sister, did everything you could. I'm just real proud of both of you."

The smiles on their faces warmed his heart, and he hated to bring up the next subject but had to know how it went down. "So, when you weren't able to get hold of me for the doctor, you got hold of your mom?" Cindy and Trevor's eyes cut toward each other, and Ryan felt their hesitation. "Guys, I know how your mom is. I need you to be honest with me so I know what I'm dealing with."

Trevor sighed and said, "I got hold of her and told her what was going on. I know she wasn't expecting me to call, and Mom struggles sometimes with things that just happen. Anyway, I handed the phone to Doctor

Foster. They talked for a moment, but I think Mom kept saying that you usually handle these things. I got the feeling that Doctor Foster was frustrated with Mom. She put Mom on speakerphone so that the nurse could listen as Mom gave permission. As soon as she got that, she handed the phone back to me. Mom wanted me to give Cindy her love, and that was pretty much it."

Hiding his irritation at Leslie, Ryan simply nodded. "Okay, Trevor, it sounds like you did everything you could. I'm real proud of you."

Turning to Cindy, he wanted to ask what Judith had given her and why she'd handed her a business card with her personal phone number on it. Suddenly uncertain, he snapped his mouth shut and decided he'd ask Judith when he contacted her. He still needed to thank her, and knowing she had a poor opinion of both him and Leslie, he discovered he wanted the chance to explain.

"Why don't you turn in early, sweetheart," he encouraged.

"I have just a little homework to do, Dad," Cindy said.

"Tell you what. Get ready for bed, and then do whatever you feel like doing. I'll send a note to your teachers tomorrow, letting them know what happened."

She nodded, her sweet smile wrapping around his heart as her arms wrapped around his neck. Hugging his daughter tight, he kissed the top of her head, watching as she left the room. Looking over at Trevor, he said, "I'll talk to your mom, but I don't want you to worry about it."

"Dad, it's okay. We know Mom loves us. She just has a hard time understanding what to do or say to us."

"I get that, Son. Believe me, I've known for many years how your mom is, but I need to make sure she understands that if I'm not available, she has to step up. But I'm going to say it one more time, Trev. You really handled things well today. Couldn't be prouder of you."

Trevor grinned, and as he started out of the room, he stopped and turned to look over his shoulder. "By the way, Dad. I think Doctor Foster is not only pretty, but she's cool. She was great with Cindy, and the way she handled Mom was perfect. Personally, I think you've got a little groveling to do." Laughing, Trevor jogged up the steps before Ryan had a chance to reply.

Huffing as he leaned back in his chair, he thought of the cute, curly-headed little girl who'd followed Brad and him around. That image morphed into the pretty teenage bookworm who'd once looked at him as though he put the stars in the sky. And now she was a beautiful, kind doctor who thought he was a jerk.

A doctor. He wasn't surprised at her choice of career or that she'd completed all the educational require-ments. After all, he remembered her being very smart. Brad used to joke that he got the brawn and she got the brains in the family. Ryan knew that wasn't true consid-ering Brad did well in school, also. But what was surprising was that she'd come back to the Eastern Shore when neither her parents nor Brad were in the area.

He remembered their house, a large, older, historic, brick home outside of Baytown that had several acres surrounding it. She'd probably bought it. Hell, probably was given the home by her parents. *Foster... she's not married. Or is she?* Just because she kept her maiden name didn't mean she wasn't married. He couldn't imagine someone with her intelligence and beauty would be single. Now, the idea of her sharing a large family home with her significant other moved through him.

Standing, he carried his plate to the sink, noting the worn countertops and older-model refrigerator. Battling the burst of envy that filled him, he was embarrassed to even acknowledge that emotion. With his fists planted on the edge of the sink, he dropped his chin and squeezed his eyes tightly shut. He wasn't ashamed of the home he was providing Trevor and Cindy, but it was tight quarters for him and two teens. But on his salary and still helping Leslie get on her feet several years after the divorce, he was doing the best he could. *And being envious of an old acquaintance that I don't even know anymore is ridiculous.*

Securing the house for the evening, he made his way upstairs, refusing to give Judith Foster any more of his thoughts other than to thank her for helping Cindy. The flash in her angry eyes moved through his memory again. *Yeah, Trevor's right. I've got some groveling to do.*

Grateful the next several days at work were more routine, Ryan took the opportunity to walk from the harbor to Main Street, heading into Jillian's Coffee

Shop. Jillian and her husband, Grant, a police officer for Baytown, had also graduated from Baytown High School, but they were several years behind him. In many ways, though, they'd started out like him and Leslie, joined at the hip, homecoming king and queen, the couple everyone assumed would get together and stay a couple. In their case, it seemed they'd broken up for several years before finally getting back together. Now, happily married with a baby, they still fulfilled the Baytown ideal couple.

Leslie had wanted that for her and Ryan. She'd been in love with the idea of love. Infatuated with the idea that everyone envied them. *At least, she thought they did. I always figured no one gave a shit about whether we looked good as a couple.* Looking back, he sometimes wondered if they'd ever really been in love. Certainly not the kind of love that two people who planned on staying married forever should've had. For himself, he would have stayed married if the only thing she struggled with was figuring out how to be a good wife. He would even have dealt with her spending habits and lack of motivation. But not the way she focused more on herself than the kids. And when they felt her disinterest in a way that was detrimental when it was in their face all the time, he'd chosen to protect the kids. He knew Leslie wouldn't like the financial constraints that came with the divorce, but he'd convinced himself that she would want to make changes for the kids. But her true colors showed when she walked away easily from them, as well.

Now, standing in Jillian's, he spied several shelves of

jewelry, remembering that Jillian showcased local artists. Walking over, he looked at them, wondering if Cindy would soon be to the age where she'd want her ears pierced. Up until now, she hadn't, and he'd dreaded the day when she would ask. Glancing at the price tag, he blinked in surprise. *Damn, they're pricey.* His daughter had thankfully never shown to have Leslie's tendencies to want or ask for things that were out of their family's price range. But looking at the beautiful sea glass earrings, he decided that when Cindy did get her ears pierced, he would buy her a nice pair.

Aware of a presence nearby, he shifted slightly to give the newcomer more room to look at the jewelry. Glancing down, he was surprised to see the tumble of curls and the delicate fingers of the woman who reached out to touch one of the necklaces. So involved in looking, she hadn't seemed to realize he was near.

"Judith?"

She jerked slightly, turning and lifting her gaze up to him. "Oh. Ryan. I'm sorry, I didn't notice you. I was, well, mesmerized by the sea glass."

"Yeah, I was looking at the jewelry, also."

Her lips curved upward but the smile didn't reach her eyes. She dipped her chin in a silent goodbye and began to turn away.

"Judith, please. I'm glad I ran into you. I've been meaning to call, but... anyway, I really wanted to thank you for the other night. For taking care of Cindy."

"You don't have to thank me, Ryan. It's my job. It's what I love to do. I'm just very sorry that I had to meet her because she was hurt."

"It might be your job, but she told me how nice you were. I know she was scared and she... well, both she and Trevor sang your praises. I know I wasn't very polite when I got there."

She waved her hand to the side. "You're a parent. A parent with an injured child. Believe me, I understand that your first concern was for her."

"Regardless, I want you to know how much I appreciate it. I also want to apologize for my distracted behavior when you were talking to Trevor. Normally, I'm completely tuned in to what's going on with my kids, but my only excuse is that I knew the sports physical was routine, and just before you came into the room, I got hit with a situation from work that had to be dealt with. I assure you that if Trevor had been unwell or injured, I would have shut the phone off, shoved it in my pocket, and not looked at it."

She stared for a moment, seeming to weigh his words, and then nodded, her smile a little wider.

Continuing, he added, "I was surprised, pleasantly so, to find you back in town."

Her eyes lit, her smile no longer appearing forced. She dropped her gaze back to the jewelry, and he took the opportunity to take her in. Light makeup. Hair falling naturally down her back, held away from her face with a headband. A light pink blouse and black pants, her doctor's white coat nowhere in sight. Flat ballet-looking shoes that appeared chosen for comfort rather than squeezing her toes together or forcing her heels up four inches. The delicate scent of vanilla, reminding him of sugar cookies, wafted past. And for a few seconds, he wanted her to look up at him the way she had that night many years ago when he'd given her a ride after her disastrous prom. It had been many years since a woman had looked at him that way. In fact, he wasn't sure any woman ever had since then, not even Leslie.

As though she could hear his thoughts, she lifted her chin, the pretty smile still on her face, and her eyes met his. "Well, if you ever want to catch up, let me know. I'd love to get together sometime."

While she wasn't looking at him with stars in her eyes, he should have been thrilled with the open friendliness she was now bestowing. And yet, he hesitated, glancing between her and the designer jewelry she'd been considering. *A doctor. Definitely above my pay grade.* And while that thought no longer made him envious, he'd spent years with a woman who'd demanded more than they could comfortably afford. And even though Judith would be able to afford things on her own, he didn't get the feeling they'd have much to talk about.

His hesitancy and doubt must've been written clearly on his face because her smile wobbled. Continuing to throw up more barriers, he mumbled, "Not sure we have much in common to talk about."

Her smile completely dropped, and the light in her eyes dimmed. "Goodbye, Ryan," she said, her words dripping with ice. She turned and walked away before he had a chance to say anything.

Christ, what a dick thing to say to her. Watching her leave the shop, he knew Trevor would tell him to pull his head out of his ass. Heaving a sigh, he felt weary.

Too many conflicting, tumultuous thoughts hit him all at one time. *If this is the best I can do even trying to have a conversation, I'm better off alone.*

Walking over to the counter, he accepted his coffee and offered a chin lift toward Jillian. Stepping out into the sunshine, he glanced around, but Judith was out of sight. *Yeah, probably for the best.*

9

Dipping her paddle into the water, Judith glided along the coast of the Bay. She tilted her head back and closed her eyes, letting the sun soak her eyelids, basking in the warmth. *Finally, a day off.* The clinic was open on Saturday for only a half-day and the three doctors rotated. Today was a day just for her, and she was determined to enjoy it. And by enjoying it, she was equally determined that thoughts of an arrogant, overbearing, oaf of a man—namely, Ryan Coates—would not fill her thoughts.

She sighed and opened her eyes. Of course, he was filling her thoughts. She hadn't seen him in fifteen years, and now, three days this past week, she'd seen him three times. And each time, he'd managed to infuriate her as well as intrigue her.

She hated to admit it, but after their last run-in, she'd snooped a little into his life. The only person at the clinic who'd lived in Baytown for years besides Doctor Preston was Rosa. They'd left the clinic at the same time yesterday, and she'd casually managed to ask if Rosa knew anything about Ryan.

Rosa, intuitive as always, had lifted a brow and asked, "Interested, are you?"

"Oh, I grew up with him. He and my brother were best friends."

That tidbit seemed to take Rosa off the scent that Judith was asking for more personal reasons, for which she was glad. The last thing she wanted was for someone to think she was interested. Because she wasn't. Absolutely not. Forcing her expression to stay blank, she'd smiled at Rosa, waiting.

"I've seen him at the clinic since he came back to Baytown from the Navy. Let's see, that would have been about ten years ago or so. He joined the VMP—"

"The what?"

"The Virginia Marine Police."

"Oh," she'd said but had no other response considering Rosa was warming to her subject.

"He's the head honcho. The captain. Anyway, he'd always come in whenever the kids needed to see the doctor. Cindy and Trevor were in preschool. The kids have always been real healthy, but I always noticed that whenever they were sick or needed physicals for school, it was Ryan who brought them in. The only time I ever saw the mom was when she was coming to the doctor herself. I honestly didn't even know they were married for a long time even though they had the same last name!"

"I wonder why," Judith had wondered aloud.

"Honey, some women are born maternal. Lots of

women aren't very maternal until they have children of their own, and then watch out, because they'll develop every maternal instinct in the book! Some women aren't very maternal and unfortunately fall into the category of neglectful or abusive. Now, that wasn't Leslie, but she definitely wasn't very maternal. I always thought she was just plain selfish. Not in an overt, in-your-face, it's-all-about-me kind of way. No, she was just what I call clueless. Clueless about what her kids needed. Clueless about how to be maternal. Clueless about putting their needs ahead of her own."

Nodding slowly, Judith understood what Rosa was saying and she'd only had one phone conversation with Leslie.

Leaning closer, Rosa added, "I also heard that woman knew how to spend money. Way more money than poor Ryan could ever afford. And when her habits finally started interfering with what the kids needed, he put his foot down."

While Rosa's tidbits of information and gossip had answered some of Judith's questions, she was now filled with shame that she had snooped. Whatever was going on in Ryan's life, it was his business. She patted Rosa's arm and quickly said goodbye, climbing into her car to drive home.

At least she now understood Leslie's relationship with Cindy and Trevor, and considering she would be their doctor for a while, she was glad to have that knowledge. *And it explains a lot about Ryan's actions. Except for the coffee shop.* When his polite apology and explanation had turned into a curt dismissal, she'd wanted to throw her hands up in frustration.

Now, she was determined to enjoy her morning and looked around to gain her bearings. A small, uninhabited island was nearby in the Bay. She'd kayaked there once with some high school friends and remembered it as a particularly beautiful place to look for oyster shells. It didn't take long although her arms were getting tired by the time she dragged her kayak up on the shore. Uncertain if there would be lots of other visitors, she was pleased to see just a few kayaks tied off nearby.

Walking along the beach, she finally felt the tension leave her body as she relaxed for what felt like the first time in a long time. Not quite ready to paddle back home, she sat on the beach with her legs stretched out in front of her, her arms braced behind her and her head lifted toward the sky.

"Doctor Foster!"

Surprised to hear a girl's voice call her name, she twisted toward the sound and lifted her hand to shade her eyes. It took a few seconds for her vision to focus, and she stared in dumb silence at the sight of Cindy and Trevor walking toward her, Ryan following along a little slower.

Cindy's bright smile beamed her way, and it was impossible to not respond in kind. "Hello, Cindy. You must be feeling better to have come out here today."

Cindy plopped down next to her and nodded as she held up her bandaged finger. "It's so much better, but I was in the two-seater kayak with Dad. He didn't want me to hurt my hand."

"Well, your dad is right." She gazed up to Ryan, seeing him stand awkwardly to the side, his hands on his hips. Shifting her gaze over, she smiled as Trevor plopped down next to Cindy. "How are you doing? Has practice started?"

"Yeah, it is going great."

"You're a freshman, right? So you're playing junior varsity?"

He nodded, then shrugged. "Actually, the coach is looking at me to possibly play varsity even as a freshman."

Her chin jerked back as her eyes bugged. "Wow, that's impressive! You must be really good!"

Grinning, he shrugged again, pride showing on his face.

"Trevor usually shouts from the rooftop when he's excited," Cindy said. "I think he's afraid of jinxing it if he talks about it too much."

Trevor scowled toward his sister. "I'm not afraid of jinxing anything."

Before the siblings could devolve into an argument, she said, "I totally get that. I was always afraid to hope for something when I was younger. It was like the more I really wanted something, the more it was going to hurt if I didn't get it."

Cindy and Trevor stared at her, wide-eyed and open-mouthed. He nodded, and Cindy said, "Yeah, you do get it. I'm that way about things in school, too."

"Are you still that way?" Trevor asked.

She noticed the blush tinging the tips of his ears and assumed he would never ask that question if his friends were around. Appreciating his honesty, she said, "Not so much anymore. By now, I've learned a lot of life's lessons that you still have to learn."

"Like what?" Cindy asked, her attention pinpointed on Judith.

"Things like we don't always get what we want. Sometimes, we have to make sacrifices for other people. Sometimes, the things we thought were important turn out to be not quite so important. Sometimes, we have to alter our goals, or change our dreams, or even come up with a backup plan. And I guess I've learned that if I work hard at something, I can probably make things happen the way I'd like, but sometimes, it doesn't work out that way. But most of all, I've learned that I can be happy in life even if every dream doesn't come true."

Once again, the two teens stared at her as though she'd just imparted words of wisdom that they needed to absorb.

"I'm impressed," Ryan said.

For a few seconds, she'd almost forgotten that he was there. Now, at the sound of his deep voice, her gaze shot back up to where he stood nearby.

"You've managed to succinctly tell the kids what I've been hoping to get them to understand for a long time. Thank you for that, Doctor Foster."

The sincerity in his voice moved through her, and she found it impossible to stay angry with him. Inclining her head toward the sand, hoping he'd take her silent invitation, she said, "I think it's fine if you call me Judith." Looking toward Cindy and Trevor as their dad sat down next to them, she added, "I knew your father a long time ago."

"He told us," Trevor said. "Dad and your brother were best friends."

Surprised he'd told them that, she nodded, but considering how he'd run hot and cold—mostly cold with her—uncertainty filled her as she forced her gaze to stay on the kids and not him. "Well, it was nice seeing you all again, but I think I'll head back home. I'm unused to being in the sun for so long."

"We've got sunscreen," Cindy said, already pulling out a bottle from her backpack.

"Oh, thanks, but I need to get back. See you around," she said, standing and brushing the sand off her backside. Unable to keep from sneaking a glance his way, it appeared his gaze was on her ass, but with his reflector sunglasses, she couldn't be sure. *I have been in the sun too long.*

She bent over her kayak to pull it into the water when Ryan's voice met her ears. "We're heading back now, too. We can all go together."

She stood and plopped her hands onto her hips, wanting to accuse him of having a split personality, but the kids' enthusiastic endorsement of their dad's suggestion kept her mouth shut.

Trevor was the first in the water, followed by her, with Cindy and Ryan right behind. With his strength, it only took a few seconds for him to paddle along next to her. Hating what she felt was surely going to be an awkward interlude, she should've known with Trevor around, the conversation wouldn't lag. For the next hour, she laughed at his stories and antics and had the chance to observe that while Cindy was much quieter than her brother, still waters ran deep. Even Ryan participated in the conversation, offering stories of him and Brad, peppering them with remembrances of her when she'd tag along.

By the time they neared her inlet, she hated to see them leave. She'd started work at the clinic as soon as she'd gotten hired and hadn't had a chance to make new friends outside the office.

"This is where I'll leave you," she called out. "My place is just down this inlet."

"No way!" Trevor shouted in return. "Our house is down Old Creek inlet, also."

The three kayaks continued paddling close to each other, passing lots with private docks, some with large motorboats and many with smaller rowboats, canoes, and kayaks.

She slowed down and inclined her head toward one of the smaller ones. "This is me."

"You live in that little cottage?" Cindy breathed, her words and expression holding awe. "It looks like it belongs in a fairy tale."

"Here?" Ryan asked.

Turning to look at him, he'd pulled his sunglasses off and stuck the arm in the neck of his T-shirt. He was staring through the trees at the back of her property toward the cottage.

"Yes. It's just a rental, but it's great because it backs to the water. And I'm at the end of the street with few houses, so there's lots of privacy." By then, she'd bumped her kayak to the edge of her pier, leaned over to climb up the short wooden ladder, and bent to pull her kayak up.

"Why are you living here?"

Straightening, she peered down at Ryan, her hands on her hips. "What do you mean, why am I living here?"

"Why aren't you in your family home?"

Her chin jerked back. "Um... my parents' old house? Where I grew up?"

He nodded, his gaze boring into hers.

"They sold it several years ago when they moved to North Carolina to live near Brad. He's married with kids, and they wanted to be close. I wasn't planning on returning, so they sold the house, packed up, and moved."

"Oh."

Lifting her brows, she stared at his one-word utterance, now wondering if Ryan had always been so hot and cold even in high school but she'd been too infatuated to notice. Cocking her head to the side, she tried to figure out what was going through his mind. "Is there a problem with living here?" She loved her cottage and hoped he wasn't going to inform her that a suspected serial killer lived nearby.

"Can we see it?"

Swinging her gaze down to Cindy, she smiled. "Of course—"

"No—" Ryan said at the same time.

Cindy looked over her shoulder at her dad, and he said, "Honey, we don't ask to see other people's houses."

Relief flooded Judith at his reason instead of it just

being him running hot and cold again. "No, it's fine. Come on, and I can get everyone something to drink."

Trevor, not giving his dad a chance to argue, climbed from his kayak and hauled it onto the pier, then turned to assist Cindy up the wooden ladder. Hiding her grin, Judith watched as Ryan followed suit.

Leading the way, they walked along the oyster shell path through the pine trees. The back of the cottage had two Adirondack chairs around the fire pit. "So far, I haven't had any visitors, so I haven't needed more chairs."

"We can always sit on the ground," Trevor said with ease.

Pressing her lips together again to keep her smile from slipping out, she pulled her keys from her pocket as they walked around to the front. Stepping onto the porch, she unlocked the front door. "Come on in. Make yourself at home, and I'll get us something to drink."

Cindy gasped as she looked around, wide-eyed. "It's so perfect," she whispered. Turning to Judith, she added, "I'm sorry I invited us over, but I have to tell you that I'm so glad to see your place. It looks like it belongs in a storybook."

She walked over and stood in front of the awestruck teen, then reached out and took both of Cindy's hands in her own. Leaning close, she smiled. "That's what I thought the first time I saw it, too. And as long as your dad says it's okay, you're welcome anytime, honey."

Without glancing at Ryan, not wanting to ruin the moment by seeing him possibly grumble, she turned and moved into the kitchen, staying busy as she pulled down glasses and grabbed a pitcher of lemonade from the refrigerator. Once the glasses were filled, she set them on the counter and turned to face the trio. Cindy still had an expression of wonder on her face. Trevor grinned widely. And finally, looking toward Ryan, she saw his warm gaze staring back at her, his lips curved upward ever so slightly. *What the hell is he smiling at?*

10

She probably thinks I'm crazy. As Ryan watched Judith move around her tiny kitchen to get his kids some lemonade, he realized in the past two hours she'd talked more with them, listened more to them, and connected more with them than their mom had in a long time. And as much as he'd tried to convince himself that he wasn't interested in her, the fact remained that Judith was as genuine now as his memories were of her in their younger years. And now, when she finally lifted her gaze to his, he was smiling.

She would have to be completely clueless to not have noticed his hot and cold reactions to her, and he had no doubt Judith was not clueless. *One more thing I need to apologize to her for.*

He'd noticed everything about her today. Her mass of curls was barely tamed into a ponytail, lots of tendrils waving about her face. Wearing a T-shirt with what looked to be a sports bra underneath did little to hide her curves. Her legs were toned, not very tanned, and starting to turn pink on top from the sun. Her face was devoid of makeup, and now that her sunglasses were off, her expressive eyes reminded him of long ago.

"So, um, do you guys want the grand tour?" she asked, her focus on the kids. "It will only take about one minute!"

"I'd love to," Cindy confessed, her eyes bright.

Walking from behind the kitchen counter, Judith stood next to them and waved her arm to the front. "This is obviously the living room. The unique fireplace is decorated with oyster shells."

Now, waving her hand toward the furniture, she laughed, "The apartment that I had when I was doing my residency was only an efficiency so I didn't have a lot of furniture. This was a perfect place since it didn't have a lot of room." Turning, she waved her arms like a game show hostess and said, "And here is my eat-in kitchen, just perfect for a table for two. Since it's only me, I get to choose my seat." She smiled as the kids laughed along with her.

She passed between them, and Ryan stepped to the side, allowing Cindy and Trevor to go first as he brought up the rear.

"There's only one bedroom, but it does have a nice bathroom. Across the hall are a pantry and laundry room. And then, out the back door, is the yard that you saw when we came from the inlet."

While Cindy was gushing over the quaint, storybook, fairytale qualities of the house, Trevor was shaking his head and muttering, "I'd be running into stuff all the time if I lived here, but at least it would be easy to clean."

Ryan chuckled, clapped his hand on the back of Trevor's neck, and steered him back into the hall after having peeked into her bedroom. His kids went through the back door and were walking around the yard when she stepped into the hall, coming to a halt when she saw him standing there.

She looked straight at him, her brow furrowed. "Why were you surprised that I live here? If you know anything weird about my neighbors, should I be worried?"

He hated that his reaction had caused concern and quickly shook his head. "No, no, nothing like that. We live not too far from here, and I've always found it pretty quiet."

"So..."

Sighing, he said, "Look, Judith, I feel like we've gotten off on the wrong foot ever since I first saw you the other day. And I'm completely willing to admit that most of the time, my foot has been in my mouth. I pride myself on that particular trait not being what I usually do, so I'd really like to make it up to you. And then, I could explain a little bit more as we have a chance to catch up."

She held his gaze for a moment, not saying anything. Finally, she scrunched her nose, giving her head a little shake. "I have to admit, you've been very confusing to me. When I suggested we get together to talk, you made it plain that wasn't something you wanted to do."

"I was an idiot."

Her chin jerked, and she blinked, then a barking laugh erupted. And her smile was brilliant. "Well, that might be the first thing we agree on!"

Grumbling, he tried to keep from smiling. "Smartass." Holding her gaze, he said, "So, how about it? Would you be willing to have dinner with me?"

She looked upward, her lips sucked in, obviously giving great thought to his question. His breath halted, finding he wanted her to acquiesce but was afraid he'd squandered his last chance.

She smiled softly, her gaze remaining on his face as she nodded. "Yeah, Ryan, I'd like that. I usually finish at the clinic each day with patients by four and am out of there by five if I hurry. You can let me know which day works best for you."

"How about tomorrow?"

She jerked again. "Oh, wow. Well, okay. I can't think of a reason not to."

"I normally don't work on Sundays, but I'm down an officer. I'm only on the schedule until two o'clock. That'll give me time to get home, shower, and come pick you up. How about five o'clock? The Seafood Shack and the Pub can get pretty crowded on the weekends. We can get away from everybody's eyes in Baytown and head to Easton. It's not far, and there's a quiet restaurant there."

"That sounds lovely. Thank you." She turned and glanced out to where the kids were in the backyard. "Um… do you want the kids to come too? They might like to hear some of the old stories."

"Tomorrow is their afternoon and evening with

their mom. But I'm not going to hide that I'm taking you out. They know that we knew each other in high school and that your brother was my best friend. They'll be glad that I'm doing something fun like catching up with an old acquaintance."

Nodding, she smiled. "Sounds good." Turning, she walked through the back door, and he followed.

He remembered how she was always so calm, so rational as a teenager. *Same as now.* She hadn't made him grovel for being an ass. Wasn't sulking. Wasn't looking for payback. She'd accepted his apology with grace. His breathing eased as he thought about going out with her. *Catch up on the past. Explain what's going on now. And maybe, just maybe, plan for a future date, as well.* With a grin, he stepped out into the sunshine where his kids were sitting in the grass and sat in one of the Adirondack chairs next to Judith.

"No. No excuses," Ryan growled into the phone.

"I know this is my day with the kids," Leslie said. "I didn't forget, but I'd made lunch plans with a friend. She's driving, and we're going to Virginia Beach. I don't know that she can bring me back in time for me to get the kids for dinner. I can get them next week, Ryan. It's no big deal. They probably have other things they'd rather do anyway."

"Leslie, we are not having this conversation. If you made lunch plans knowing that you were supposed to pick up the kids about one o'clock and spend the afternoon and evening with them, then you fucked up. Especially planning something in Virginia Beach. There are plenty of places to have lunch close by, so you've got no excuse. Just be at the house to pick the kids up when you said you were going to."

The familiar huff met his ears. "There's nothing nice right around here. And Marjorie was going to take me somewhere nice in Virginia Beach to celebrate me getting a job."

"A, you've only been working a few days, haven't gotten a paycheck yet, so spending money at a *nice* restaurant isn't the smart play. B, unless Marjorie's changed greatly, she likes to have quite a few martinis with lunch. Are you seriously going to let her drive you all the way from Virginia Beach, knowing that she's been drinking? And C, why don't you celebrate the new job with the kids? Cindy and Trevor care about you. They want to know how you're doing. You can tell them about this new job and... hell, Leslie, just talk to them!"

The next familiar response met his ears—silence for a moment. But the days were long gone when he'd give in just to not argue, so his silence met hers.

"Fine! I'll cancel with Marjorie," she said as though she were being asked to donate a kidney. "You always make me feel like I don't want to spend time with the kids. I do, but it's just that they've reached the age I don't know what to talk to them about. It always feels so forced and awkward."

It was on the tip of his tongue to tell her that her comment was bullshit considering that Trevor could enjoy talking to anybody about anything, and that included his mom. And while Cindy tended to clam up, that was only because she always felt like her mom didn't understand her. Sighing, he decided to drop the sarcastic comment and instead said, "The most important thing, Leslie, is that the kids will have a good time with their mom. It doesn't have to be over the top. It can be something simple for you to just have a chance to catch up with them and chat. Ask about school. Ask about their friends. And act like you care when they answer. You can do this. I know you can."

Her voice small, she agreed. "I know I can. It's just hard, Ryan. You were always so much better with them than I was."

Deciding he was done with the conversation, he said, "Okay, pick them up when they're expecting you, and have a good time."

Disconnecting, he shoved his phone into his pocket and squeezed his eyes shut, pushing her out of his mind. Instead, the image that flooded his thoughts was of wavy curls, blue eyes, and a bright smile—and the opportunity to spend time with Judith. *Now, let me just get through the rest of this shift.*

An hour later, fury rolled through him. "Christ!" Ryan bit out, surveying the damage. When the emergency call had come in about a skiff colliding with a motorboat and a child was involved, his pulse kicked into overdrive. Glad the incident was not too far out in the Bay, his team had arrived quickly with Coast Guard backup.

The sight that greeted them was enough to chill the heart of any parent, seeing the child unresponsive with blood running from a head injury. The skiff was mostly demolished, and the child had been pulled onto the motorboat by the occupants and the boy's uncle.

The uncle was crying, kneeling over the child, holding a compress onto the wound, but his emotional state was making his efforts ineffective. Jared moved him to the side and began immediate assessment and treatment while Beth readied the gurney to get the child to the harbor where the ambulance was ready and waiting.

Once the boy was on the backboard and strapped in, Callan and Jared transferred him to one of their boats, and with Jared taking charge, Beth steered them away.

Ryan checked the motorboat and skiff, noting the motorboat damage to be significant, as well. He moved the boat driver and uncle to his vessel, giving the Coast Guard the clearance and opportunity to attach lines to the motorboat for towing.

Nodding toward Andy, who was both interviewing and consoling the uncle, Ryan turned to the visibly shaken driver.

"Sir, we're going to need a statement from you, verbal now and then written when we get back to the station."

"I never saw them until they darted out from the inlet over there," he said, pointing to a small inlet. "I couldn't even see who was steering until I was almost upon them. I tried to turn away, but they were too close." He shot a gaze toward the boy's uncle and leaned closer to Ryan, lowering his voice. "It was the boy. It was the boy who was steering."

Lifting his brows, Ryan twisted to look at the man Andy was sitting with. "He wasn't at the wheel?"

"No, no. I shouted as soon as I saw them and was trying to turn, but it was clearly the boy at the back with the motor, and this man was sitting at the front."

"Okay, sir, when we arrive at the station, you'll be taken to a room where you'll be formally interviewed and write your description of what happened. I know the events of today are upsetting, but we'll need as many details and as much information as you can give us."

He waited until the man nodded and moved over to take a seat before Ryan walked over to Andy and the uncle. Before he had a chance to speak, Andy stepped closer to Ryan and, keeping his voice low, said, "Suspect BWI."

Fuckin' hell... drinking and letting a kid steer the boat. Stepping closer to the man, he leaned down and said, "Your nephew has arrived at the Baytown harbor and been transferred to an ambulance. The officer with him has contacted his parents, and they'll meet him at the hospital."

The man lifted his red-rimmed eyes up to Ryan and nodded. "I just can't believe we were hit like that. The man came out of nowhere and just hit us!"

"Were you on the Bay or coming from one of the inlets?"

"Um... we had just entered the... um... Bay," he said, his brow furrowing. "Yeah, yeah, just entering the Bay."

"And did you attempt to steer away from the boat as soon as you saw it?"

"Uh... yeah... of course... sure I did!"

"Sir, how much did you have to drink either before you were in the boat or during?"

"Drink?" The man's eyes widened, and he sat up a little straighter.

"Yes, sir, I can smell alcohol on your breath. Boating while intoxicated is against the law in Virginia, and we're going to administer a breathalyzer test."

He immediately began waving his hands back and forth, protesting. "No, no, Officer. I just had a little bit to drink, but I've done that before, and it's no problem."

"Done what before?" Ryan asked, knowing the man would soon give him the answer he was looking for.

"Drink while in a boat. That's not against the law. Lots of people drink when they're out on boats." By then, the man had stood, waving his arms around, and Andy moved closer to him.

"That's true that it's not against the law to consume alcohol when in a boat. But it does apply to anyone operating a watercraft, and since you were the person in charge of this skiff, then the law applies to you."

"No, no, David was steering, not me!"

"So, your eight-year-old nephew was steering the boat while you were sitting toward the front, not operating the boat at all, and drinking? It's important that we get this straight."

The man's brow furrowed as though attempting to noodle through the answer that would work out best for him, but finally, his shoulders slumped, and he shook his head. "David wanted to drive the boat. I didn't see any harm in that. Hell, the kid has grown up around boats."

"So, when you left the inlet, David was steering. And you were at the front?"

"Yeah, but it's not like I was just sitting up there doing nothing but drinking. I was looking around, helping him out."

Ryan crossed his arms over his chest, leveling his hard stare at the other man. "And you didn't see that your nephew had steered the boat right into the path of an oncoming motorboat?"

The man's face contorted as he plopped back down onto the seat, shaking his head. "This is all fucked up, man."

By that time, their craft had pulled into the Baytown harbor, and as they alighted from the boat, Andy placed the man in handcuffs, reading him his rights. Ryan placed a call to the dispatcher at the North Heron Sheriff's department to send a unit over while another VMP officer administered the breathalyzer, proving what Ryan already knew they'd find—a blood alcohol concentration level over the legal limit.

The uncle had just been driven away to the county jail by the deputy when a call came in from Callan. Connecting, he said, "Please tell me something good."

The silence from Callan caused Ryan's heart to plummet.

"I'm sorry to report that David died on the trip to the hospital and was pronounced DOA."

His legs gave out from under him, and Ryan fell backward into his chair, the air rushing from his lungs as his chest squeezed.

Callan continued, "His parents were there when we arrived."

As anger filled Ryan, he knew that Callan was affected more simply from having been with the child from the time they'd moved them onto the VMP vessel, then into the ambulance, and to the hospital. "Fuckin' hell, Callan, I'm sorry. Shit."

Callan cleared his throat, and a heavy sigh met Ryan's ear. Finally, Callan said, "Did you find out what happened?"

"It turns out David was steering the skiff while his uncle was sitting in the front drinking—"

"Goddammit!" Callan growled.

"I know, man, I know." They were silent for a moment before Ryan added, "Get back here, write up what you can, then cut out of here and go home. Hug your wife."

"Sophie's pregnant. I hadn't even told anyone. I don't even have a baby yet, Ryan, but I can't imagine losing my child."

Ryan squeezed his eyes closed, his heart once again aching. "I hear you, Callan. I've got two, and the mere idea guts me. I pray that I never have to experience what David's parents are going through. Maybe the timing seems fucked, but congratulations, man."

Disconnecting, he sat for a few more minutes, then glanced at the time. He was almost off the clock and then would head home to shower. For the past twenty-four hours, at least until the boating accident, his mind had been filled with Judith and how much he was looking forward to taking her out tonight. Now,

Callan's news about David made him wonder what kind of company he would be. *Jesus, I've been a dick to Judith several times already and really wanted a chance to be with her.*

Heaving another sigh, he dialed her number. She answered with such enthusiasm, he dropped his chin and pinched the bridge of his nose with his thumb and forefinger, willing the burgeoning headache to abate. "Judith, I think I'm going to have to take a rain check."

"Ryan, what's wrong? Are you okay? You sound terrible."

Her voice had immediately softened, concern radiating through her words. Shaking his head, he couldn't remember Leslie ever responding to him having a difficult day by asking how he was. Not one to beat around the bush, he blurted, "Boating accident. An eight-year-old little boy was killed."

"Oh, my God! I can't imagine how horrible for the family. Oh, God, eight years old... still such a baby." She was silent for a few seconds, then added, "What can I do?"

Stunned silent for a few seconds, he tried to wrap his mind around her concerned words, a strange feeling moving through him. Lifting his free hand to his chest, he massaged the area over his heart that had ached but now was easing. When he had dialed, he'd intended to break their dinner date, but hearing her soft voice, he desperately wanted to see her. "I'm not sure that tonight is a good night for dinner. I wanted it to be nice, but..."

"I understand, believe me. Whenever I've lost a patient, it's hard. Ryan, if you need to be alone, I completely understand. But if you'd like company, then why don't you come over to my place? I've got plenty of food, wine, and we can keep each other company. We don't have to get into anything heavy, but we can still catch up or just sit quietly, and you won't have to be alone."

His heart leaped at the idea that he could see her, stunned that she adapted so quickly to a change in plans. "Are you sure? Because I still want to take you out to dinner sometime."

"It's not the place where you gather that's important. It's the people that you're with. So, come over any time. I'll be here for you."

Her words scored through him, followed by a warmth that soothed the edges of his tumultuous day. He thought of Callan arriving home to Sophie, who would do what Ryan had only dreamed about. And just the thought of seeing Judith caused his lips to curve upward.

11

Judith stood by the window, waiting for Ryan to appear. As soon as his SUV rumbled along the oyster shell drive leading to her house, she flung open the front door and stepped out onto the porch, her hand lifted in a wave. His sunglasses kept her from seeing his eyes, but there was no mistaking his smile. She bounced slightly on her toes as he alighted from behind the wheel and walked straight to her, shoving his glasses into his front pocket.

She searched his face, hoping to ascertain his state of mind. As he stepped onto the porch, she placed her hand on his arm, still holding his gaze. "How are you? I've been so worried about you since you called."

He didn't hesitate in placing his hand over hers, giving a little squeeze. "I'm glad it doesn't often happen in my job, but you can't be in law enforcement and not face death."

"And for it to be a child," she said, nodding. "I understand."

"In your line of work, I'm sure you do. And for that, Judith, I'm really sorry."

She jerked her head toward the door. "Come on in. I had no idea what you would feel like eating or drinking but decided to go with something comforting. I hope it's okay."

He reached around her and held open the screen door, allowing her to duck under his arm.

"Considering that I expected to take you to dinner and ended up here with you offering me food, believe me, I'd eat anything. But especially if it's comforting, I'm on board." They had just stepped inside when he groaned, "Oh, my God! Bacon!"

She laughed and looked over her shoulder as she rounded the counter in the kitchen, waving her hands in front of her. "I know it's been many years, but I still remember how you liked to come over when my mom did breakfast food for dinner. I've got scrambled eggs, hash brown potatoes, bacon, sausage, biscuits, grits, orange juice, coffee, and fruit." She held her breath as his gaze moved over the counter, breathing a sigh of relief that she'd made the right choice when his smile widened and his shoulders relaxed as though the weight of the world had just lifted.

"Grab a plate and get whatever you want. I'll pour the juice and coffee."

Soon, they were settled at her small table and both dug in. She'd skipped lunch in anticipation of their dinner and had a feeling he probably hadn't eaten either. She filled him in on Brad and her parents, giving him the quick rundown on their lives in North Carolina.

It didn't take long for their forks to scrape the bottom of the plates, both leaning back in their seats, sighs of satisfaction leaving their lips at the same time. She met his eyes, and they both started laughing.

"I suppose I should've eaten daintily, but in medical school and my residency, I often missed meals and ate on the run. It's embarrassing, but I've learned to eat heartily whenever I can," she confessed.

"Don't apologize on my account," he said. "The food was perfect. A perfect choice and perfectly cooked. Considering I was shoveling it in, I would've felt weird if you had eaten daintily."

They stood and took the plates to the sink, working side-by-side as they cleaned the dishes and put the extra food away. Pouring fresh cups of coffee, she nodded toward the living room. "We can sit outside, or we can sit in there. Wherever you think you'll be comfortable, Ryan, is fine with me."

"I think I'd like to sit in here if you don't mind," he said, leading the way into her living room. He hesitated once they were there, and she settled on one end of the sofa, giving him the chance to claim the comfy chair. When he sat on the other end of the sofa, she was surprised considering it wasn't very large, and that left a small space between them. Wanting to give her full attention to him, she twisted, tucked her foot up under her booty, and faced him.

While he didn't tuck his feet up under him, he twisted his body to angle toward her, as well. She had soft music playing in the background, not romantic but calming. Wanting to take pressure off him, she said, "I know that originally you said you wanted to catch up and explain some things, but you've had a really rough day. We don't have to talk about anything if you don't want to. Or, if you want to talk about what happened today, I'm a good listener."

"You always were."

Her brow crinkled in confusion. "I always was what?"

"A good listener." She remained quiet, and he continued. "It was probably one of the reasons that Brad and I never minded you hanging around. You didn't talk on and on about nonsense or shit we didn't care about. You watched, you listened, and if you had something important to say, you did. I see that particular trait is still with you."

"I guess it is. I have to listen a lot as a doctor, and it always came naturally to me."

They sipped their coffee for several minutes, the calming music playing in the background, neither speaking.

"I don't regret marrying Leslie."

She jerked slightly, then quickly blanked her expression, hoping she covered her surprise at his opening statement. Having no idea where he was going with this thought, she simply waited as he stared toward the fireplace.

Suddenly, he swung his gaze back to hers and repeated, "I don't regret marrying Leslie... for only one reason. I got

Trevor and Cindy. Fatherhood didn't happen the way I always thought it would nor with the person I thought I'd be with, but it came nonetheless, and I wouldn't trade one moment of being their father for anything."

Her heart warmed at his words, her smile genuine. "I know I've only met them a few times, but they seem wonderful. And while I don't know Leslie, I can only imagine that having you as their father is one of the biggest reasons they're as wonderful as they are."

"Thank you for saying that. God knows I'm not perfect by a long shot, but I'd like to think that I'm a good dad."

She took another sip and waited. Now that he'd begun talking, she hoped he'd keep going. She was curious. Curious about the man she'd loved as a boy. Curious about the man he'd become. But she knew it was his story to tell and wanted him to tell her whatever he was comfortable divulging. He didn't make her wait long.

"The only reason Leslie and I got married was because she was pregnant. I had already received orders that I'd be shipping out for six months. She'd been complaining, wanting me to get out of the Navy, not understanding that I had a commitment. By then, I realized our teenage relationship was hardly an adult, long-term, meant-for-marriage, happily ever after. As I was getting ready to break up, she informed me she was pregnant. I felt a ton of different emotions, but the bottom line was I had a responsibility. She wanted a big wedding, but I refused, something her parents probably never forgave me for. We had a small wedding, and two weeks later, I shipped out."

"I can imagine that was hard for both of you."

He nodded and admitted, "I'm not saying it was easy on either of us, but she lived with her parents. By the time I got back and we moved into a small apartment near the naval base, I discovered how much money she'd been spending. Not just things for the baby but things for her. And when I tried to tell her how much money I actually made, she'd cry and say that I wasn't providing enough."

Judith's cup halted on the way to her lips, and she blinked. "You weren't providing enough? Was she working during this time?"

Shaking his head, he admitted, "No. She didn't want to go to college because she said it was pointless for someone who was going to be a housewife. She was living with her parents, and whether or not she had a job didn't affect me since we were just dating. But I already saw the handwriting on the wall. I tried to encourage her to find even a part-time job to help out with our bills, but she didn't want to work, especially being pregnant. That would've been fine if we were living within our means, but she spent money as though she had no concept of balancing a checkbook."

"I'm so sorry about that, Ryan. I can't imagine the stress that put on you."

He shrugged and sighed. "I was just back from the tour and tried to make things easier on her. We barely had time for just us before Trevor came. Gotta tell you, though, holding him made me forget all the concerns I had about her. It was as though everything that was wrong with the marriage was right with him. So, I pushed all the negative to the side and did what I could to make things better."

"But it takes two people working together, both sacrificing, both compromising to make a marriage work," she said softly, knowing she was telling him something he already knew.

He nodded slowly and didn't speak for another moment. Finally, he said, "She got pregnant again quickly. I thought she was on the pill, but she later told me that she'd wanted another baby. She loved Trevor when he was a tiny baby. Or rather, she loved dressing him up, taking him out, having people fawn over her. But when he had trouble sleeping, it was me that rocked him. When he was teething, it was me that soothed him. She always said that it was hard on her nerves to deal with him." Shrugging, he said, "I just accepted that. Looking back, I can see she got pregnant again because she simply wanted another newborn."

Eyes wide, Judith was unable to keep the snort of surprise from slipping out. "Was that her plan for motherhood? Just keep having newborns?"

Chuckling, he admitted, "I have no idea." Sighing, he continued. "Listen, I didn't come over here to give you the whole rundown of my marriage. Suffice it to say, things did not get better. I finally gave in to getting out of the Navy and taking a job with the VMP here on the Eastern Shore so she could be close to her family. That was fine because it gave me a chance to be back here with my family, too. I moved up in rank, something that seemed to make her happy."

"And were you happy?"

His gaze stayed pinned on her but he was silent as he slowly shook his head. Finally, as though the words were pulled from him, he said, "I swear, Judith, I think you're the only person outside of my family who's ever asked me that."

His comment was bad enough, but it was the guttural tone of his words that caused her heart to ache. "And the answer?"

"I've got a great job. Eventually became captain. Love my kids. They're the highlight of my life. But other than my job and my kids, no, I wasn't happy." He scrubbed his hand over his face, a heavy sigh leaving his lips. "I hadn't planned on a divorce. As far as I was concerned, Leslie was simply Leslie, and I just had to put up with her and make sure the kids were okay. But things got worse. She'd made friends with a group of women from the country club who must've felt sorry for her for being married to a man who didn't have the money or the inclination to join. She'd be at lunch or playing tennis and forget to pick the kids up from school. It got to where the teachers just called me if they needed something. She never helped the kids with homework. Never checked to see if the homework was done. Never bothered signing their school notes. They always bought school lunches because she didn't take the time to pack them what they would've preferred eating but then forgot to give them lunch money. I had to take away all her credit cards, and then she turned around and opened another one. I sat down with the checkbook each month and couldn't believe the shit she was buying and hiding. Christ, I was working a demanding full-time job, taking care of the kids, taking care of the house, and was not getting a break from the one person who was supposed to have my back."

He sighed heavily again, and she asked, "What was the breaking point?"

"I had a two-day, out-on-the-water training to attend. It was planned for, and I made sure Leslie and the kids had everything they needed. Trevor was eleven, and Cindy was nine or so. I got home at the end of the second day and found out that the kids had missed both days of school because Leslie couldn't manage to get them ready and out the door in time, they missed the bus, and she didn't take them. It's not like they were left alone because she was there. But they watched TV, ordered takeout, played games while she talked on the phone to her friends. When I got home, I blew my stack. She just didn't get it. She kept saying that I was always trying to get her to spend more time with the kids, and when she finally did it, I was angry. She couldn't understand, saying that I was always telling her to spend more time with the kids and she thought she'd fulfilled that by not taking them to school."

"So, you were done." She made the statement, knowing there was no reason to ask the question. His story had made that plain.

Nodding, he confirmed. "I was done. I filed for divorce, and she wasn't that upset about it. She said she'd known we hadn't felt like a couple in a long time.

She didn't fight me on custody, but she wasn't happy when my lawyer presented all the evidence of her spending over the years, and so she got very little in alimony, and it's about to run out." He drained the last of his coffee and set the empty mug on the coffee table. Leaning forward, he clasped his hands together, resting his forearms on his knees. Twisting his head to look at her, he continued. "I talked a lot to the kids about it, but they assured me that they were happy with me. They know their mom loves them but get frustrated with her, as well. In many ways, it was always just the three of us, so now, it still is. We just don't have the contentious feeling in the house that we used to."

"I find it hard to know what to say, Ryan," she admitted. "I want to say that I'm so sorry for everything you and the kids had to go through. And I'm sorry that Leslie couldn't be the woman you deserve."

He snorted and shook his head. "I don't know about what I deserve, but I sure as hell know that Cindy and Trevor deserved better."

She leaned forward and placed her hand on his arm, holding his gaze. "I always thought a good guy like you deserved the best."

They stared, not speaking for a long moment. Finally, when she wasn't sure if he was going to speak more, he said, "I sure as fuck didn't mean to come over here and unload all this on you. I guess I just wanted you to understand why I showed up the way I did to the clinic. The first night with Trevor, I'd just gotten an important text from work on top of having to deal with some of Leslie's shit when you walked into the room.

So, you got a bad impression of me as a dad being disinterested. Then, I was in a panic when Trevor got hold of me about Cindy and found out how Leslie didn't help matters, and I took my bad mood out on you. That didn't make sense considering I just realized who you were and had always remembered you fondly. Acting like an ass just made me more of one. Anyway, I know that was strike two."

She had no problem understanding his reasons now that she was privy to how difficult Leslie made things for him and the kids. Her top teeth landed on her bottom lip, and she scrunched her nose slightly.

His gaze dropped to her mouth before lifting, and his lips curved. "I can tell you want to ask a question." Laughing, he added, "It's weird since we haven't been around each other in many years, and yet I can still look at your face and recognize expressions."

She laughed, as well, and rolled her eyes. "Well, you certainly explained the past and apologized for the times from the clinic. But what about the comment that we wouldn't have anything in common to talk about? I really didn't understand that."

He winced, and she wanted to smooth the wrinkle in his brow, tell him it didn't matter what he meant, and let him know she was just glad that he was sitting with her. But before she had a chance, he shifted on the sofa to face her more fully, his hand reaching out to take hers.

12

Ryan stared into Judith's eyes, stunned that she'd listened to his long-ass tale, especially bizarre considering he hadn't ever told anyone that much about his life. He'd never told his parents everything he'd just shared, and he was close to them.

Sure, his coworkers and family knew of Leslie's foibles as his marriage disintegrated, all offering encouragement, but he'd never just sat with anyone and blurted out the last fifteen years of his life to anyone. And yet, Judith had listened, understood, and didn't make him feel as though he hadn't done enough. But then, he remembered that about her... she'd always looked at him as though he could do no wrong when they were younger. *Christ, those days were so long ago.*

Now, he had one more thing to explain and apologize for, and then he hoped they could stop focusing on him and turn their attention to her. "To be honest, Judith, this is embarrassing. I consider myself to be a secure man, comfortable with who I am and what I am in life. As stupid as this sounds, it's occasionally hard to get past the many complaints and comments Leslie voiced over the years about me not providing enough. Somehow, when I found out you were a doctor, I fucked up when I made dumbass assumptions. You were looking at earrings that I wondered if I could afford to get for Cindy when she has her next birthday. I figured you'd probably moved into the big family home and had a high standard of living. I have no idea why I did that with you considering I've got friends from all walks of life. But that's on me. I fucked up, and I'm sorry. It wouldn't matter if you were rolling in money or buried under student loans. First of all, it's your business, and second of all, I wouldn't care. You've got a job. You're working. You're out busting your ass every day. So what you earn and what you spend it on is completely up to you, and I was a dick for letting my insecurity jump up and bite us in the ass."

She burst out laughing, and he stared, surprised, but also thought how beautiful she was when she laughed. When she was younger, her laughter was soft, much like Cindy's. But now, this mirth seemed to come from deep inside, and he couldn't help but grin in return.

"I was just going to say that you give the best explanations and the most amazing apologies of anyone I've ever heard!"

Still chuckling, he shook his head. "I was just thinking that I haven't talked this much to anyone in… well, ever. You make it easy to confide in you."

Her gaze dropped to where his hand was holding hers, and when she lifted her head, her eyes were twinkling. The desire to lean closer and see if her lips tasted as good as they looked ran through him and his fingers spasmed on hers. "Um... let's talk about you now," he blurted, refusing to take advantage of their proximity to each other on her small sofa. A flash moved through her eyes, replacing the twinkle, and he hated not being able to read her.

Her shoulders lifted in a small shrug. "There's not much to tell. I went to college, got into medical school, internships and residencies... and here I am."

"Okay, what's the deal?" he asked, shaking his head. "Really?"

She jerked slightly. "What do you mean?"

"I give you long dissertations about the last fifteen years, and you managed to squeeze all of the years into one sentence? That's hardly fair!"

"Oh, I didn't know you wanted all my deep dark secrets!" she laughed. "Honestly, Ryan, I don't have any. As you know, Brad got married and moved to North Carolina. My parents moved down there several years ago. I didn't have any plans of coming back to Baytown, but I was tired of living in a big city and preferred small-town medicine. When the job at the Baytown Family Clinic was advertised, at first, I couldn't believe that I was considering it."

"Why did you?"

She looked down at their hands still clasped together and smiled. "As soon as I drove into town, it felt like home. I interviewed with Doctor Preston and loved the clinic. Of all the places I've lived, none of them felt like they were right. But here? I just knew."

"And... a special guy? Someone that'll be joining you here?" He didn't bother apologizing for fishing for information. He was interested and didn't mind her knowing.

"No. No special guy."

"Was there one at one time?"

She cocked her head to the side, her brow crinkled. "Are you asking if I've ever been involved with someone?"

"Yeah, I am," he said firmly.

Licking her lips, she slowly shook her head. "No. Never married. Never engaged. Not currently dating anyone. There wasn't a lot of time while I was focused on my studies. My last long-term relationship was over three years ago, and it had only lasted six months."

"Why?"

She blinked several times as though not under-standing his question. "Um... why?"

"Yeah. Why is someone as kind and beautiful as you not snatched up by a man who realizes how lucky he'd be?"

A little snort slipped out, and she tried to pull her hand back, but he held firm. Huffing, she said, "You knew me a long time ago, Ryan. I've changed very little. I'd still rather have my nose in a book than go clubbing."

"I did know you a long time ago and thought you were sweet and pretty back then, as well. But you're wrong. The woman I see in front of me is not the same shy girl from days gone by."

The breath left her lungs, sending a warm puff across his face. "I grew up."

He remained silent, hoping she'd offer what he'd begun to crave in her presence: more of her.

"I focused on becoming a doctor. I made decisions that were best for me and my goals. I gave up on childish dreams and decided that I had to make my own way without waiting for the handsome hero on the white horse to carry me off to his castle."

"Who was *the* hero?"

Her fingers twitched in his hands. "What?"

"You said *the* hero, not just *a* hero," he prodded.

"I… didn't mean—"

"Who, Judith? Who was *the* hero you stopped waiting for?" He knew it was dangerous to keep pushing, the fear of her shutting down almost causing him to stop. But he remembered all the times that she'd trail after him and Brad, the times that she'd manage to sit next to him when he had dinner with her family, and times that he'd greet her at her locker between classes where her smile always made him happy. And he remembered another event—when he knew she wasn't too young for him to notice her, but life had intervened in a way that kept him from acting on the feelings that had assaulted him that night. "Who?"

She pressed her lips together and cut her eyes away, but he squeezed her fingers gently, drawing her gaze back to him. "The…" She wheezed slightly, then she cleared her throat and began again. "The hero of my childhood was you, Ryan. But the night of my senior prom is when I realized it was time to put that childish dream away." She shrugged her shoulders as though her words didn't carry much weight. "So, I did. I grew up."

Her voice attempted nonchalance, but he felt her words were anything but casual. They were pulled from deep inside of her and resonated deep within him.

Swallowing deeply, he leaned forward ever so slightly. "I remember that night." Her wide eyes stayed pinned on him, and he continued. "I remember staring at you, no longer thinking of you as a child but knowing there was nothing I could do about what I felt. I remember regret punching me in the gut but thought maybe it was just me. And then Brad blurted out about me and Leslie, and I saw the look on your face before you turned and ran into the house. Cold reality slammed into me with the knowledge that maybe you'd felt something, too, but my life course was now on a different trajectory. I got on the ship, and you went to college, and I pushed all thoughts away other than what I needed to do."

No words passed between them, but the air thickened with emotion. His gaze remained firmly on hers, entranced as her pupils widened. *With lust?* Uncertain if he was the only one longing to kiss, he leaned forward slightly then halted, giving her the decision.

Her movements mirrored his, only halting when their lips were a breath away. It took every ounce of willpower to remain perfectly still, refusing to give in to the overwhelming urges, handing all control over to her. What may have only been a few seconds stretched into eternity. Then, with a little sigh that puffed her sweet breath over his face, she erased the space between them, her lips meeting his.

For a moment, he continued to remain still even though the simple touch had lust racing through every nerve of his body, firing his blood, swelling his cock. Focusing on the moment, he reveled in the feel of her soft lips as she angled her head and moved her mouth over his. Finally, her tongue darted out and traced around his lips, and his control snapped like a rubber band pulled too tight.

His hands left hers only to slide up and cup her face. The petal-soft skin underneath his palms had him wonder what the rest of her body would feel like. Then, like a flame to tinder, the kiss took on a life force all its own. Tongues tangled as he plunged into her mouth, exploring her warmth, memorizing her taste. The velvet softness as her tongue dragged over his had him swell even more, and he was forced to drop one hand to his crotch to try to adjust his cock.

Needing more room, he leaned forward, pressing her back while wrapping his arms around her and rolling. Not wanting to bury her under his weight, he made sure he was mostly to the side with one thigh over her legs and one arm under her head. Their lips had barely separated, and he quickly sealed his mouth over hers again. This advantageous position not only allowed him to press his hips against hers but it freed up one hand to roam.

As his fingers moved slowly from her jaw down her body, his thumb skimmed the side of her breasts, halting just underneath. For a second, he hesitated, uncertain, but she moaned into his mouth and pressed her body toward his and all doubt fled. He gently cupped her breast, his palm filled with the weight, the pebble of her nipple felt through the silky cups of her bra.

She groaned again, and this time her hips undulated, the pressure against his cock creating a nirvana he never thought possible fully clothed. His hand continued its downward path, slipping underneath her shirt, his fingertips skimming her skin that he found to be just as soft as her face. She jerked slightly, and he grinned as he mumbled against her lips, "Ticklish." Moving upward, he dragged the material along as he once again palmed her breasts, this time the silky bra creating the only barrier.

Gently pulling the cup down, his thumb swept over her nipple, eliciting more groans from deep inside her. His mouth remained sealed over hers, and he swallowed each groan, feeling them in his dick. Barely aware that her fingers were digging into his shoulder, he was now completely focused on her hand as it traveled down to his waist, to his hip, and slid between them, squeezing the length of him.

At that moment, he had no idea where the evening was going to end, but his cock was aching to bury itself deep inside her body. He jerked at that thought. *Jesus, this is Judith! Not some bar pickup to fulfill a physical need.* As much as he hated to admit it, he needed to stop. *She deserves so much more than what I can offer.*

She pulled back, her gaze moving between his eyes, searching. "What happened, Ryan? Where'd you go?"

He wanted to deny that anything had pulled him out of the moment, but the reality was he couldn't lie to her. Maybe to himself but not her. "When I came over tonight, I didn't expect this." She winced, and he quickly amended, "I didn't expect this, but I very much want it."

She hesitated, then prodded, "But…"

"You deserve so much more."

She blinked, her chin pulling back slightly. "Seriously? That's what you're giving me? That's why you fell into your head?" Her hand moved to his chest where she started to push away.

He held tight, wanting her to understand. "It's just that I'm not in a place to give you what you should have."

She shrugged again, this time managing to sit up halfway, her glare pinpointed on him. She may have thought she was intimidating, but the expression only made him want her more. "I'm not eighteen years old anymore! I'm not looking for *the* hero of my teenage dreams. Hell, I'm not even looking for *a* hero. I don't need a man to take care of me. I'm almost thirty-four years old, a professional woman with a demanding career. I'm not trying to get into your pants to trap you or tie you to me. I'm not demanding the white picket fence. And I assure you that I'm not lost in some adolescent fantasy of thinking sex with you will make all my dreams come true! And furthermore—umph," she grunted as he pulled her back down to him.

"Got it, babe," he said, his lips landing on hers again.

Her laying it out for him was the sexiest thing he'd ever heard in his life. With her kiss-swollen lips, wild curls in disarray, flushed face, and flashing eyes, he'd nearly come in his pants. And the fact that she'd put him in his place, reminding him that she wasn't asking for more than he could give, was the icing on the cake. He knew it was selfish as fuck, but to think he could have this slice of happiness that he never thought he'd experience and that she was one hundred percent on board, he wanted to take from her and give to her whatever he could.

This time, it wasn't just his hand that was roaming. Her hand slipped under the bottom of his shirt, her fingers tracing along the muscles of his back before curving around to drag along the ridges of his abs. Their arms crisscrossed as his fingers were doing the same on her body, trailing a path upward and over her breasts. Pushing the material up as he went, he kissed his way down her jaw, moving past the cotton now shoved to her upper chest, and latched on to her nipple through the silky cup of her bra.

She groaned and the sound shot straight through him. The scrap of material, which a few seconds ago had felt so good on his mouth, was now in his way. He tugged the cups down, exposing her breasts, taking only a few seconds to admire her perfect form, circling her nipple with his forefinger before placing his lips on her soft skin, sucking deeply. Her hips began undulating again, pressing against his aching cock. Fumbling worse than a teenager, he managed to get her bra unsnapped before rolling her to her back, now moving between both breasts as her bra landed on the coffee table.

Her hands alternated between clutching at his biceps and grabbing his shirt, trying to push it upward. He shifted up to his knees just long enough to reach behind his back, snag the material, and drag it over his head, tossing it to the side. Rolling over on top of her again, they were now naked chest to chest, and the feel of her full breasts pressed against his skin had his senses spiraling out of control.

The kisses flamed hot as their tongues skated along each other's, heads twisting and turning, noses bumping. He felt sure he'd had more finesse as a teenager but seemed incapable of caring about anything other than her taste and feel. And with her fingernails digging into the skin on his back, she must have felt the same. He couldn't remember the last time he'd been so intoxicated by a kiss. Once divorced, casual hookups had been few and far between, and kissing was not anything he wanted to engage in. Kissing had always implied intimacy, something his couple of hookups didn't include. And it seemed like years before the divorce since he and Leslie had really kissed.

But now, he knew that if he and Judith did nothing more than just what they were doing at the moment, he'd walk away a satisfied man. Then her hands slid down to his ass, squeezing as her legs lifted to circle his hips. His jean-clad cock was nestled against her core as she pressed upward.

She pushed him back slightly to suck in a ragged breath, and he looked down to see if she wanted to stop, knowing it would test the last thought he'd just had. Instead, she looked up, and said, "Too many clothes!"

Grinning as he shifted to his knees, hooking his hands into the top of her yoga pants and sliding them down over her hips, he couldn't wait to get her naked. *Okay, I'd be satisfied no matter what, but sliding into home base with Judith would be perfect.*

13

As Ryan peeled off the rest of her clothes, Judith stared up at the most gorgeous man she'd ever known in her life. She'd held that opinion when she'd first seen him over twenty years earlier, and the statement was still true today.

His gaze raked down her entire body, and she wiggled in anticipation, her core screaming for friction, her soul shaking with need. She reached up and managed to get his buckle undone as he toed off his boots. Without undressing more, he bent and scooped her off the sofa, eliciting a squeal of surprise. He stalked to her bedroom, and when she blinked up at him in question, he held her gaze.

Laying her gently on the bed, he said, "Our first time isn't going to be on your sofa. I might not give you everything you deserve, but you'll be comfortable in your bed."

At that moment, she fell a little more in love with Ryan Coates. To be honest, she'd never really fallen out of love with him. She'd walked away when she was eighteen years old, knowing that his life was with another woman. She'd managed to put him in the emotional box that she'd tucked away into the corner of her heart. He wasn't hers. He'd never been hers. And it had been time to give up youthful dreams. And if he hadn't been divorced when they'd met again, he would've stayed in that little decorative box, locked away.

Now, as he loomed over her, his gaze gliding from her face down to her core where her legs lay shamelessly open, she watched as a slow smile curved his lips. And for an instant, she wondered if she was about to make a colossal mistake. The kind of miscalculation that stayed with you so that when you lay on your deathbed it was one of your biggest regrets. He'd made it plain that he couldn't give her more than what they were doing right now. *Can I be happy with that? Stolen kisses, furtive glances, fuck buddies?* She knew he'd stop if she asked, but unbidden, her lips curled into a smile, also. *Not having tonight with him would be my biggest regret ever.*

Lifting her hands, she thought he'd climb onto the bed with her, but he instead dropped to his knees, settling her thighs over his shoulders. Before she could blink, he dove in as a man starved. It took a second for her brain to catch up to what she was feeling between her legs, then she gasped, flinging her head back to the mattress. *Holy moly, what that man can do with his mouth!*

He licked and sucked, tonguing her clit as he inserted a finger deep inside. A pulsating need grew deep within, and all thoughts, reason, concerns, and ideas flew out of her mind. He worked her sex until she considered singing hallelujah, only stopping at the realization that her singing might kill the mood. The coil tightened inside as though wound by a key, each lick and suck from him bringing her closer to the edge. Inserting another finger, he hit the exact spot that made her cry out, her fingers digging into his scalp as her entire body shivered when the coils sprung loose.

Wondering if she'd lost consciousness for a few seconds, she slowly became aware of his continuing to lick before he kissed over her mound, up her ticklish belly, and nuzzled her sensitive breasts before reaching her mouth. He plunged his tongue in, allowing her to taste her essence. Still struggling to draw in oxygen, she was glad he kept the kiss light, desperately needing to breathe but uncertain if she cared. *Dying in Ryan's arms... what a way to go.*

She felt the mattress dip, and her eyes flew open to see him shift to a stand. His gaze held hers and a cold panic begin to sliver through her veins, pushing out the warmth at the thought that he was leaving. But his hands went to his zipper, and he quickly shucked his jeans and boxers down. Bending, he pulled off his socks and snagged a condom from his wallet, rolling it on.

The warmth filled her again, chasing out the cold doubt. Lifting her hands, she wiggled her fingers, beckoning him to her. Her gaze traveled to his impressive cock, her smile widening.

"Damn, babe, you're good for my ego," he growled,

crawling onto the bed, nestling his cock at the apex of her thighs again.

"If you haven't had others worship your dick, then I can't say much for the women you've been hanging out with."

He barked out a laugh as he held his chest off hers with his forearms planted on either side of her, his hands cupping her face. Kissing her lightly, he shook his head. "For the record, there haven't been that many. It's a small town, and I'm usually at work or with my kids, and that's fine with me. Only had a couple of out-of-town hookups, nothing more than physical and sure as hell nothing like this."

His words speared through her, causing the warmth from earlier to flame into an inferno. "I really need you inside me now," she said, not embarrassed with the need that filled her voice.

Grinning again, he nodded slowly. "Whatever the lady wants, the lady'll get." His hips settled between her thighs, the tip of his cock nudging her entrance.

She lifted her feet and wrapped her legs around his hips, her ankles digging in slightly, urging him on. He entered her gently, easing in until fully seated. She wanted him to hurry. She wanted him to go slow. She wanted it hard and fast and also to drag it out to make it last. As he began to move, thrusting his hips, more force with each one, she decided however he gave it to her was the perfect way. For a moment, time ceased to matter as their bodies danced to the rhythm of lovers down through the ages.

"Christ, you're tight. Tight, slick, fuckin' heaven," he ground out, his breath hot against the side of her face.

Her breasts bounced in rhythm until he lowered himself, their bodies now fully flush together. She closed her eyes and gave over to the sensations assaulting her, both praying this was not going to be the only time they were together but knowing she now had new memories to go into her heart's little box in case it was. Soon, all thoughts left her as she gave over to the electricity shooting through her nerves, the heat of her blood racing through her veins, and the feel of his cock dragging against her inner muscles. Once again, the coil tightened, finally springing loose as she clung to him, crying out his name.

He continued to thrust, and she accepted his body with welcome until finally, he shuddered as he roared through his own release. He continued to pump until he slowly pulled from her, laying to the side, tucking her in close. She opened her eyes and stared into his, unable to read whatever emotion he was feeling but knowing she'd never be the same. You can't experience receiving the gift that you wanted for much of your life and walk away unchanged. But right now, at this moment, she simply wanted to enjoy the gift in her arms.

Lifting her hand, she wiped his brow, dragging her fingers down his face, feeling the rough scruff where he usually shaved, memorizing everything her senses were discovering.

He lowered his face, kissing her lightly, one arm tucked under her head and the other hand clutching her face. He finally dragged his lips from hers and sighed. "I'll be right back. Gotta deal with the condom."

She watched as he walked away, disappearing through her bathroom door. A moment later, she heard the flush, water running in the sink, and another small sliver of fear moved through her at what would greet her when he walked out. *Casual indifference? A cocky smile, ready to go again? Blowing out a comment about how great it was while he got dressed to leave?*

Before she had a chance to wonder anymore, he walked toward her and all thoughts left her other than what a beautiful man he was. Not just physically but in every way. He worked to save and protect and loved his job. His kids were the light of his life, and anyone who knew him understood that. To just call him a friend was an honor.

She slid off the bed, ready to get dressed, when he reached around her and jerked the covers down. "The kids are with their mom tonight. She'll get them to school tomorrow."

She glanced behind her, the covers pulled back making it look like he wanted to crawl in. Jerking back to stare at him, she cocked her head to the side. "Are you sure she will?"

Snorting, he nodded. "The kids will set their own alarms and know that if she's not up, they'll get her up. So, yeah, they'll make it to school on time."

Sucking in her lips, she sighed. "And you're sure because they're able to take care of it themselves now."

"Yeah."

That was the only word he spoke, but she knew it

was a constant battle for him to make sure Leslie stepped up. She held his gaze, wishing she had the words to comfort but not wanting to mar their post-coital bliss with talk of his ex-wife.

As she remained quiet, doubt shot through his eyes as he asked, "Is it okay if I stay?"

This dream keeps getting better. She tried to keep the grin from her face, but as his gaze shot to her mouth, she knew she hadn't hidden her excitement. "I didn't know if you needed to get back."

"I appreciate that, babe. But no. No one's at home expecting me."

She nodded as she climbed into bed, and he followed her, pulling the covers up. Sex with Ryan had been amazing. Spending the night with him in the same bed would be a dream come true. *And when he walks away from this, it might make things harder, but I'm willing to take a chance.*

He flipped off the lamp, but the room was not plunged into darkness. The full moon outside cast beams through her blinds and the small nightlight from the bathroom sent a bit of illumination in, as well. She was glad because as they lay facing each other, she wanted to see his face... wanted to continue to memo-rize everything about him at this moment in time... a moment she had never thought she'd experience.

They cuddled, arms and legs wrapped around each other, which was fine by her, but she was uncertain if he was a post-sex talker or just wanted quiet. Then he opened his mouth, shocking her with his words.

"Babe, right now, we'll keep this quiet, just between

us. I don't want it in the kids' faces until I'm sure they're at a place to understand what's happening. We'll ease into things with them. And we'll start by you coming over for dinner as soon as you can this week. In fact, tomorrow. I don't want to go too long before I see you again, so come for dinner."

Her whole body jerked, and his attention homed in on her face. Her brain had been unable to keep up with what he was saying, and she blurted, "Um... keep *what* quiet? I assure you, Ryan, I wasn't going to tell anyone we'd hooked up. And dinner? At your place?"

The instant the words *hooked up* left her mouth, his brow lowered and his countenance darkened. "Hooked up?"

"Um... yeah... I mean, I thought that you said earlier that..." She huffed, frustrated that she had no idea where his head was. "I thought that we were just doing this... you know, sex. You said you couldn't give me what you thought I deserved, so I figured that meant we were just having sex." He was quiet, and she sighed. "Ryan, I'm not into games. I don't play them, and I don't understand them. So, perhaps you need to speak plainly."

Reaching around behind him, he turned on the lamp by the bed, illuminating the room with soft light again. He shifted slightly so that his elbow was bent, his head resting on his palm, his other hand cupping her face, smoothing his thumb over her cheek. "I like that you don't play games. You never did. I remember that about you. Judith, I fucked up a long time ago, not taking a shot with you when I could have. If I hadn't pussied out, our lives would have been very different. But then, as I told you, I can't regret the past because I've got Cindy and Trevor. But if you think for one second that I've got a shot at having you in my life and I'm not gonna take it, then you'd be wrong."

"You fucked up? A long time ago?" She had no idea what he was talking about, but with the intense gaze he'd settled on her, she knew he was serious. *"But if you think for one second that I've got a shot at having you in my life and I'm not gonna take it, then you'd be wrong."* Focusing on the last words he said, she had a feeling her life was about to change. And almost afraid to breathe at the thought of a long-buried dream coming true, she clung to his shoulders, waiting to see what he needed to say.

14

Ryan hated that Judith thought what they'd just experienced together was nothing more than a hookup. And he hated that he hadn't been clear about what he wanted. *But hell, I had no idea what I wanted or how this was going to go.* But now, lying sated, naked and tangled with her, he wasn't going to let another moment pass where she didn't know exactly what he was thinking. He nodded slowly, memories flooding back that he'd kept at bay but were imprinted on his brain and his heart. "You remember spring break of your senior year?"

Her brow furrowed as she stared. "My spring break?"

"Yeah."

Her brow furrowed. "Um… yes."

"I do, too."

She smoothed her fingers over his jaw slowly as though memories were moving through her. "I remember seeing you at the beach."

"Yep, that's exactly what I remember. I had a weekend of leave and came home to Baytown. Brad came home from college, and he and I were hanging out. I told him that I was shipping out and had decided that Leslie and I needed to break up. We were better off not together. Brad was fuckin' ecstatic considering that he'd always thought Leslie dragged me down anyway. We ended up at the beach, and there you were, sitting on a beach towel under an umbrella, reading a book. But it was the first time I'd seen you in a year. You stood up and walked toward the water, and I know my fuckin' jaw hit the sand. You were drop-dead gorgeous, with a killer body and a knockout smile. You were alone. I couldn't believe you weren't surrounded by guys. I'd always known you were a cute kid, then a pretty girl, and I knew you had just turned eighteen, so I didn't feel like a perv staring at you. Hell, I couldn't even hide it from Brad. He knew I was checking you out and just laughed. The only warning he gave me was that if I was out to play, then you were hands-off. I wanted to punch him. Because if there was one thing I was never going to do, it would be to jerk you around. Not you. It was crazy. I was just getting out from under the weight of my relationship with Leslie and thinking of freedom, but one look at you then, and I was ready to throw down. But there wasn't anything I could do with everyone around, so we just hung out. But the vision of you that day stayed with me all these years."

"I remember thinking that for the first time, it felt as though you were looking at me, the real woman, not just a kid. Of course, looking back, we were both just kids. But that day, the way you hung around and made me feel special, you had to have known how much I cared for you all those years. You were the stuff of all my teenage dreams." A little giggle slipped out as she shook her head. "I probably should be embarrassed, but there's nothing wrong with dreaming."

"I knew you had a thing for me, but you were too young so I never went there. Not even in my mind. But that spring, I began to think, as well. You asked me about the Navy, where I was going, what I was doing. Leslie had never done that. Not once. So, I spent the day trying to get up the courage to ask you out on a date. But I only had the weekend, and I knew I was going to be shipping out. I suppose I could've told you and asked you to wait, but that wouldn't have been fair. Like you said, looking back, we were both kids. We had a lot of life in front of us we needed to live." He sighed heavily, the memory of that day as clear as the two other most important days in his life, the births of Trevor and Cindy.

"But everything changed the next day. Leslie called and said we had to talk. And she told me she was pregnant. About six weeks along at that time. She'd always been real irregular, so she hadn't realized it. And that was right about the last time we'd been together."

"I'm surprised Brad didn't say anything between then and prom," she said, a faraway expression in her eyes as though casting her mind back to those days.

"I asked him not to tell anybody. Our parents were the only ones who knew. When you called and needed help at prom a month later, I was sober, so I was driving

Brad. When I stared at you, all dressed up in that gorgeous evening gown, hair and makeup out of this world, I remember staring into your eyes and thinking *if only*. And regret hit me so hard, Judith, I'm not sure how I kept standing. We stared into each other's eyes under the moonlight, and I could swear what I felt was mirrored in yours."

She held his gaze, her voice soft. "And then Brad blurted everything out."

"Yeah. I saw the light dim in your eyes, and I was fuckin' gutted, babe. I realized that I was never going to hold you in my arms. You were never going to chase after me and Brad again. You were never going to look at me with stars in your eyes again. You were going to go off to college, do great things, and chances were, I was never going to see you again. And I was fuckin' gutted."

Barely whispering, she admitted, "I was destroyed. Oh, I know, I was so young. But I cried for days, then finally put those feelings to the side and realized that my life had to go on."

They were silent for a moment, each lost in the past. She blinked and her lips curved slightly as she smoothed her fingers over his face again. "As you said, Ryan, you can't have regrets because the life you led has given you Cindy and Trevor. And while Leslie didn't turn out to be the wife you deserved, there must've been some good times in there somewhere. And I had the freedom to go wherever I wanted to college, medical school, and residency, not tied down by anything. If we'd gotten together, who's to say that our lives would have been rosy? Perhaps we were simply two people who needed to be apart so that when we came back together, we could truly appreciate what we have."

"I'm glad to hear you say that. When I said I couldn't give you what you deserved, it's true. You deserve someone who's going to wine and dine you, and right now I don't have wining and dining in my budget. You deserve someone who will proudly hold your hand around town, and right now I don't want to shove anything in my kids' faces. You deserve someone who can focus all their attention on you, and right now I've got two kids who need me, an ex-wife who has to be reminded to spend time with her kids, and a job that can have unpredictable hours. But what I didn't mean was that we were just a casual hookup that wasn't going to go anywhere. At least, not the moment our bodies joined."

"So, you want to see me again," she said, her smile wide and her eyes lit, punching him in the gut again, but this time, in a good way.

"Oh, yeah. And after we sleep tangled together and wake up for more lovin', we'll head to work and then you'll come over for dinner."

"How will that… I mean, what… oh. What will you tell the kids? Won't they wonder why I'm over?"

"We're old friends. They know that. We've chatted and reconnected. We'll get them used to seeing us together, then ease them into us dating. Don't worry. We've got this. Okay?"

She let out a huge breath, then grinned. "Okay. If you say so, big guy. We've got this."

"So, are you two dating now?" Trevor asked, cocking his head to the side as his hands wrapped around a taco as he struggled to eat it without spilling all the contents as soon as he took a bite.

Ryan jerked, glanced first toward his son, who appeared oblivious while he shoved his taco into his mouth, then glanced toward Judith, seeing her wide eyes, then toward Cindy, who appeared nonplussed as she broke her taco into pieces so she could spear it with a fork.

"Of course, they are, Trevor," Cindy said, matter-of-fact in her soft voice.

Trying not to choke on his taco, Ryan took a swig of beer. Clearing his throat, he started to speak but Cindy jumped in again.

"Dad doesn't have friends who are girls that he invites to dinner. Plus, he's known Judith since she was younger than me."

"That's what I figured," Trevor said after managing to swallow the massive bite. He grabbed his soda and drank thirstily before looking up, seemingly just now aware that his dad and Judith were staring at him. "What?" He grabbed the napkin and wiped his mouth. "Do I have food on my face?"

"When do you not have food on your face?" Cindy laughed. "Boys always eat like pigs." She leaned toward Judith and whispered as though imparting great knowledge, "You should see the school cafeteria table where football players sit. It's a mess!"

Feeling the need to wrangle control of the conversation back, Ryan leveled Trevor with a steely-eyed expression. "First of all, Son, think before you speak. Your question put me and Judith on the spot. I could've handled that myself, but that makes it embarrassing for the other person. Second, I told you that Judith and I are friends."

"Just friends?" Seeing Ryan's scowl, Trevor quickly winced as he looked toward Judith. "Sorry."

"Yes, right now, we're just friends. Spending a lot of time together, getting reacquainted, and we enjoy each other's company."

"So, isn't that like dating?" Cindy asked, her head cocked to the side. "It's not like you're seeing anybody else."

Ryan wanted to throw in the towel, crying defeat, but seeing Judith trying to hide her mirth, he simply rolled his eyes while he shook his head. "You two should be trying to make a good impression on Judith instead of acting like knuckleheads."

A giggle burst forth, and Judith clapped her hand over her mouth. "I'm sorry, I shouldn't laugh. But seriously, guys, your dad and I are friends. Yes, we're enjoying getting to know each other again and spending time together. As far as anything beyond that, we don't know. We're certainly not ready to slap a label on anything."

"That makes sense," Cindy said, smiling while nodding. "Although, I really hope you do start dating."

"Me too," Trevor threw out. "Just think, free medical care!"

"Boy," Ryan belted out. "You've just got KP duty!"

Trevor's brow scrunched but he knew better than to complain. Shrugging, he dug back into his third taco, completely missing Ryan and Judith's grin across the table.

"Well, that was unexpected," she said later as they sat outside in his backyard.

Trevor had put away the dishes, and much to Ryan's surprise, Cindy had volunteered to help, something he suspected was to give Judith and him more time to themselves. "Honest to God, I never expected that, Judith. If I had, I'd have warned you and been more prepared myself. Maybe I should have talked to them first."

"They love you."

He knew her words were true, but it felt good to hear them from someone else.

She wasn't finished as she continued, "And you're a phenomenal dad."

He shook his head and sighed. "Parenting is crazy. One minute, I feel like dad of the universe, and the next minute, I feel like a failure."

"I think everybody feels that at certain times, but believe me when I say that I've seen lots of parenting styles, and you're a great dad."

Their chairs were next to each other, but he suddenly wished that she was in his lap instead of a foot away. "You can't say shit like that to me when I can't pull you into my arms and kiss you," he announced.

She laughed, her eyes sparkling. "Is that a Ryan law?"

"It is now, babe." Her hand was resting on the arm of

her chair, and he reached over, linking fingers with her. Her brows lifted, but he shook his head. "I know it's soon, but it's not like we're having sex in the middle of the backyard," he said, eliciting another bark of laughter from her. "The kids know we're friends and have a pretty good idea that we're seeing where this goes, so there's no reason not to hold hands."

Her fingers squeezed his, then her expression sobered. "You know, this is moving really fast. We just met again recently, and you didn't seem all that keen on being around me. Then we have a heart-to-heart and end up jumping each other, which led to spending the night, which led to dinner with your kids, which has us here declaring that we're possibly dating before we've gone on a date."

He understood where she was coming from but needed her to understand him. "It seems fast, but it's not. I've known you since Brad and I first became best friends. My feet were often tucked under your parents' kitchen table next to you. Yeah, you were just Brad's little sister, but that didn't mean we didn't know each other. Being two years older than you was a huge difference when we were teenagers. By the time I started noticing you as something other than just Brad's sister, I was almost eighteen years old, still dating Leslie, and getting ready to graduate and join the Navy. I was young, stupid, and never really thought much beyond the moment. I knew even then that Leslie was never going to be my forever woman, but she was there, and she put out. To a young man thinking with his dick, that was good enough. We broke up a couple of times after I joined the Navy, then we'd get back together. Looking back, it was a fucked-up, dysfunctional relationship. And by the time I realized that, I was getting out of it, and finally, you were of an age that I could pursue, and everything changed. I'm not trying to rehash the same old shit, but the point is, Judith, that I've had feelings for you for a really long time. I couldn't do anything about them when we were younger, and then we were out of each other's lives for years, going our own way. So, while it seems fast now, it feels to me like we're just coming into our own time."

Her smile rivaled the sunset in the distance, and he hoped she got where he was coming from.

She squeezed his fingers again and said, "You know, for a man, you have a great way of expressing yourself."

He smiled in return. "I can bark out an order and expect my subordinates to obey. I can talk till I'm blue in the face with Leslie and never get through. With Trevor, I explain things fairly quickly and he gets me. With Cindy," he shrugged, "it takes a little more conversation."

"And with me?"

"With you, right now I need to make sure you understand that I'm not moving too quickly without thinking things through. And if that takes a helluva lot more explanations, that's exactly what I'll do."

They settled into an easy silence for a few minutes, still enjoying the sunset. He thought the kids might come out and join them, but it appeared they were giving him and Judith plenty of time to be alone. It seemed as though things had settled into a comfortable norm between them almost immediately, and he let out a sigh of relief.

"Did Cindy talk to you about what I gave her the other evening at the clinic?"

Blinking, he felt his comfortable ease disappear. "Um… no. Do I need to be concerned?"

"I don't want to betray a confidence, but I feel like you need to know that I gave her samples of feminine products along with basic information and my phone number."

Ryan considered himself to be a modern man, but at the words *feminine products* in the context of his daughter, he grimaced. Pulling himself together, he asked, "Don't they get that information in school?"

Judith leveled him with a narrow-eyed glare. "Seriously? I don't think health or sex education has changed much since we were in school."

"Shit," he grumbled under his breath.

"The only reason I'm telling you this is because she had basic questions, and I answered them both as a physician and a woman. I just don't want there to be secrets between you and me, but I told her that she could come to me. But I think it's important, Ryan, for you to understand that this is not something that Leslie has talked to her about, and Cindy doesn't feel comfortable discussing it with her mom."

He held tightly with the hand that was linked with hers and scrubbed his other hand over his face as another sigh escaped. "Okay, here's the deal. I should have anticipated that Leslie hasn't talked with Cindy about all of this, but honestly, it never entered my mind.

I want my daughter to be informed and make smart choices, and she sure as hell isn't gonna come to me about this, and quite frankly, I'm glad. But I'm pleased that she felt like she could open up to you."

"I've made it clear to her that I'm available, but I'm not going to come to you every time she confides in me unless it's something that I feel you need to know."

"I trust you, Judith. We're developing a partnership. And I know it still seems fast to you, but you're going to be in my kids' lives. You're going to have fun conversations with them and serious conversations. You can enjoy them because they're great kids. But sometimes, you're going to have to tell them when they're doing something wrong or being stupid." He shifted in his chair and leaned closer, holding her gaze. "I trust you to handle my kids with care and let me know if there's something I need to handle."

She shifted her body toward his and leaned forward. "Is it wrong that I really want to jump you right now?"

"Not any more than I want to jump you."

"Then will you just settle for me squeezing my hand again?" she asked.

"No," he replied, smiling when her eyes widened. "But I will settle for a kiss."

"Really?"

"Hell, yeah." He leaned forward and touched his lips to hers, his tongue darting out just enough to quickly slide over hers. Shifting back into his seat, his fingers still linked with hers, he figured if his kids were watching, they'd be happy for him.

"This feels like peeking," Cindy said, her eyes trained to the two people sitting next to each other in the backyard.

"No one is keeping you here," Trevor retorted, his gaze out the window.

They were quiet as they watched their dad kiss Judith. Turning to each other, they grinned.

15

Two weeks. Judith walked through the clinic with a smile on her face. It had been two weeks since she and Ryan decided they were starting something new. Two weeks that included lots of quick kisses, several dinners at his house, a kayak picnic with him, Cindy, and Trevor, and even a Sunday lunch at his parents' house. They'd managed another sleepover at her house when the kids spent the night with their mom.

Of all of those, it was the Sunday lunch that had nerves firing through her body—until she'd arrived and discovered that Ryan's parents were as delighted about them dating as his kids were.

Cora and Roger Coates had become acquainted with her parents when Brad and Ryan became friends in middle school. Judith remembered all of them sitting together watching the boys play ball, but she'd never been to their house and certainly hadn't seen them since Brad and Ryan graduated.

Arriving at the modest brick home on the outskirts

of Baytown, she'd peered out the passenger window as Cindy bounded from the back seat and skip-jogged up the front walk to greet her grandparents as they stepped from their house. Trevor had followed with a more casual I'm-a-cool-guy air, thrusting his hand out to shake with his grandfather before enveloping his grandmother in a hug.

"You okay, babe?" Ryan asked.

"At my age, you'd think I wouldn't be nervous. But it's just dawned on me that I haven't met the parents of someone I was involved with since college."

"They're not strangers, and I promise they won't bite."

Rolling her eyes, she waited as he climbed from behind the wheel, rounded the front of his SUV, and assisted her down. Walking toward the porch, she wasn't sure what Ryan had told his parents, but Cindy was already offering introductions.

"Grandma, Grandpa, this is Dad's girlfriend, Judith. She's a doctor at the clinic here in town. Her brother was Dad's best friend in high school."

Ryan had one arm around Judith's shoulders but maneuvered so that his free arm could loop around Cindy, pulling her gently back into his embrace, as well. "You want to let your old man handle the introductions?"

Cindy twisted her head around to look up at him and crinkled her nose. Judith didn't want Cindy to be embarrassed, so she quickly said, "I don't know, Ryan. I think Cindy managed to do a very succinct job with her introductions." She was rewarded with a huge smile from Cindy before she turned her attention to Ryan's parents. With her hand extended toward them, she greeted, "It's nice to meet you officially again after so long."

Cora Coates brushed past her extended hand and pulled Judith in for a hug. "Oh, my dear, we can't wait to spend time with you. And, of course, find out how Brad is doing as well as your parents. I'm embarrassed to say that we've only sent Christmas cards the past few years since they've been gone, but we have kept up on social media."

Ryan's father, Roger, shook her hand warmly before ushering them all inside. The meal was simple and delicious, the conversation flowing and easy, and her nerves quickly dissipated. It wasn't until Roger, Trevor, Cindy, and Ryan headed outside while she stayed inside to help Cora that his mother caught her off guard.

After the dishes were put away and the leftovers stored in the refrigerator, Cora leaned against the counter and said, "I was never Leslie's biggest fan, but I tried to be a good mother-in-law."

Jerking slightly at the sudden change in topic, Judith said nothing but mimicked Cora's stance, leaning against the opposite counter.

"I hope you don't think I'm being presumptuous bringing her up, and I certainly don't want to make you uncomfortable."

Shaking her head, Judith still had no idea where Cora was going with the conversation, but the pained expression on his mom's face made Judith feel that whatever it was, Cora needed to talk. "No, it's fine."

Cora sighed, seeming relieved. "When she and Ryan were in high school, I could never quite put my finger on what it was about her that seemed off. It was actually your brother that put a fine point on what I noticed."

Very curious as to what Brad had said, she continued to give her full attention to Cora.

"He was over here for dinner with us one night, and afterward, Ryan hurried out of the room in frustration because Leslie had called. Brad looked over at Roger and me and said, 'Leslie is so self-involved, it's like she forgets Ryan has anything else to do except be there for her.' Roger then wondered aloud if her parents had raised her to be so selfish. Then Brad shook his head and said, 'Leslie's not selfish. She's self-involved.' Well, before we had a chance to question him further, Ryan came back in and nothing else was said. Later that evening, out of curiosity, I looked up the definition of selfish and self-involved. Now you might think with me and Roger both working in education, we'd know the difference, but truthfully, we hadn't thought about it. And what we discovered was Brad hit the nail on the head."

"I confess, Cora, I'm intrigued. I don't think I've ever really thought of the difference. What did you learn?"

"Well, it's so interesting. The easiest definition would be examples. A selfish person eats all the french fries on the plate. A self-involved person doesn't eat all the fries and might even let other people eat them. But then they'll talk at great length about how they didn't get any fries, something besides fries should have been offered, or everyone should've noticed how they felt about fries."

"So, while the selfish person demands that everything is about them, the self-involved person is completely absorbed in how everything affects them?"

Cora nodded emphatically. "Exactly! It was amazing how Brad, even as a teenager, picked up on that. Leslie loved Ryan, or thought she did, but the relationship revolved around what she needed. I don't doubt that she loves her children, but again, motherhood to her is how it affects *her*. Occasionally, Roger and I mentioned this to Ryan, but he'd already learned it for himself and had no desire to put the kids through a divorce just because he felt like the marriage wasn't right for him. But when it affected the kids detrimentally, he had to put a stop to that. And I think it says a lot that Cindy and Trevor understand that about their mom and wanted to live with their dad."

"I know they love their mom," Judith agreed. "I hope that Leslie can continue to forge a relationship with them that's beneficial for all."

"You're a very special woman, Judith," Cora said, eyeing her intently. "The feelings you and my son have are not particularly new, are they?"

"I fell in love with him when I was younger than Cindy." Judith hadn't intended to blurt out such a confession, but Cora was so easy to talk to and the smile aimed at her made her feel as though the news wasn't a complete surprise or at least not unwelcome. "I'm not sure that makes me special, but it's the truth. But the time wasn't right, life intervened, and we grew up to be the people we were meant to be. And by pure luck, we happened to have met again at a time in our lives when we can explore these feelings."

Cora blinked several times rapidly, moisture gathering in her eyes. She stepped forward, her arms spread out, and pulled Judith into a hug, rocking her back and forth. "I'm so happy that you've come back into his life. So thrilled that you're in Cindy and Trevor's lives."

"Everything in here okay?" Ryan's voice cut through their moment.

"Absolutely," Judith said, smiling.

"And why wouldn't it be?" Cora asked, her smile just as wide. "We were just getting ready to come out and enjoy the afternoon sunshine with the rest of you." With that, she walked by him, patting his shoulder as she moved through the door.

He'd cocked his brow as she walked to him, their arms wrapped around each other. "We're fine. Let's just say I was getting your mom's seal of approval."

"I never doubted that for a moment, babe. She was never a fan of Leslie's, and while she tried not to let that show, I knew it. Considering you're the complete opposite in every way, I knew she'd love you."

They walked outside together, her heart singing.

Now, sitting in her office, she looked down at her phone and chuckled. She'd talked to her parents last night and let them know she was dating Ryan, much to their delight. Seeing Brad's name on her screen, she wasn't surprised he was calling this morning.

"Hello, brother dear."

"Seriously, Judith? That's all you've got to say?"

"Well, you hardly have given me a chance to say anything yet!"

There were a few seconds of silence before he jumped in. "So, you and Ryan Coates?"

"Yep."

"Come on, Sis, this is me. Give me more than that. Do I need to come to Baytown and kick his ass? Come there to congratulate him for finally getting his head out of his ass about his ex? Give me something to go on here," Brad complained.

"We're dating, but before you say anything, just know that it's new. We're seeing where things go."

"According to Mom, you've met his kids and had dinner with his parents."

Laughing burst forth. "What's the matter? Feel left out?"

"Hell, yeah. I gotta say that I never liked him with Leslie and was glad when he finally got divorced. I feel guilty that he and I mostly just communicate at the holidays. I'll plan on coming up in a couple of weeks. See your place and reconnect with him."

"I'd love that, and so would he. Check your schedule and let me know. I'll get you and your family reservations at one of the cute inns in town. In fact, Mitch Evans' wife owns one."

"Sounds good. Okay, I've got to get back to work, and I'm sure you're already in the clinic. Tell Ryan I said I'll kick his ass when I see him if he doesn't treat my kid sister right."

He disconnected before she had a chance to retort but rolled her eyes nonetheless, unable to keep the grin off her face. Still smiling while walking through the clinic, Natalie met her in the lab and lifted a brow toward her.

"Rumor is you've got a gorgeous, silver-fox police captain hooked, and by the smile on your face, I'd say the rumor is true," Natalie laughed.

"Well, I don't know about hooked, but I have to admit the smile on my face is there for a good reason," she quipped in return.

"Don't know him well, but I know he's a good man. His kids are good, too. And since I've gotten to know you, I think y'all make a great team."

Before she had a chance to reply, Sam popped his head in. "Sorry, Dr. Foster. You've got a drop-in in room four. She insisted she had to see you and only you even though I told her that you were just about to leave. And I swear, she wouldn't go into her problem with me. Sorry!"

Glancing at her watch, she sighed. "Lucky for this patient, I can see them before I leave." Heading down the hall, she clicked her tablet to see the patient's information just as she walked in. Halting, she lifted her head to blink in surprise at the woman sitting in the chair. "Leslie?" Quickly recovering, she asked, "Are you okay?"

Leslie sucked in her lips, her gaze moving from Judith's face, dropping down to her hands clasped in her lap. "I just needed to talk."

Judith took a moment to look at the woman she remembered so well from high school. Trim body. Meticulous hair, makeup, and manicure. Pressed slacks paired with a short-sleeved blue sweater. High heel pumps on her feet with a matching purse sitting on the floor next to them. It was hard not to remember how put-together Leslie was in high school with her cheerleading outfit or cute clothes and makeup and hair model-perfect at a time when most girls were trying outlandish attempts at both. Judith had always felt so immature and frumpy compared to her. Glancing down at her white coat covering her scrubs, stubby fingernails, and rubber shoes, she didn't need a mirror to know her unruly curls were sprouting from her ponytail. It had been that kind of day—wrestling toddlers with snotty noses, giving vaccinations to crying babies, stitches in an older man who'd had a farm accident, and a host of other patients that walked through the doors. Now, face to face with Ryan's ex, her joy was quickly replaced with irritation.

"Do you need to talk to me as a physician? If so, that's great although you might be more comfortable with Dr. Martinez or Dr. Preston—"

"I need to talk to you."

Judith tried to hide her jerk but was sure she failed. Lifting her hand, she shook her head. "No, no, Leslie. Not here. Not now—"

"I need your help. Surely you owe me that."

Irritation morphed into anger, and Judith forced her legs to walk forward and lowered herself onto the stool when what she wanted to do was kick Leslie out. Leaning forward so that she could be front and center in Leslie's vision, she dug deep to find the patience needed and tried to keep her voice steady. "Leslie, first, I don't owe you anything. Secondly, if you need help with your children, you need to bring this up to Ryan, not me. And thirdly, this is a doctor's office. My place of work. This is not the correct place for a personal visit. Now, I'll ask you to leave and—"

"But you're the only one who can help me. And I don't have your phone number so I can't just call you. This was the only way I can think to get you to talk to me. To help me."

Sighing heavily, Judith decided that perhaps the quickest way to get rid of Leslie was to hear what she had to say. "Okay, what do you need to know?"

"For the past couple of weeks when the kids come over, all I hear is how wonderful you are. You're smart and funny and a doctor and live in a cute cottage. You like to kayak and go on picnics—"

"Leslie, we're already off-track."

"I need to ask about Trevor."

Jerking, she rushed, "Trevor? Is he okay?"

"I need to talk to you about his birthday and what to get."

She blinked, uncertain she'd heard correctly. "You need to know what to get Trevor for his birthday?"

Leslie huffed, twisting her hands together. "He's going to turn fifteen next month, and it's hard for me."

Oh, my God. Heaving a sigh, Judith asked, "What's hard for you? Not knowing what to get him?"

"I don't know what he wants. I don't know what fifteen-year-old boys like. You obviously know what he likes because he always seems to have a good time when you're around. So, I figured you were the person to ask."

"Have you asked him?"

Leslie blinked, her brow furrowing as she stared back at Judith. "Ask him? Then it wouldn't be a surprise. It wouldn't be special—"

"Leslie, he's not five years old and ready to wake up to see what Santa brought. If you asked him to give you a list of some things that he'd like, then he'll be thrilled with anything off that list that you get him. And he will be more thrilled that you were the one who got it for him and that you cared enough to find out from him what he'd like to have."

She lifted a hand and rubbed her brow, her lips pressed together. "I don't have... I don't have a lot of money to spend. I started a new job but have only gotten one paycheck. Ryan has—"

Lifting her hand quickly again, Judith shook her head, wondering if Leslie was always this difficult to keep on track. Remembering what Cora had said about Brad's observation, she knew her brother was right. Self-involved—everything tracked back to Leslie. "We're not going to discuss the money situation between you and Ryan. That's not my business, and I don't want to know. If you're concerned that Trevor's list is going to have nothing on it that you can afford, I assure you, he's a smart young man. He'll give you a list of things that he'd like to have that he knows you'd be able to get. In fact, if you and he just had a taco night where the two of you talked, he'd like that."

"Tacos?"

"I know he loves them. I know he could eat a dozen of them. If you and he just shared a taco dinner with a birthday cake, he'd be happy."

"That has so many calories. I don't think I could enjoy that."

Judith stared at the woman in front of her, and for the first time felt sorry for Leslie. It was obvious she truly wanted to do something for her son but was not only clueless about him but she also couldn't seem to take herself out of the equation. No longer wanting to continue, she stood. "Leslie, this isn't about you. If you can't enjoy some cake with your son without worrying about the calories, then you have more issues to deal with than what to get him for his birthday. But that has nothing to do with me, and we're not going to discuss it. Spend some time with your son. Ask him what he'd like for his birthday. Pick out one of the things and get it for him. He'll be thrilled that you did this. That's it, Leslie. That's all you need to do. Now, I have work I need to take care of, and please remember, don't use this office for a personal conversation with me in the future."

She turned and had made it to the door, her hand on the knob when Leslie stood and spoke once again, her voice barely above a whisper.

"If you and Ryan get married, the kids will have you and I'll be left with nothing."

Judith looked over her shoulder and shook her head. "If you're left with nothing, Leslie, you'll have no one to blame but yourself. Cindy and Trevor are *your* kids. They love *you*. They want a relationship with *their* mom. You know, humans can love lots of different people and accept love from many. It doesn't come down to either one or the other. So do everything you can to show your kids how much you love them, and you'll get that back tenfold from them." With that, she opened the door and walked out, the smile no longer on her face, her heart no longer light. Once inside her office, she shut the door and sat at her desk. As a physician, she'd learned to compartmentalize and did that now.

Opening her computer, she typed in her records, reviewed lab reports, and looked at the next day's schedule. When finished, she walked outside after saying goodbye to the remaining staff, climbed into her car, and drove home. Once there, she kicked off her shoes, poured a huge glass of wine, and sat in her tiny living room, watching the sun set over the horizon, wondering how life became so complicated when she finally had the man of her dreams.

16

"Babe, I hope you have a better day than yesterday," Ryan said, having called Judith before she left for work. He was already on the road, heading to the North Heron Sheriff's Department for the monthly law enforcement leaders meeting. The previous evening, he'd nearly hit the roof, pissed as hell when she'd told him about Leslie's visit to the clinic. He'd gone outside to rant so the kids wouldn't hear him, ready to call his ex and rip her a new one. The only reason he hadn't was because Judith had talked him down.

"Ryan, I didn't get the feeling that Leslie was trying to ambush me. She's just clueless about what to do with the kids but recognized that I might know. She wasn't bitchy. She wasn't nasty."

"No, she's never been," he'd argued back. "She just has always made it about her."

Judith admitted that had been her assessment, also. "Please give her this one," Judith had begged. "I made it clear that she wasn't to come to the clinic anymore for this reason. I also made it clear that I wasn't going to listen to the situation between you and her. And I also explained that the kids will have the benefit of lots of people who love them and that she's not being pushed out."

"I told her the same fuckin' thing, she just doesn't get it."

"Well, let's see if she gets it this time. Let's give her this one pass. If it happens again, then you do what you've got to do and say what you've got to say to her."

He'd fumed the rest of the evening and lost count of how many times his fingers had gone to his phone to call Leslie, each time Judith's calm voice of reason sounding in his ears.

Pulling into the parking lot, he glanced down as a text came into his phone. Hoping it wasn't one of the kids who'd forgotten something, he sucked in a quick breath seeing Brad's name.

WTH – dating my sister and I don't get a text. I know it's not x-mas, but still...

Shaking his head and grinning, he didn't have time to text back before another one came in.

Wife is already planning a trip to the Shore. Get ready for a Foster invasion. My kids, your kids, and probably our folks as well.

The grin stayed on his face as he typed,

Bring it on. Sounds like old times.

Old is right... but I can still kick your ass if you don't treat J right.

No worries... I've waited a long time for her.

Good. Talk to you soon and hope to see you in a few weeks.

He climbed from his VMP vehicle and waved at several others as they entered the building. Walking into the conference room, he headed straight to the coffee pot, pouring his third cup of the day and wishing it was spiked. Offering chin lifts to Mitch, Colt, Dylan, Wyatt, Hannah, and Liam, he settled at the table, and they soon began. Mitch, Wyatt, Dylan, and Hannah were all police chiefs of tiny towns on the eastern shore. Colt was the Sheriff of North Heron County, and Liam was the Sheriff of the only other Virginia county on the Eastern Shore, Acawmacke.

As usual, some of the reports did not pertain to him specifically, but he was always interested in what the others had to say. Since the meetings typically reported on items that weren't just specific to their jurisdiction but pertained to the Eastern Shore as a whole, it behooved him to stay abreast of any concerns, especially if they might involve the waterways.

When it was his time, he handed out copies of the latest Coast Guard report that he'd received. "The Coast Guard is constantly monitoring the ships in the Bay, especially those anchored as they await permission to move up to Baltimore. I know at our last meeting, I talked about their concerns, but in the last month, the problems with speedboats around the cargo and transport ships have increased. The concern is smuggling, but not having caught anyone yet, it's hard to say."

"You talked about drug running last time," Mitch said. "I asked the Baytown harbor master to keep an eye on our harbor, but he says he hasn't noted any new activity."

Dylan and Wyatt nodded simultaneously. "Same at Manteague," Wyatt said. "I've got my harbor master on the lookout, plus our regular fishermen. None report any new activity in the harbor although if things are happening at night, fishermen wouldn't be around to notice. I confess I haven't gone back and looked at any of the surveillance recordings."

"The harbor master at Seaside has a part-time assistant who was keeping an eye on things," Dylan reported. "No unusual activity."

"I figured as much," Ryan said, rolling his shoulders and hearing his back crack. "But to be honest, this doesn't really surprise me."

"What are you thinking?" Colt asked.

"The Coast Guard is investigating smuggling coming from the ships that have traveled around the world. They can drop the load to the motorboats, and then the goods can be transported anywhere. In fact, they probably avoid the known harbors around, even the small ones."

"Are you working with the Coast Guard on this?" Mitch asked.

"Yes and no. They have jurisdiction over the cargo and transport ships in the Bay. They can also deal with any motorboats they deem necessary to check on. But we can stop them, check them, and board them, as well. So, if they're in our jurisdiction, yes, but I'd call the CG if we find something suspicious that we think they need to deal with."

As the meeting wound down, they chatted for a moment about the latest practices for the American Legion youth games. "I thought about getting a few of the teens who play for Baytown High School to see if they'd like some community service by helping at the games or practices," he said. "I know Trevor would volunteer."

"Good idea," Colt agreed. "Some of us get spread thin during the tourist season, and maybe the teens can help out as long as they're supervised."

"Okay, I'll bring it up at the next meeting," Ryan said, standing to leave.

"I hear someone is dating the pretty new doctor," Dylan said, wiggling his eyebrows, eliciting a shoulder slap from his wife, Hannah.

"Considering we're all happily married or engaged, that only leaves one of us in the middle of this rumor," Liam grinned.

Ryan cut his gaze toward the others as they chuckled. "No point in denying it."

Hannah cocked her head to the side and held his gaze. "Dylan told me that she grew up here. Did you guys know each other back then?"

"Hell, Hannah, you've been around long enough to know what it's like here. Everybody knew everybody on the Eastern shore," Mitch laughed.

"Her brother was my best friend growing up. She was a couple of years behind, so I knew her, but the timing was all wrong back then. Now, it's better."

Each of them offered their congratulations, and he knew it came from a good place. He'd never been one to air his dirty laundry, but his troubles with Leslie weren't exactly secret. "I appreciate it. It's new, and yet after knowing her so long ago, it's not. But what it is feels right."

Driving back to the VMP station in Baytown, his mood was significantly better than when he'd left that morning. He'd agreed with Judith, deciding to not go ballistic on Leslie for cornering Judith at work. *This time.* As far as he was concerned, it was her one free pass. Now, focused on the rest of his day, he looked forward to dinner at the cottage. Considering Trevor had late practice and Cindy was studying at a friend's house, he hoped he and Judith could shorten the meal or skip it altogether to give them enough time to hit the bedroom. Just the thought of her naked underneath him had him adjusting his crotch. *Shit, I can't get to the station with my dick leading the way.*

Thinking of something to get his mind off her naked body, he didn't have to wait long when the radio called in a situation off the Baytown beach. He'd just pulled into the parking lot and had enough time to grab his equipment before he jumped onto the boat with Callan, heading out of the harbor. *Nothing like people acting like shits with jet skis to knock sex right out of my brain!*

The next hour was spent hauling over three jet skis, two being driven by teenagers and one young adult. All three had alcohol on their breath although it was still under the legal limit. Considering that none of them were of legal drinking age, the two teenagers were not registered on the jet ski rental agreement, and they were violating the Baytown Public Beach ordinance banning jet skis to a certain distance, they were hauled onto the VMP boat, their jet skis towed by one of the other VMP vessels and taken back to the station.

Calls to their parents were made, and the responses from some of them when they got to the station pissed Ryan off even more. The eighteen-year-old was cited as an adult, and he was glad Jared was dealing with him. Ryan and Callan dealt with the parents of the two younger teens. One set, apologetic, polite, and furious with their son, accepted the responsibility, telling their son he'd be working extra hours to pay off the tickets.

Nodding as they left, he turned to deal with the other set of parents, the ones he'd purposely made wait when they walked into the station as though they owned it. He made his way around his desk and sat down, staring at them as they sputtered excuses, the son slumped in the seat next to them. Finally having enough, he lifted his hand. "There were families, young people, small children in the water. If one of them had been killed, your son would be sitting in jail right now and the district attorney would already be pressing for him to be tried as an adult for murder at most, manslaughter at the least."

That seemed to shut the parents up for a few seconds as their mouths dropped open and their eyes widened. When the father started to open his mouth again, Ryan cut him off. "As it is, your son has the opportunity to learn the lesson of a lifetime. Obey the law. Take responsibility. Don't make excuses. Stop acting like a jackass. I hope he takes this opportunity and learns that." Turning toward the young man who was now staring at him with a look of surprise on his face, he continued. "I hope *you* have to work hard to pay off the fines, still knowing that you have a record. And I hope you learn from this major fuck up because you see, this wasn't a minor, teenage indiscretion. This was a major fuck up of colossal proportion. But because I sat here and listened to your parents make excuses and throw out thinly-veiled threats about bringing a lawyer, I'm not sure you'll learn that lesson because your parents sure as hell haven't. But maybe, just maybe, you can rise above your upbringing and be a decent young man. For your sake, I hope so." He was so pissed that Ryan almost missed the flash of respect that moved through the boy's eyes before his attention swung back to the red-faced, spitting-mad parents. Lifting his hand again, he shook his head. "This is over." Calling for Joseph, he stood and waited at the door. "This officer will take you out and get everything processed."

The mother walked out, clutching her purse, blinking back tears while her husband continued to fume. "You haven't heard the last of this yet." Looking down at his son, he barked, "Let's get out of here!"

The teen followed his dad, then looked over his shoulder toward Ryan, his mouth twisted in a grimace. Swallowing deeply, he nodded.

Sitting down at his desk again, Ryan scrubbed his hand over his face and sighed. Hopefully, the kid not only heard and listened but would be able to claw his way away from the asshole his dad proved to be.

His phone vibrated, and pulling it from his pocket,

he grinned, forcing his breathing to steady. "Hey, Trev. What's up?"

"Hey, Dad. I know I've got late practice today, but Chuck's parents asked if I could go to their house afterward. I had volunteered to help Chuck with his geometry, and his mom said that she'd feed me dinner. I wanted to know if that was okay."

Ryan's heart swelled with pride. "It's absolutely okay, Trev. I'm having dinner with Judith, and I'll swing by Chuck's and pick you up afterward."

"Thanks, Dad! Tell Judith I said hi."

"I will. Have a good practice, and I'll see you later." Disconnecting, he lifted a prayer in thanks for his kids. They were normal, typical, healthy kids who could sometimes drive him crazy, but there was no doubt they were good kids.

Glancing at the clock, he realized it was almost time to check out. A grin spread across his face, now knowing he had extra time with Judith at the cottage.

"Can you take it?"

"Honey, I'll take whatever you've got to give."

Ryan grinned, his hands on Judith's heart-shaped ass, both on their knees. Her hands clutched the headboard as he took her from behind. Sweat dripped from his forehead. "Tight and slick. Damn, babe, you feel so good."

He'd called her on the way, telling her they had extra time since the kids would be home a little late. As soon as he walked in her door, she'd jumped into his arms, wrapping her legs around his waist and planting her lips on his. His cock had been ready to play most of the day, and with her greeting, it was tired of waiting.

Kicking the door shut, he'd managed to flip the lock with one hand while holding on to her booty with the other. Stalking into her bedroom, they'd barely made it in when he set her feet on the floor and clothes began flying. Stripping each other in record time, they fell back onto the bed, laughing. Soon, the sound of mirth was replaced with kisses, panting, grunting, and little escaping moans. They'd started with him on top, then he'd flipped her, giving her a chance to be in control as she rode his cock with her curls bouncing around her shoulders and his hands were filled with her breasts. She'd come hard, and he'd watched that beauty explode in front of him, not remembering seeing anything as sexy as Judith riding out her orgasm on him.

Just as she'd collapsed on his chest, he'd flipped them again, pulled out as she'd mewled her displeasure, then rolled her to her stomach, pulled her hips up, and slid into her from behind.

Now, he wanted her to come again and was determined to make it good for her. Sliding his hands to her breasts, he captured the full globes as they moved beneath her, tweaking her nipples. "Are you close?" he growled, his words dragged over gravel as they were pulled from his lungs. She moaned but didn't answer. "Babe?"

"Yes, yes, I'm close," she grunted, her body moving with each thrust.

His balls were on fire and the feel of her inner muscles pulling on him let him know he was close. "Touch yourself," he ordered as he rolled one nipple between his fingers and gripped her ass with his other hand.

Still holding onto the headboard with one hand, she slid the other down to her clit. Suddenly, her body tensed underneath his, and she turned her head to the side so he could see her profile, her face flush and her eyes squeezed tightly shut. Her whole body shuddered as she cried out his name, and that was the last hold he had on his resolve. Hoping his grip was not bruising, every muscle in his body tightened as he thrust through his release, stars exploding behind his closed eyelids. He continued to pump until every last drop had been wrung from his body.

Judith's legs slid out, and she flopped face down onto the bed, his body landing on top of hers, eliciting an 'oof' as his weight pressed down. Uncertain he could move, it was the awareness that he didn't want her uncomfortable that forced his muscles to obey as his cock slid from her slick sex and he shifted to the side.

They lay for long minutes until their ragged breaths eased, their sweat-slicked bodies cooled, and their racing heartbeats steadied.

Rolling his head to the side so that he faced her, their gazes held as their lips curled into wide smiles.

"Thanks for coming over for dinner," she said, her eyes twinkling.

"Thanks for greeting me at the door the way you did."

"Thanks for catching me when I jumped you."

"Babe, you jump, and I'll catch you anytime."

Her soft giggle met his ears, one of the sweetest sounds he'd ever heard. He reached over and brushed her damp curls away from her face. "You are so beautiful. I can't believe I'm here with you. I can't believe you've given me this chance. I thought I'd given up all hope of being in a happy, healthy relationship. So, thank you, babe, for the chance to fall in love with you."

Her quick gasp and wide eyes gave evidence that his words surprised her. Uncertain of her response, his breath halted in his chest squeezed, waiting.

Her expression softened as she lifted her hand and ran her fingers through his hair, her thumb sweeping over the stubble on his jaw. "I fell in love with you when I was twelve years old. I gave up that dream, but I'm not sure I ever stopped loving you. And now, the dream is real, and so is my love."

Her words scored through him, leaving a brand on his heart. Sealing his lips over hers, his tongue swept through her warm mouth, their bodies pressing together again. Determined to make love again, this time slower, more gentle, full of emotion and not just passion, he mumbled, "We've got just enough time before I have to pick up the kids to make love, but I'm afraid we won't have time to eat. Hope that's okay, babe."

Still kissing, she mumbled in return, "With you in my bed, who needs to eat?"

A woman after my own heart... hell, a woman who has my heart. With that thought, they made love again.

17

"Dad, I don't want to. Why can't I stay here?"

Ryan pinched the bridge of his nose with one hand, the other hand resting on his hip as Cindy's whiny voice came from the living room. His normally soft-spoken, reasonable daughter had turned into a young woman with mercurial mood swings, smiling and happy one moment, angry and fussy the next. He thought back to what Judith had told him and grimaced. Cindy was only thirteen, but he knew he was facing her full-blown adolescent years. If ever there was a time that he wished Leslie was a more-together, cognizant, with-it mother, it was now. *God, grant me patience.* Of course, he had Judith in his life now, so, taking a deep breath and letting it out slowly, he acknowledged that God had already answered his prayers.

Hoping his face did not show the irritation he felt when Cindy walked into the kitchen, he said, "I told you that I have to go to work this morning even though it's Saturday because I'm down an officer. Trevor has volunteered to help with the AL game this morning, and I'm dropping him off at the ball field. He'll catch a ride back afterward, but that'll be several hours away. I called your mom to see if you could spend the morning with her, but she's also working—"

"Working?" Cindy's eyes narrowed, her hands thrown up into the air. "Since when does Mom work on a Saturday morning?"

"I know this is new for everyone, but you know your mom is working with Sophie Ward in her interior design business." He could see that Cindy was gearing up for another smartass comment that normally he would agree with, but his conversation with Leslie a few minutes ago had him trying to give her the benefit of the doubt.

"Oh, Ryan, I'm so sorry, but I have to work this morning."

"Seriously? You're working on the weekend?"

"I know this is something new for me, but I'm trying to do the right thing with this job." Her voice softened, and she added, *"I really like Sophie, and I'm really glad she's giving me this chance. I like the work she does, and she's in a rush to get a house ready at The Dunes Resort for a magazine shoot. I'm learning a lot, Ryan. And, for the first time in my life, I get a steady paycheck."*

He'd winced, frustrated that she wouldn't be able to spend the morning with Cindy but couldn't fault Leslie's reasons for being busy. For the first time in years, they were having a conversation that wasn't devolving immediately. "I'm glad things are going well with the job. Really, I am."

"Cindy's going to be mad at me though, isn't she?"

He heard the concern in Leslie's voice, something else that was new. "She has to learn that she has two parents that are working, and she can't always get her way."

"Something you always said that I hadn't learned." Before he could retort, she said, "Not that I disagree with you. I guess it's better late than never. Please tell her I'm sorry, and I'll try to do something special with her this week."

"I will, and thank you. She'll like that."

He disconnected, and while he knew he was facing the wrath of a thirteen-year-old, not having to argue with Leslie had been a welcome relief.

Now, he was looking at the hard set of Cindy's face as she glared out the window. "Cindy, look at me." He waited until he had her eyes, then continued, "Your mother was sorry, and I believe her. I know you don't want to go to the game with your brother, and while you're old enough to stay by yourself, I don't want you to when your brother can't have his phone right with him and I might be out on the water."

Her shoulders slumped for a few seconds, then she suddenly startled and looked up, her eyes bright. "I'll call Judith! She doesn't work on Saturday mornings!"

Cindy was pulling out her phone. He reached out and put his hand on her shoulder, shaking his head. "No, you're not calling Judith. She has her own life and has things that she's going to want to do on a day off."

"She's your girlfriend, which practically makes her like a sort-of mom to us—"

"Whoa, don't get ahead of yourself, Cindy. It's not up to you to put labels and titles on what she is and what we are."

"She said I could call her anytime," Cindy continued to argue.

"Yes, if there's a reason. You throwin' a childish fit because you're not getting your way is not a good enough reason." He expected anger, but instead, her chin quivered as her eyes filled with tears. Once more, he prayed for God's grace, thinking how much easier it was with Trevor, who'd just walked into the room, his wide-eyed gaze going between his sister and his dad.

Ryan's phone vibrated, and he pulled it out of his pocket, seeing Judith's picture on caller ID. "Hey, babe."

"Wow. Somehow, with that greeting, I can tell you're not in a good mood. Everything okay?"

"Yeah, just fine. We're trying to get out the door and having a few issues."

"I know you're working this morning, and I think you said Trevor has a game?"

"Yeah, I'm getting ready to drop the kids off the field. Cindy's going to hang at the game until Trevor is finished, and I'll have someone bring them home."

"I was going to go kayaking this morning and was going to ask if the kids wanted to come. I forgot that Trevor was doing volunteer coaching today. If it would make it easier, I can go to the game and bring the kids home."

"Not going to ask that of you, babe, but thanks."

"Do you think Cindy would want to go kayaking instead of hanging out at the game? Oh, she's probably got friends she wants to be with—"

"You really want company that much?" he asked, torn between thinking that Cindy needed to sit at the game as a lesson learned about not always getting her way and thinking that she'd love to spend some time with Judith.

"Absolutely! I never mind being by myself, but I'd love to go kayaking with Cindy if she wants."

He didn't bother asking, knowing what the response would be. With his gaze pinned on Cindy staring at him with a confused expression, he replied, "She wants."

"Great! Since I'm not ready yet and you guys are running late, take Cindy to the game and tell her I'll come to pick her up in about thirty minutes. Just make sure she packs her bathing suit, and I've got plenty of sunscreen."

"I owe you, Judith. You've just made a teenage girl very happy and my morning a little easier."

Laughter met his ears, and she whispered, "I'll get very creative for your payback, big guy."

His heart lighter, loving the sound of Judith's mirth, he grinned. "I'm counting on it. You can drop her off at home when you get finished since Trevor will be here. And I'll see you later." Disconnecting, he watched Cindy almost vibrating with eager anticipation. "You've got two minutes to get your suit, towel, and whatever you need to go kayaking with Judith."

She threw her hands into the air and screamed, whirling to race out of the room. She'd barely taken two steps when she whirled around again, this time racing to Ryan, slinging her arms around him. He hugged his daughter and kissed the top of her head, glad that her crisis had ended well while knowing it wouldn't always be that way.

As she raced upstairs to grab what she needed, Trevor looked over at Ryan, his brows raised. "One day, Dad, I hope I meet a woman like Judith. When I do, I'm gonna tie her down, marry her, and pray to God that we have nothing but boys!"

Since there wasn't a word that came out of his son's mouth that he disagreed with, he chuckled and nodded. "Do that, and you'll be a happy man, Trev. Now, grab your stuff, and let's get going."

Judith looked over her shoulder while dipping the paddle into the water, grinning at Cindy. It hadn't missed her attention that when she'd arrived at the Baytown ball field, she was aware of lots of friendly yet curious smiles directed toward her as she greeted those she knew when she made her way through the stands. When Cindy had yelled her name and waved, bounding down the steps to her, she knew even more curious eyes were focused on them. Trevor must've heard his sister because he jogged over, greeting her, as well.

She'd chatted with him for a moment, then casually draped her arm around Cindy's shoulders as they walked back toward the parking lot. The girl who'd seemed so shy when she first met her appeared to blossom more each time they were together.

Cindy had thanked her profusely for taking her out today, filling her in on her dad's reasons for not wanting her to stay in the house by herself even though she was thirteen. They'd made it to Judith's house, where she waited as Cindy changed into her bathing suit, pulling on shorts and a T-shirt over the top. They'd walked down the path to the water and pushed off from the pier with their kayaks, made their way out into the Bay, and then paddled side-by-side.

"I'm glad you were able to come out with me today," Judith said, smiling as Cindy moved her kayak alongside hers.

"I'm glad you asked me!"

"Do you not like going to the baseball games?"

Cindy scrunched her nose and shrugged. "Most of the kids play, and I suppose it makes me a weirdo, but I don't like playing baseball. I don't like having that ball thrown at me. It makes me nervous, and when I get nervous, I swing at anything and yet almost never hit the ball. I don't like to throw, and I don't like to practice." Her shoulders slumped.

"Honey, if it's not your thing, then it's not your thing."

"I guess. Trevor's really good at it. And so many of the kids play, and they don't seem to mind if they're not good at all. I watch them, Judith. They laugh and have fun. And when I get out there, I just turn into a nervous wreck, my stomach hurts, and I don't like it. Dad's cool about it. He doesn't make me play, but then I have to sit in the stands. I don't mind because I usually take a book to read, but then I look like a dork who's sitting in the stands of a baseball game with my nose in a book."

Judith barked out a laugh, then immediately felt contrite when she saw the hurt pass through Cindy's gaze. "Oh, sweetie, I'm not laughing at you! Quite the contrary. I'm laughing because you sound exactly like me when I was your age."

"No way!"

"Cross my heart, it's the honest truth. My older brother was so athletic."

"That's Brad, right? Dad's best friend?" Cindy asked, a smile on her lips.

"That's right. They were both on the baseball teams and did all kinds of sports together. I tried tennis, volleyball, softball... and hated them all. Just like you, they made me nervous."

Cindy's eyes widened, "Did it make your stomach feel weird? Like you wanted to be sick?"

"Oh, yeah! I tried running track, thinking that would be a sport I would be good at and wouldn't mind, but even that wasn't my thing. I wasn't artistic and wasn't particularly musical. I love to read. If I hadn't gone into medicine, I think I would've majored in literature."

They glided along, the sun warming their bodies as they gently moved through the water, enjoying their conversation more than the exercise.

"I thought about going into English, or maybe history. I'd love to teach in elementary school. I think it would be nice to make sure that young children fall in love with learning."

Heart squeezing, Judith smiled and held Cindy's gaze. "Oh, honey, I think that's wonderful. You would make an inspiring teacher. And I think your biggest gift to children would be letting them know that everyone is special, no matter what they like to do."

They were quiet for another moment, continuing to

paddle as they made their way around several inlets, peninsulas, and small islands. They'd just come to the small beach on the island where she'd met Ryan, Cindy, and Trevor weeks ago. "Let's stop here for a little bit." They paddled closer, then walked up on the shore, dragging their kayaks with them before plopping down on the warm sand side-by-side. Judith leaned back with her palms resting behind her, her face turned toward the sun.

"I just don't want to be like my mom."

At Cindy's soft confession, Judith jolted. Her initial response was to rush to confirm that she couldn't see Cindy turning into Leslie, but she remained quiet, hoping that Cindy would continue to express her thoughts.

"It's just that Mom never worked. But it wasn't that she didn't just work outside the home, she didn't do a lot inside, either. She'd cook but then complain that she didn't enjoy it. She'd clean but then complain that we made a mess and so it was harder on her. She'd take Trevor and me places but then complain that she was missing a chance to play tennis or be with her friends." She sighed and looked out over the water for a moment before turning her attention back to Judith. "I'd hear her... with Dad. He'd go over the bills at night after Trevor and I had gone to bed, but sometimes if I couldn't sleep, I'd hear. If he brought up that she needed to watch her spending, she'd complain that he didn't make enough money. And when he suggested she get a job to help out, she'd say he wasn't being fair to her."

Feeling the need to tread very carefully, she said,

"You know, your mom loves you, but perhaps she's always had a hard time finding her way, both as a wife and a mom."

"Dad once said it was because of her parents. He said Grandma was hard on her, often belittling her efforts, and that Grandpa pretty much just gave her anything she wanted. So, she never had to do things on her own and has never learned how." Cindy sighed, "But that doesn't explain why she didn't want to learn with me and Trevor."

"It's very hard to change once you're an adult, but it's important for you to understand that you can. Just like your mom can change. And it certainly sounds like with her new job, she's trying. But that's another way that if you become a teacher, you can help young people understand how to find their way in life even if their parents don't show them."

Cindy appeared to weigh Judith's words carefully, nodding slowly. Her lips curved slightly, and she said, "I'm really glad you're with Dad. He's super happy now that you're around." She ducked her head and tucked her hair behind her ears. "And I'm really happy that you're around, too."

Reaching over, she wrapped an arm around Cindy's shoulders and squeezed. "I gotta admit, I'm really happy, too. Not only am I getting a chance to get to know your dad again after so many years, I'm also getting a chance to know you and Trevor."

Cindy scrunched her nose and held Judith's gaze. "Are we in the way? I mean, kind of like extra baggage?"

"Oh, beautiful girl, you and Trevor are the cherry on

top of the sprinkles on top of whipped cream on top of the best ice cream sundae!" Cindy giggled, and the smile on the teen's face matched her own. "Now, we'd better get back or your dad's going to think we got lost!"

Nodding, Cindy jumped to her feet, and they pushed their kayaks back into the water. They hadn't gone very far when she spied a boat floating just ahead, no motor attached and no person visible. It didn't appear to be anchored, and Judith wondered if it had floated away from someone's pier.

Curious, she pulled ahead of Cindy as she approached the boat, then gasped loudly as a bare foot lifted over the side, then disappeared to the bottom of the boat again. Calling over her shoulder, she shouted, "Stay where you are, Cindy! I've got to check this out, but I don't want you to come any closer. And make sure you have your phone ready, just in case."

Approaching, she reached her hand out to the side of the boat and peered into the bottom. The sight that met her eyes caused a squeaking gasp as she attempted to hold back her cry of alarm. Looking back to make sure Cindy wasn't approaching, she yelled, "Call 9-1-1! Tell them to send the police and medical to your phone's location!"

Seeing Cindy nod while grabbing her phone, Judith turned back to the boat.

18

Using her line, she tied her kayak to the side of the boat, then tried to slide her leg over the edge to climb in. The sight that had met her eyes was a man, still breathing but with what appeared to be a gunshot wound through his chest.

The boat wobbled as she ungracefully climbed inside, terrified she was making his situation worse. With little room and no medical supplies, she knelt to the side and tried to assess his condition. Eyes closed. Still breathing but barely, with blood seeping from his mouth and nose. Bluish tint to his skin. She lifted the edge of his shirt and was faced with the evidence that her first assessment of a gunshot wound was correct. *Christ, he's lost so much blood!*

Frustration filled her at being unable to provide medical attention that might save his life. Wondering if she could make him more comfortable, she realized his arms were tucked under him. Gently sliding her hand to his biceps, she discovered she couldn't budge his arms.

Shifting him ever so slightly, she knelt further and looked down, gasping in horror once again as she observed his wrists tied together.

Feeling as though her brain was moving through molasses, the realization he was the victim of a crime and not an attempted suicide slammed into her. Looking up, she spied Cindy on the phone, her eyes pinned on Judith. "Are they coming?"

Cindy nodded and yelled, "Do you need me?"

"No!" she shouted, hating the way Cindy jumped at her tone. "Honey, it's bad. So please stay over there." Cindy paled, but it was much better than if she came near and saw what Judith was dealing with.

Hearing a gurgling noise, she looked down and saw the man staring up at her. Bending low, she said, "I'm a doctor, but there's not much I can do right now. I've called for help. Just hang on and we'll get you to a hospital." She wasn't sure if he could hear her or even see her, but she hoped her voice gave him some peace.

His lips moved, and more bloody spittle slid from his mouth. He seemed to want to speak, so she leaned closer. "I'm sorry, I can't hear you."

"Mo... ther... s... heart."

She looked down, this time his eyes appearing more focused on her face. "Mother's heart?" He blinked. Knowing that people near death often see their loved ones, she wasn't surprised at his words. She'd heard similar whisperings during her rotation in emergency medicine. "Do you see your mother?" He blinked again. Tears stung her eyes as his body shuddered, the hiss of his last breath leaving his lungs before he stilled. "Oh, God," she cried, a tear sliding down her cheek.

His body looked so awkward with his hands still tied, but she shifted back to the end of the boat near his feet to wait. As heart-wrenching as the scene was, she knew it was a crime scene, forcing herself to not touch anything else until the police arrived.

She lifted a hand to push the curls that had escaped her ponytail back, then heard a cry from Cindy. Looking over, Cindy was staring wide-eyed.

"Judith... blood!"

Jerking out of her stupor, she lowered her hand quickly, realizing it was covered in the man's blood. "It's not mine, honey. I'm okay. But we can't move or leave until the police get here."

She pulled out her phone that was in its waterproof case around her neck. Dialing 9-1-1, she quickly told the dispatcher that the injured man was now deceased due to a gunshot wound and, having looked around, gave a description of where they were. The dispatcher assured her that Captain Coates was on his way. Disconnecting, she looked back to Cindy.

"I'm scared," the teen said, her voice much softer but still carrying over the water.

"I'm right here, Cindy, it's okay. We're going to be fine. We just have to wait for a little while. I need you to hang tight, sweetheart. Can you do that for me?"

Cindy nodded, still holding her phone and her paddle while the two women locked gazes in silence, drawing strength from each other.

Ryan stood on the deck of the VMP boat, his heart in his throat, his mind racing, and his stomach clenching. When the call had come in about a report of an injured body found in a boat north of Baytown, he'd raced out with Jared, Beth, and Joseph. When the dispatcher ran to tell him that the call came from his daughter, he'd nearly collapsed. She'd informed him that the location was coming from Cindy's phone and that Judith was with the injured.

As Jared steered the vessel out of the harbor, the dispatcher relayed Judith's information: the man was deceased from a gunshot wound. *God, please don't let Cindy have seen the victim.*

He'd called Callan, who was at the AL game, and told him to get Trevor and for them to come to the location the dispatcher was sending them to. Not knowing what he was going to face when he got there, he knew Trevor would need to be with his sister, and he might need Callan to take charge of the investigation if Ryan needed to be there for Judith and Cindy.

It didn't take long for the two VMP vessels and the CG vessel following to round one of the bends on the shore leading to one of the hundreds of inlets and observe two kayaks in the distance, one next to a small motorboat. Jared slowed, and as they approached, he shot Cindy a hard look, ascertaining that she was at a reasonable distance to stay safe. Looking down, his heart stumbled again at the sight of Judith sitting on the end of the boat, some blood on her arms and the dead man lying at her feet. She looked up and offered a weak smile in greeting that more resembled a grimace.

"Dr. Foster," Joseph called out, gaining her attention. "I'm going to have Officer Dobson pull us alongside the boat. You'll feel a bump, but I need you to stay still and where you are. Once we get tied to the boat, we'll assist you over."

"Okay, I've got it," she said, nodding.

Ryan held her gaze as Jared adeptly maneuvered the craft. She wasn't panicked, but he assumed a medical doctor had seen a lot, even in her young career. Her gaze kept shifting over to Cindy, and in the middle of a fucked-up situation, his heart warmed at how she was worried about his daughter.

It only took a moment before Joseph secured the boat to the VMP vessel as the other VMP and CG boats stayed nearby. Ryan had wanted to focus on Judith, but now, his attention remained on the man's body lying awkwardly in the boat.

"He was still alive when I discovered him," Judith said, speaking clearly and loudly so that the others could hear her. "I tied my kayak to the boat and crawled over. He appeared to have a gunshot wound to his chest, and when I tried to make him more comfortable, I realized his arms were tied behind his back."

At those words, Ryan jerked. *Fuckin' hell... a murder... a fuckin' assassination.* Tapping his radio, he called into BobbieJean. "Contact the medical examiner. We've just come across a murder victim, possible assassination. Give the details that you know of our location, tell them that we'll be coming into the Baytown harbor. ETA to follow."

At his words clearly heard by everyone, they waited to see what directions he was going to order. "Beth, start taking pictures. Everything. Every angle. Zoom in and distance. Don't leave one fuckin' thing undocumented."

She already had the camera with her and immediately began doing as he ordered.

"Once he took his last breath, I knew I couldn't move him," Judith said, still sitting at the man's feet. "I know it's a crime scene, and I'm assuming the medical examiner comes out of the Eastern Shore Hospital. Does he need to come out here, or can I certify that the man is deceased?"

"As a licensed medical practitioner, you can certify that the man is deceased, and we can bring him back to the harbor. What do you need?"

"Do you have a stethoscope on board?"

He looked toward Joseph, who was already pulling out the medical kit. Taking the stethoscope, Ryan knelt beside the boat and handed it to Judith. Speaking softly, he asked, "Are you okay, babe?"

She held his gaze, then offered a curt nod. "As much as I hate to admit it, I've seen worse in the ER. But I sure as hell wasn't expecting this today, and I'm worried about Cindy."

He'd sent the other VMP vessel over to where Cindy was still sitting in her kayak and had watched as one of his officers gently helped her aboard then wrapped a blanket around her shoulders. His gut clenched, but he looked back at Judith. "They know to keep her over there. Has she seen any of this?"

"God, no! I made her stay back, even when I wasn't sure what was happening. As soon as I saw it, I haven't let her near."

"Christ, thank you, babe."

She didn't reply but instead took the stethoscope and gently shifted around so that she could place the diaphragm on the man's ankle. She listened for a moment, then moved up and wrapped her fingers around his wrist for another moment. Moving up further still, she placed the stethoscope diaphragm against his chest in several places and then again against his neck. Shifting back, she looked over her shoulder and nodded. "I can certify that he's deceased. Cause of death will be determined by autopsy by the medical examiner, of course, but I can also confirm that he has a gunshot wound to the chest. And, as I said, when I found him, his hands were bound behind his back. Also, he was still breathing, and I checked the time on my phone when he stopped breathing and it was eleven twenty-seven."

The sound of a fast-approaching vessel caught their attention, and Ryan turned to see another VMP boat in the distance, slowing down as they neared so they wouldn't disturb the water. Andy was at the wheel and Callan stood on the deck, his hand on Trevor's shoulder. The wide-eyed expression on Trevor's face didn't ease as he searched the gatherings on the other boats. Ryan could tell Trevor's gaze had landed on Cindy when relief flooded his being and the air rushed from his lungs.

"Trev," Ryan called out, gaining his son's attention. Jerking his head to the side toward the other boat where Cindy sat, Trevor offered a chin lift. Andy maneuvered their craft toward the one Cindy was on, and Trevor deftly jumped over to the other boat, his arms surrounding his sister. He held her tightly, whispering in her ear. Cindy nodded, then leaned back and looked up at her brother, her arms encircling his waist. Trevor shifted slightly so that he was facing the scene, keeping Cindy's back to what was going on. Ryan's heart squeezed in his chest at the sight of his kids comforting each other.

Seeing that they were okay, he jerked his gaze back down to the boat, finding Judith's eyes pinned on Cindy and Trevor, as well. "Babe?"

She twisted around and looked up at him.

"Let's get you out of there so we can deal with what we need to."

She nodded, silent, and he watched her carefully. She was a physician, but he had no doubt today had been shocking, and her feeling responsible for Cindy added a layer of stress. Judith carefully crawled back to the end of the small boat, her movements indicating she did not want to disturb any possible evidence. As she moved to a squat, she leaned forward to place her hands on the side of the VMP boat for balance, but Ryan was already there to assist her up. As light as she was, he lifted her easily, setting her feet onto the deck.

He started to pull her into his embrace, but she stiffened. "I've still got some blood on me."

"Sweetheart, don't think for one minute that's going to keep me from wrapping my arms around you so that I can feel that you're here with me." He felt her body relax, and he hugged her tightly. Glancing over her head to the other boat, he and Trevor made eye contact, their stances mirroring each other. Offering a chin lift to his son, he turned his attention back to Judith. "How are you doing?"

She lifted her gaze to him and sighed. "A bit shocked. Okay, a lot shocked. It's one thing to work in the ER and know what might come in or work in the hospital with a terminal patient. With Cindy and I having such a great morning, having it end this way is disturbing." She turned her head and looked down at the activity now taking place. "What do you need me to do, Ryan?

"I'm going to have you transfer over to the boat with Trevor and Cindy. Callan will stay here with me, and I'll have someone take you back. You'll need to be interviewed. So will Cindy, which I fuckin' hate for both of you."

"Honey, don't worry about me. I've been interviewed by the police before. And while Cindy can describe anything she saw in the area, she didn't see the man either before or after he died."

"Thank God for that," he breathed. "I'm going to be tied up here for a while. Once we have all the pictures, we can lift his boat onto our vessel and will head back to the station. The medical examiner has already been called for and will meet us at the harbor. Once the body is transferred to him, then I'll get your statements."

"Can I get Cindy back to your house so that she can change clothes and have something to eat? Then I can bring her to the station?"

Nodding, he said, "That would be great." Pulling her close again, he kissed the top of her head. "All I keep thinking about is what if she and Trevor were out here by themselves. They don't kayak often without me around, but they do sometimes."

"Your kids are great. It would've been horrible, but they would've handled it. You should be so proud of Cindy. She stayed back when I told her, she called 9-1-1 when I told her, she did everything I asked. If she had freaked out or not obeyed, it would've been a mess."

"I'll make sure I let her know how proud I am," he assured. He shifted them to the side and radioed for Callan to bring his vessel onto the other side, telling Trevor to keep Cindy facing the shore. With a little maneuvering, the two vessels were soon side by side. Cupping Judith's face, he kissed her, both to infuse warmth into her cold lips and to carry her essence with him.

She offered a tiny smile, squeezed his hands, and said, "Don't worry about me. And don't worry about the kids, I've got them."

He held onto her as she maneuvered with Callan's help to the other vessel, then Callan jumped over to stand next to Ryan.

Andy called out, "I'll get them to Dr. Foster's place and then come back."

Waving his agreement, he watched as the vessel moved away, heading along the coast. Knowing that Cindy and Trevor were with Judith and none of them were near the murder scene anymore, he breathed a little easier.

Turning back to his officers, he said, "Okay, let's work together and get this man back to the harbor. We've got a murder to investigate."

19

It had been a long day, and the end wasn't in sight. A gathering met them at the harbor, and Ryan was glad for the private docking for his boats. Mitch and Colt were already there, waiting to assist with the investigation along with Jeff Monroe, the local Coast Guard station chief. Zac had the ambulance backed as close as he could, and the long-time medical examiner, Dr. Warner, had arrived. He quickly made the apparent concurrence with Judith's assessment that the man was indeed deceased, reminding them that while the obvious gunshot wound to the chest was evident, the official cause of death would be determined by the autopsy.

Once Dr. Warner finished his initial evaluation at the site, they could move the body to various positions to continue to take photographs and begin the assessment of the evidence. After finishing, Zac and the other EMT moved the body to their ambulance to transport the man to Eastern Shore Hospital's morgue.

Ryan stepped over to talk to Mitch and Colt, glad that both were providing assistance and dispersing the small crowd gathered at the public side of the harbor.

"Already have the Gazette and someone here from the Virginia Beach newspaper and television station here ready to get statements," Colt grumbled.

Ryan shook his head. "I'm not even going to give a statement until we have a little bit more information."

"I'll go over and tell them that," Mitch said. "I'll let them know that you'll call a press conference when you have any information." Sighing, he added, "Mayor Banks is itching for information, as well. I'll tell him that you'll brief him when you brief the news."

Clapping Mitch on the shoulder, Ryan nodded. "Appreciate it." Looking to the side where Beth made a motion, he lifted his chin toward her before turning back to the other men. "So far, this is what I can tell you. Unidentified man, hands restrained behind his back, gunshot wound to the chest, floating in a boat with no motor or oars."

Colt shook his head slowly. "Execution."

Mitch and Ryan nodded, and Ryan said, "Yeah. Fuckin' execution." Scrubbing his hand over his face, he sighed. "We'll start processing the evidence, and I'll see what the medical examiner comes up with. Chances are, even with central, VMP, and Coast Guard, I'll be calling in the FBI."

"Definitely something beyond the few murders we've had to investigate out here, that's for sure," Mitch said. "I know it goes without saying, but I'll say it anyway. Anything you need, just give me a call."

"Same here," Colt agreed.

"I'll keep both of you informed on the investigation." With that, Ryan shook their hands and headed back into the station. He stalked into his office first, pulling out his phone, glad when Judith picked up on the first ring. "Babe, how are you? How's Cindy?"

"We're both fine, honey. Andy took us right to my back pier and let us off. I changed quickly, then drove Cindy and Trevor back to your place, and that's where we are now. I'm keeping a pulse on Cindy, but I think it all feels very surreal to her since she didn't see the man's body. Trevor is twitchy. He's keeping a close eye on Cindy but mentioned privately to me that he keeps thinking about what if she and I had stumbled upon the scene earlier."

"Christ," Ryan growled. "I'd thought about that but should have known he would, too."

"I need to tell you that I encouraged Cindy to call her mom and let her know what was happening. I hope I wasn't overstepping my bounds, but rumors travel fast in a small town, and I didn't want Leslie to hear from someone else."

With the phone still held to his ear, he dropped his chin and stared at his boots, heaving another sigh. "Thank you, babe. That was good thinking on your part. I'm not sure when I would've gotten around to that with everything going on here. But I hate to ask, how did it go?"

"Well, I wasn't privy to the whole conversation, but I think it went okay. Actually, Trevor made the call, explained the basics to Leslie, and then Cindy got on to assure her that she was fine. It didn't sound like Leslie asked a lot of questions and certainly didn't offer to rush over here, but she certainly seemed glad that the kids called."

"With her, that's about the best we can hope for."

"How are you doing?"

Once again, he was struck by the question from Judith that he couldn't remember ever having heard from Leslie. His kids would ask, but it never seemed to enter his ex-wife's mind to see how he was doing. The simple question soothed the ragged edges. "I'm doing okay, more worried about you. Which is another reason I needed to call."

"You need Cindy and me to come in, don't you?"

"Yeah, I do. Have Trevor come, as well. He can show you how to get to the parking lot we use that's behind the gate. There's a small crowd of reporters and just curious folk already gathering, and I don't want them bothering you or Cindy as you come in."

"Okay, honey. Give us about five minutes to get ready, and then we'll head out. See you soon."

Disconnecting, he squeezed his eyes tight and sucked in a deep, cleansing breath. Hearing voices in the hall, he let the air rush out of his lungs and popped his eyes open. He had a murder to investigate, and his two girls were coming to be interviewed. Not the afternoon he'd envisioned when he got up this morning.

"And then, he managed to speak. He said, 'Mother's heart.'"

Ryan stared at Judith, his brows lifted. They had started with Cindy, and he'd had Beth conduct the interview, thinking that she might be more comfortable with a female. As her parent, he'd stayed in the room but remained quiet. *Well, mostly quiet.* The desire to growl numerous times had been difficult, but what Judith had said was true. Cindy had not seen anything other than the boat drifting in the water. During the time that she'd been waiting for Judith to check on it and then while they waited for the police, she hadn't noticed anything unusual. No activity on the shore. No activity beyond the shore. No other boats around. In fact, she'd mentioned that the Bay had been very quiet for a Saturday morning.

Now, sitting in as Callan interviewed Judith, listening to her describe what she'd found, what she'd done, and how she'd handled the situation—including Cindy—he wasn't surprised at her professionalism, and his heart squeezed at how she'd taken care of his girl.

But with her last statement, he jolted slightly. Judith had told them that the man was still living when she'd discovered him but that his injury was too great, and she wasn't surprised when he took a last shuddering breath and died. What had surprised him was that the man had spoken.

Before he had a chance to question further, Callan jumped in. "Mother's heart? You're sure that's what he said?"

Judith nodded, her mannerisms and tone of voice

exuding certainty. "When his eyes first opened, I identified myself and gave him assurances, but I have no way of knowing if he could hear me or understood. He tried to speak at first, but it was very weak, and I wasn't in a position to hear. Also, it was my opinion that there was blood in his lungs, and his chest rattled, making it difficult to breathe or speak. When I saw his lips moving, I leaned so that my ear was closer to his mouth and asked him to please say it again. His breath was once again weak, and his speech was halting. But he said, 'Mo... ther... s... heart'. Just like that."

Callan looked over at Ryan, who offered a slight shake of his head, indicating he didn't immediately recognize what the man might have been trying to indicate.

Judith continued, "During my medical school rotations, I was around people who were dying in both the hospital settings and those brought into the ER. People who were dying would say all kinds of things. Some are angry and cursing. Some are crying and pleading. But there seems to be a point where many people, when the acceptance of impending death hits them, will call out a loved one's name, call on God or whatever deity they worship, ask for forgiveness. Sometimes they will look at one of the doctors or nurses and think we're someone else... a mother, a father, a sister, a spouse."

"So, when he said, 'mother's heart,' it didn't strike you as unusual?" Callan asked.

Shaking her head, Judith held Ryan's gaze before shifting over to Callan. "No. Although, I will say that was a part of me that was a little disappointed. I hoped he might give me a name—either his or maybe whoever had shot him. When I first saw the gunshot wound, I didn't realize his hands were tied behind him and wondered if he had tried to commit suicide, possibly tossing the weapon overboard. When I realized that his hands were secured behind him, I knew that I was looking at a crime scene."

Her eyes shut momentarily as she winced, pain slashing across her face, and Ryan wanted to reach out and take her in his arms. Softly, he asked, "Do you need a break, Judith?"

Her eyes opened, and her expression gentled as she looked at him. "No, it's okay. I so wanted to cut the ties from his wrists to make him more comfortable, but I had nothing with me. My bag had my cell phone, sunscreen, and a copy of my ID. That's all I took." She shook her head slightly and her voice filled with frustration. "I'm a doctor. You'd think I would go out with basic medical supplies! Gauze, scissors, band-aids, antibiotic cream! I didn't have anything—"

"Judith," Callan cut in. "You couldn't have helped him even if you had a small medical kit."

"But I could've had scissors to have released his arms—"

"No, you couldn't. The average person would have tried, but you knew you were looking at a crime scene and couldn't tamper with anything. I know it's hard, but we're lucky that you're the one who found him. If the average person had found him, God only knows what they would've done to have contaminated the crime scene, and the man still wouldn't have lived. We would have just been that much further behind in trying to find his murderer."

Her gaze sought Ryan's, and he nodded slowly, fighting the urge to reach out and take her hand. "You know Callan is right."

She dragged in a breath and let it out slowly. "I know. I think as soon as I realized he'd been shot by someone else, not possibly a suicide, I felt so helpless. And when he was trying to speak, I just wanted to make sure his last words were heard by someone. And when he said, 'mother's heart,' I assumed he was calling for his mother, going to join his mother, saw his mother, or just remembered his mother."

"And while you were there, you didn't see anyone on shore, any other boats, or activity anywhere?" Callan asked.

Shaking her head, Judith confirmed, "No, not at all. We didn't go very far as I told you. Just from my inlet, then turned north once we came out on the Bay, paddled for about twenty minutes, stopped on the small island for a short rest, and then were on our way back. It was a very quiet morning, and we didn't pass any other watercraft during that time."

Callan shared another glance with Ryan, then turned back to Judith and nodded. "Okay, I think that's it. Obviously, if you think of anything else, let us know. I'd like to say that we can keep your name out of it, but this is a small town. It won't take long for someone to ferret out that you and Cindy were the ones who found the body. Ryan will talk to the press later, but we won't release your name, and certainly not Cindy's, either."

As they stood, Judith said, "Thank you. I'm well aware that I'm not to say anything to the press if they come to me."

Walking out, he wrapped his arm around her, stopping just before they got to the reception area. "Hate like hell this happened, babe."

"Sweetie, all I did was come across a man that I was unable to help but maybe eased his last thoughts before he passed. I'm glad it was me, someone who had some training, and not a child, or a teenager, or person who wouldn't know what to do. On top of that, you're the one who must deal with everything now, so I'm sorry it happened for you. And, of course, I'm sorry about whatever happened to him. I can't imagine the horror of being restrained and having someone shoot point-blank."

Once again stunned at how she was taking care of him, he wrapped his arms around her and pulled her tightly against his chest. Her head tucked under his chin, and he pressed his lips to her hair, the feel of her in his arms offering comfort. "How were things with Cindy earlier? Before you found the man?"

"They were great. We had fun. I think she needed some girl time. She reminds me a lot of me at that age."

"I've thought that, too."

She leaned her head back and smiled up at him. "Really?"

"Yeah. Quiet. Thoughtful. Smart. Sometimes shy, and yet you know there's a lot there."

"My grandmother used to say, 'Still waters run deep.'"

He nodded. "It's true with you and sure as hell true with Cindy." They were silent for another moment, then he squeezed her slightly. "I really hate to ask, but can you go back to my place and stay with the kids?"

"There's nowhere else I'd rather be. I'll stay until you get home so you don't have to worry about the kids."

Kissing her lightly, he reluctantly loosened his arms but kept one around her shoulder so they walked out together. Hugging and kissing Cindy, then clapping Trevor on the shoulder, he watched as the three of them left the station and climbed into her car. He breathed a sigh of relief at not having to worry about his kids.

Turning, he was surprised to see Callan, Jared, Beth, and BobbieJean standing nearby with slight smiles on their faces. Lifting a brow, he waited.

"It's just nice to see you've got someone taking care of you now," Callan said.

Beth added, "She's a good woman. She's good for you."

Chuckling, he nodded. "Damn straight," he agreed. With that, they moved back into their workroom, hours to go before they could call it a day.

20

"Man, I'm so glad the Chicken Coop delivers," Trevor said between bites of fried chicken.

Judith looked down at the table before looking back up at him. When she'd decided to order dinner, Cindy had mentioned she'd need to take into consideration how much Trevor packed away. Since she also ate when stressed, she'd ordered a lot, assuming they'd have tons of leftovers. Now, a bucket of chicken was two-thirds eaten. She'd ordered extra sides of french fries, macaroni and cheese, mashed potatoes, and coleslaw, figuring somewhere in all of that, she'd hopefully find some of the major food groups even if they weren't overly healthy. Plus, one of the three medium pizzas she'd ordered was now gone. "I'm glad they deliver, too, considering I might have to order again before your dad gets home," she quipped.

A soft giggle came from Cindy, and Trevor stopped mid-bite to look at her before he glanced down to the table's decimation and then back up again. Swallowing, he said, "I'm a growing boy." Then he shrugged, continuing to eat.

Grinning in return, she glanced over at Cindy, thrilled to hear her gentle laughter. "Are you getting enough, sweetheart?"

Cindy nodded and continued to grin. "I didn't realize how hungry I was until the food got here."

"Considering we didn't have lunch and, to be honest, I had a very light breakfast, I figured we needed a feast."

"I'm sorry for what you guys went through," Trevor said, stopping to take a long drink. "I wish I'd been with you."

"That's sweet, but there's nothing you could have done," Judith assured.

"Yeah, I get it. But I still hate the idea I wasn't around. I gotta tell you that when Callan called me over and told me that something was going on with you two and we had to get to the station and out on a boat, I was terrified."

"I'm so sorry you were worried," Judith said. Her gaze moved between the two and she repeated, "Really sorry."

"I never really thought about your job," Cindy said, drawing Judith's attention to her. "Because you work in a family clinic, I just thought about you dealing with runny-nosed kids, vaccinations, cuts like my finger, physicals... you know, that sort of medicine. But you were cool as a cucumber out there, dealing with what needed to be done and not freaking out."

"That had to be a mess," Trevor said, still eating.

Cindy's brows lifted at her brother's comment, and she looked wide-eyed toward Judith. "Ugh. Gross."

Judith tried to not grin but couldn't hide it. "By the time I got through medical school, I'd not only been exposed to all the education and training but also had the opportunity to work in lots of different areas. I delivered babies, worked in a cancer center, orthopedics, just to name a few. And, of course, I had a rotation in a large hospital's emergency room. So, while none of those specialties were what I wanted to further my training in, I certainly had the experience. I chose family medicine because I love the idea of treating whole families, getting to know my patients, and being able to follow them through their years."

"And the ER?" Trevor asked, finally no longer eating but resting his forearms on the table as he focused his attention on her. "Is it like the shows on TV?"

She thought for a moment and then said, "To be honest, I never watch medical dramas on TV. But, from what I've heard and read, most of those shows have real doctors as consultants, so they probably have a lot of real-life scenarios but could never portray what it's really like."

"I can't imagine," Cindy shuddered.

"That's why there's a place for everyone. Even in the medical profession, we all have different callings." Judith looked over at Trevor. "You know, I've talked to Cindy to see what she's interested in, but I never asked you."

"I really like what Dad does," Trevor admitted. "You know, he was in the Navy first—oh, yeah. I forgot that you knew him then. Anyway, I think I'd like to join the military, too. I don't know that I want to do the Navy, so Dad's letting me talk to some of his friends that were in the other services. Like Police Chief Evans in Baytown was in the Army. I figure I've got a couple more years to decide, but that's what I think I'd like to do."

She smiled at the young man sitting across from her, his face and mannerisms so like the teenage Ryan she remembered from years before. "I think that's a good idea."

"Tell us about Dad when you knew him a long time ago," Cindy said, her eyes bright. "I used to ask Mom, but even though she and Dad dated in high school, it was like she couldn't remember."

The request caught Judith off guard, and she blinked several times rapidly as she felt her pulse increase. *When I knew Ryan a long time ago.* The gates opened, and memories flooded, one right after the other. Each one so crystal clear that she closed her eyes and it was as though she was back in time, hearing him laugh with Brad. "I loved to hear him laugh," she said, feeling her lips curve upward as they had done so many times when she was young and he was around.

Opening her eyes to see Cindy and Trevor's complete attention focused on her, she stumbled, almost afraid to share her memories with anyone. But after Cindy's comment about Leslie not talking about Ryan's youth when it was normal for children to want to know about their parents, she knew she had to fill in the blanks so that they'd have a new picture of their dad.

"My older brother Brad and Ryan became friends in middle school. They probably knew each other in elementary school, but it wasn't until they were both playing baseball in middle school that they became friends. He didn't come over then, but I heard his name sometimes. The first time I met him, I was about twelve, and they were just turning fourteen. I noticed him right away. He started coming over for dinner, so it wasn't unusual for him to be at our table. Of course, Brad was at your grandparents' house, a lot, too. By the time I was in middle school and they were in high school, I noticed him more."

She laughed, looking at Trevor. "The first time I saw you in the clinic, I was dumbstruck. It was like looking at your dad all those years ago. I have no doubt that even as a freshman, you have girls chasing after you. I can certainly tell you that your father did."

Cindy giggled, and Trevor leaned back, preening.

"But he wasn't just good-looking. I remember he was smart, and it used to drive Brad crazy because Ryan didn't have to study as hard to ace tests. He was also really nice. Even nice to a gawky, geeky, thirteen-year-old."

"You can't be talking about you," Trevor said, shaking his head, disbelief on his face. "Not someone as hot—um... nice-looking as you."

"Trevor!" Cindy admonished.

"Sorry," he mumbled. "But still, it's the truth."

She laughed and shrugged. "Back then, I was more

likely to have my nose in a book than anything else. I wasn't athletic, much preferring to be in the library."

More memories slid through her, each more potent than the other. Lifting one foot onto the chair seat, she wrapped her arms around her shin and propped her chin on her knee. Closing her eyes for just a moment, she smiled, continuing to be assaulted by the past.

"I remember my first day of high school, feeling scared, and couldn't help but look for Brad and Ryan. Somehow, just knowing I'd see their familiar faces made it better. It turns out we had the same lunch period. And while I would never deign to sit at their table, Ryan always made a point to stop by my table and say hi. I think he upped my cool factor even though I was a geeky, gawky bookworm. He was so handsome, and he had the greatest laugh. It was the kind of laugh that made you feel like it was real, that whatever he found amusing was really, really funny. I started going to their ball games just to watch him—I mean *them* play. I think when he started dating Leslie, every girl was jealous of her."

Her heart ached just a bit, and she was amazed that the memory could still affect her so. She'd fallen so far into her reminisces that when she opened her eyes, she jolted slightly, seeing Cindy and Trevor's attention still riveted to her.

Clearing her throat, she continued. "By the time they were seniors and I was a sophomore, I think everyone expected your dad to go to college right after high school, the same as Brad. He could've gotten some scholarship money for his grades or for baseball, but he shocked everyone when he announced that he had joined the Navy."

"Were you shocked?" Cindy asked, a strange specter in her eyes.

Shaking her head slowly, she admitted, "No. He used to talk about his grandfather's time in the Navy. He talked about wanting to travel to other places. He talked about wanting to get life experiences that he wouldn't get from a textbook. He wasn't someone who was desperate to get away from the Eastern Shore or his family or his friends, but there were things he wanted to discover and experience that he couldn't if he stayed here or just went to college right out of high school."

"I remember, when I was really little, Mom fussing about Dad being in the Navy. I guess it was right before he got out," Trevor said. "I remember her saying, 'I can't believe this is the life you expect me to live. I never knew this is what you wanted.'" He shook his head, his voice soft. "Weird that I can remember that."

Cindy looked from her brother over to Judith. "I sometimes don't think that Mom understood Dad at all. And that statement makes it sound like she never understood him. And yet, you did." Wanting to tread carefully, Judith simply nodded, but Cindy wasn't finished. "It sounds like you understood Dad a lot better."

"I suppose maybe I just paid attention more." She wished she'd adopted a lighter tone but felt the words pulled from her. Taking a deep breath, she let it out slowly. "Anyway, I had two years left in high school when he joined and Brad went off to college. I saw him occasionally when he came home for leave. Usually, Brad would make sure he had time off then, as well. I was a senior in high school, almost graduating when I saw your dad for the last time. He was on leave, and he and your mom were planning on getting married. After that, I went to college, medical school, and you know the rest of the story. Over the years, he and Brad ended up just sending Christmas cards and occasional greetings when my parents left the Eastern Shore to move to North Carolina to be with Brad's family."

"Did you think you'd see Dad again when you moved back?" Cindy asked.

Shaking her head slowly, she stared out the window, casting her mind back. *Did I? Did I consider it, or did I just push it from my mind, thinking it would be too painful? Or did I convince myself it wouldn't matter after all this time?* Still looking out the window although not focusing on anything as her vision blurred, she sighed. "Not really. The last time I'd seen him, I was eighteen years old. That was almost fifteen years ago. In truth, I never got over him."

"You never got over him?" Cindy pressed, her voice soft, her eyes both sharp and dreamy.

Jolting, Judith's gaze shot back to the kids, and she realized her emotions had pushed their way into her reminisces. "Forgot him, I mean. I never forgot him," she rushed, her cheeks heating. Standing, she grabbed some of the platters from the table and headed into the kitchen, calling out, "I'll get these wrapped for your dad to eat when he comes home."

With her back to the table, she missed the look Cindy and Trevor shared, both smiling.

———

It was late by the time Ryan got home. Cindy and Trevor had already crashed, and Judith was hovering by the window, waiting. Seeing the headlights of his SUV pull into the drive, she hurried through the house and into the kitchen, waiting at the back door. As soon as he walked through, she hesitated for only a few seconds, her gaze roving over his face, taking in the fatigue that made the small lines at the sides of his eyes deeper, but as soon as he smiled at her, she rushed into his arms. Standing in the middle of the kitchen, tightly embraced, she breathed easier for the first time since that morning. Neither spoke for several long minutes, then finally, she leaned back and looked up, whispering, "The kids are fine. I fed them, but I confess I had no idea how much teenage boys ate. I can only imagine what your food bill is."

He burst out laughing, and she felt the rumble deep in his chest and smiled.

"Shitty-ass day, and you make me laugh as soon as I get home." He bent and touched his lips to hers before lifting his head and kissing her forehead. "Actually, I should amend. Yes, it was a shitty-ass day, but my kids are safe and cared for, and I'm met at the door by my woman, so all is good."

"It gets even better," she said, still smiling up at him, loving the fact that she was still wrapped up in his arms.

"Trevor didn't eat everything, so I've got some phenomenal leftovers. Cold fried chicken, mashed potatoes, and coleslaw from the Chicken Coop. I even ordered some pizza and had leftovers."

"Holy shit, babe, you weren't kidding about feeding my kids. And all of that sounds amazing. I'm starving."

"Then you're going to have to let go of me so I can open the refrigerator and start getting everything out."

"And you have to kiss me first before I let go of you," he quipped in return.

She lifted on her toes, still grinning, and kissed him, sliding her tongue over his. The kiss flamed as always, but she was determined to feed him, so she finally fell back on her heels and moved out of his arms, immediately feeling their loss.

"I don't want to make you wait since you've taken care of the food, but if you give me five minutes, I'll take a quick shower and be right back."

She looked at him and wondered if he realized what he'd revealed. *How many times did he come home tired and dirty, longing for a quick shower before eating, and Leslie grumbled because he'd made her wait?* "Sweetheart, take as long as you need. There's nothing that can't be heated or reheated and, for that matter, there's nothing that's as important as you feeling comfortable. So go, do what you gotta do, and don't rush on my account."

The gratitude-filled expression he bestowed on her was worth all the waiting in the world and let her know she was right about his previous relationship.

He turned and was almost out of the kitchen before he stopped and looked over his shoulder at her. "It means the world to me, Judith. The absolute fuckin' world."

She tilted her head to the side and waited for him to explain.

"Knowing I can do my job and someone was looking after my kids, putting their needs first. Having someone here when I got home who's got their own life but is helping me with mine in a time of need. It fuckin' means the world. Thank you."

She wanted to tell him he didn't have to thank her. But instead, she simply smiled and nodded, instinctively knowing they were words he needed to say. He headed to his bedroom, and she turned back to the refrigerator, pulling out the food to reheat.

He returned quickly and expressed his gratitude over the food multiple times as he chowed down, eating almost as much as Trevor had. She didn't pepper him with questions, understanding the confidentiality of the investigation, but he shared with her what he could. It would be at least another day before the medical examiner had completed the autopsy, but the ME had sent the fingerprints to the state lab. He told her that he'd given an initial brief to Baytown's Mayor Banks and had given a statement to the press.

By the time he finished eating, there weren't a lot of leftovers to wrap up and put back into the refrigerator. She was already thinking of shopping for them the next day so he wouldn't have to put that on his list of things to do.

"Don't forget to give me the receipt for all this food," he said.

With her head stuck in the refrigerator, she called out, "Don't worry about it. My treat." There was no reply, and she stood and turned around and saw the hard set of his jaw. Before he had a chance to retort, she threw both hands up in front of her. "Ryan, please don't make this into an argument. This isn't about a man taking care of *his* woman. This is about a woman who is doing something for the man she cares about—and his kids. This also isn't about keeping score. I know when we go out together, you always want to pay. That's cool. I'm not going to argue about that. When you come to my house, I'll get the food. But this was just me doing something I wanted to do for people I care about."

He held her gaze for a long time, and she wondered if he was going to capitulate when, finally, his shoulders relaxed, and he opened his arms, welcoming her into his embrace. Once more, they stood in the middle of the kitchen, arms around each other.

He kissed the top of her head and mumbled against her hair, "I get that. What you need to understand is that there are things that I'm used to doing and want to do. But you're right, and I'm not going to make this into something it's not. It's not a power play. And I appreciate the gesture more than you can know."

Her arms squeezed around his waist as her cheek rested against his steady heartbeat.

He added, "And I'm sure Trevor appreciated it, as well."

She burst out laughing and closed her eyes, taking in the feel of his body pressed against hers, the fresh smell of his soap, and the care that seemed to surround her when she was in his arms. Leaning her head back, she said, "I really hate to leave, but it's getting late, and I need to get home."

His eyes widened, and he shook his head. "Now *this*, I will insist on. I don't want you going home tonight. It's late, and I'd worry about you. For tonight, please give me this and stay here. If not, I'll need to follow you to your house to make sure everything's okay there, and then I'd have to leave my kids here, which I don't want to do."

Answering quickly, she nodded. "Okay. I don't want to put you in a position where you have to make a choice."

"Christ, you're easy," he said. "I never realized how hard I had it until now with you. Jesus, babe, thank you."

"The only thing is tomorrow morning. I need to get up to get out of here before the kids wake up."

He hesitated and then nodded. "We need to talk to them at some point. They're smart kids, savvy, and they really like you. I have no doubt they've already figured out that we're sleeping together, but you're right. There's no need to put it right in their faces now."

She glanced toward the living room. "I can sleep on the sofa."

Narrowing his eyes, he glared down at her. "No fuckin' way. The kids are asleep, both dead to the world, and on a Sunday morning, they'll sleep till at least eight. You can sleep in my bed with me, and we'll set the alarm. I know we'll just be sleeping, but I want you in my bed, wrapped up in my arms."

Grinning, a small giggle slipped out. "I like the way you think."

"Get used to it, babe," he said, kissing her lightly.

As he flipped off the lights and secured the house, they walked arm in arm to his bedroom. And she smiled the entire time.

21

Sunday morning found Ryan walking into the Eastern Shore Hospital, heading to the medical examiner's office. He'd spent the first part of the morning having breakfast with his kids, wishing that Judith hadn't slipped out early and gone back to her house. But when he called to let her know he was heading to the hospital, she immediately said she'd return to his place to hang with the kids while he went to work. It was a tribute to how much Trevor and Cindy enjoyed her company considering they would normally chafe and grumble at the idea that somebody was hanging with them at their age. But the drama of Saturday was still fresh on everyone's minds.

The medical examiner had begun the autopsy and promised Ryan he'd have information this morning, so he left his officers to continue combing over the boat even though they'd found little evidence other than a multitude of fingerprints that would take time to put through the system.

Pushing through the door, he greeted Dr. Warren, glad to see the Medical Examiner waiting for him.

"Good morning, Captain Coates. Come on in."

Ryan followed the doctor into an office and settled quickly into the chair provided. "Please, just Ryan is fine. And God, I hope you can tell me you've got something for us to go on."

"I sent the man's fingerprints off and they got a hit—"

"Damn, excellent!" Knowing the man's identity was a huge leap forward in their investigation of his murder.

"Don't know if you're gonna like it," Doctor Warren said, lifting a brow.

Ryan held his gaze, waiting.

"Hank Sutton. His name won't mean anything to you, but his occupation will. He worked for DEA."

Eyes wide, he blinked. "A DEA agent? Somebody executed a DEA agent?"

Keeping to the facts, Doctor Warren continued. "Cause of death was due to a gunshot wound to the chest. The bullet did not hit his heart but did nick his lung in the upper left quadrant. Since we have Dr. Foster's eyewitness testimony to the time of death, we know when that was, and based on the wound and amount of blood loss, I can estimate that the wound occurred less than an hour before he died. I can't pinpoint it more than that."

Ryan's mind began racing. *Was he shot, immediately placed into a boat with no motor, and drifted for an hour? Was he shot, left somewhere closer to where he was found while bleeding out, and then put in the boat and only drifted a short while before Judith discovered him? If he was shot close by, would she or Cindy have heard it?*

"I know you're already sifting through the possibilities, so let me get through the rest of this."

He nodded, giving the ME his attention.

"Thirty-five years old. Excellent health. No alcohol in his system. No drugs in his system. There were no other wounds on the body nor bruising, other than his wrists where he had struggled against his restraints and bruising due to the position he lay in the boat."

"So, he wasn't attacked or tortured first," Ryan noted.

"There was no evidence of that at all."

"So, they weren't trying to get information from him, just punish... retribution... an example."

"There was sand embedded in the fibers of his pants at the knees," Dr. Warren added, his facial muscles taut.

"Shit... they had him on his knees, hands restrained." Ryan grimaced, adding, "They wanted him to mentally suffer."

They spent the next several minutes reviewing the rest of the medical examiner's autopsy results, and Dr. Warren promised he'd get the full report to him as soon as the lab results returned. Standing, they shook hands, and with his copy of the findings, Ryan jogged out to his SUV.

First things first... talk to the DEA contact in Virginia Beach. Sighing, he knew it was going to be another long day, but the execution of a DEA agent ending up near Ryan's turf didn't sit well with him.

Calling Judith, she immediately picked up her phone

and asked, "How are you?"

Struck once again with her first concern being him and not asking when he was getting home, he felt his airways expand, his breathing easier. "I'm okay. Leaving the ME and heading back to the station. How are you and the kids?"

"We're fine. Trevor wants to go over to a friend's house to study for a history test. I told him I needed to check with you first."

"I'm going to say yes, but before we get off the phone, I want to talk to him."

"Okay, sweetie. Cindy didn't have a lot of homework, but she's finishing up what needed to be done, and we're going to have a girls' afternoon."

Brows furrowed, he wasn't sure what girls did when they had an afternoon off and was almost afraid to ask. Deciding he could no longer try to ignore what he didn't understand when it came to teenage daughters, he chuckled. "And this would entail what exactly?"

"When I tell you, you can't accuse us of being sexist. But she said she'd like me to teach her how to put on makeup, which I'm not exactly an expert in. Also, she said she'd outgrown a few of her clothes, so I'll help her sort through her closet. And then, I figure everybody will benefit if she and I get into the kitchen and bake some goodies. I don't have a clue what yet, but whatever it is, you and Trevor will get the benefit of our endeavors."

He loved hearing what she was planning with Cindy, especially knowing his daughter had never had those experiences with her mom. "First of all, babe, the last thing I would ever accuse you of is being sexist. Second of all, you going through her clothes with her to decide what needs to be given away and what needs to be put on a list to buy makes my job so much easier. And thirdly, you're drop-dead gorgeous, so whatever you want to pass on to my daughter is fine with me as long as she doesn't enhance her beauty so much that I have to beat the guys off."

"Hate to tell you, honey, but I have a feeling you and Trevor will both soon be beating them off."

"Shit, I was afraid of that."

"I know you're busy, so I'm gonna hand the phone to Trevor and say goodbye."

"Goodbye, gorgeous." He waited, hearing the noise of the phone jiggling.

"Dad, everything okay?" Trevor asked.

Heart warmed that his son was concerned, he quickly replied, "Yeah. Been to the medical examiner, and I'm heading back to the station. Who's the friend you want to study with?"

"Um... well, I don't think you know them."

"Give me their name, Trev."

"Rosanna. Um... Rosanna Dumfries."

His head jerked slightly in surprise. "*Rosanna?* This isn't a name I've heard before."

"She's a freshman, like me. Really smart and really nice. We've got like three classes together and her locker is near mine. So... um... I happened to mention the other day that if she ever wanted to study together, let me know. She said she could, but it would have to be at her house so that her parents would be there."

"Dumfries. I know a Leon Dumfries from the American Legion. Is that her father?"

"Hang on, I'll check." Ryan waited a moment, and then Trevor came back. "I texted her and she says that's her father."

"Okay, here's the deal, Trev. Text me her phone number and her dad's phone number and their address. If it's okay with Judith to drop you off, then I'll let you go over there to study. No studying in Rosanna's room, even with her parents there. My guess is that you're going to be sitting at a dining room table."

"Geez, Dad, I'm not trying to make out with her. I mean, she's pretty and all, but she's not like that. We really are just going to study."

Ryan grinned, hearing the truth in his son's voice while admiring that Trevor was already showing this girl respect. "I hear you, son, and what you're saying sounds good. Just send me the contact info, make sure Judith doesn't mind taking you, and be home by supper."

"Thanks, Dad!"

Disconnecting, he continued driving down the main highway that bisects the Eastern Shore. He was in the middle of a murder investigation, one that involved people he cared about on the periphery, and yet felt strangely at ease. His kids and Judith had his back, just as he would always have theirs. He could focus on the investigation without being pulled in too many directions. He hated that so early in his relationship with Judith that he had to rely on her to be with or run around with his kids and yet was comforted by how easy she'd slid into their family. Vowing to make it up to her as soon as he could, he flipped on a signal and turned toward Baytown. *The sooner I get to work today, the sooner I can get home.*

Once he got into the station, he saw that all his officers were there, even the ones that weren't scheduled to work that weekend. With a nod, he called out, "Conference room, five minutes. I'll go over the ME report."

It didn't take long for them to settle quickly, and he reviewed the initial findings from Doctor Warren. As soon as he mentioned the victim's identity, the response felt as though the air had been sucked from the room. "Obviously," he said, "as soon as we are finished here, I'll be notifying the nearest DEA field office in Virginia Beach."

"Do you think they even know he's missing?" Callan asked. "If Hank was working undercover, they might not yet."

"Good point. And they might not know which office he was from if he wasn't out of Virginia Beach."

"Will they take over the investigation?" Joseph asked.

In response to the rookie question, Ryan shook his head. "No, it's still our investigation. DEA won't investigate a murder, but you can be damn sure that they'll want in on every sliver of information."

"Can't say as I blame them," Beth added, and everyone nodded their agreement.

"It's a Sunday, so I'm sure I'll have to go through several layers before I can finally talk to someone who specifically knew what Hank was doing. Their information will go a long way in helping us pinpoint what he was working on, where he was working, who he was targeting, and that should get us closer to knowing where the murder occurred. I have no doubt that the FBI might step in, as well, but keep in mind, this is still our case for now." Going over the rest of the information from the medical examiner, he then turned to Callan and asked, "Anything from the boat?"

Callan grimaced, shaking his head. "There are no markings or identification on the boat at all. The murderers chose it well because there are a multitude of fingerprints on it we were unable to get lifted, and it's the type of boat that would be found anywhere. No manufacturer markings, it's old and worn, doesn't look like it's been repainted, and we've gone over it, trying to pull anything we can."

"Assuming it was chosen for just that reason and can't be identified," Andy surmised, "then would we consider that the murder was planned ahead of time?"

"Good point," Ryan agreed, nodding. "Or, if we're talking drug runners, then they would be using nondescript boats and may have quite a few at their disposal." Looking toward Jared, he asked, "What have we gotten from the Coast Guard?"

"I got tide charts and estimations, but now, with the information from the medical examiner, I can more easily pinpoint where the boat originated from," Jared replied.

Jared and Callan had both formerly served with the Coast Guard, and Ryan considered himself fortunate that they had chosen to further their career with the VMP in Baytown. Their knowledge of the currents and tides and deciphering the information the local Coast Guard offered was invaluable. "Okay, stay on that."

As the meeting disbanded, he headed into his office to begin his calls. It took several attempts to make it past the initial hierarchy at the Virginia Beach DEA office, but he eventually got hold of someone who was passing along the urgent message to their field chief who would call him back. Waiting, he reviewed the autopsy report again, then connected his call quickly when it rang.

"Chief Jorgensen? This is Virginia Marine Police Captain Ryan Coates. I'm sorry to disturb you on a Sunday and even sorrier with the news I have to pass along."

"Please, call me Harvey. What have you got for me?"

"And I'm Ryan. I'm calling about a man found in a small boat floating near the coast about four miles North of Baytown. Yesterday, our medical examiner sent his fingerprints to the state lab, and they came back identified as Hank Sutton, a DEA agent."

"Goddammit!" Harvey cursed.

"So, I take it that you knew him?"

A heavy sigh met Ryan's ears. "Yes, I knew him. Not well because he was already working here when I got here a year ago, but we'd met. He was working undercover."

"I wondered about that considering the clothing. I know you have a lot of questions. We have things to go over, but first things first. He'll need to be positively identified. Do you know if he had a family?"

"If I remember correctly, he was not married, which

would make sense considering how long he'd been undercover. I'll have to check our records, but it seems like he had a brother in the DEA, also, but not in our office. I think perhaps the Baltimore office."

"If you want to get that contact information to me, I'll give them a call. We'll have to have someone come and give a positive identification. Once we have that, then I'll need everything you can give me about what he was working on and where."

"Do you have a problem with me being the one who passes on the information to the brother?"

"No, Harvey, I don't. I understand you feel like it would be better coming from you. I'd feel the same if it was one of my own."

"If you send me the name and address of the medical examiner's office, I'll contact the brother and let him know what's happened. There's no reason why he wouldn't be able to come down from Baltimore later today or first thing in the morning. He'll understand that time is of the essence to find out who did this."

After chatting for several more minutes and exchanging pertinent information, Ryan disconnected his phone. Leaning back in his chair, he squeezed his eyes tight for a few seconds, scrubbing his hand over his face. Glancing at the clock, it was already the middle of the afternoon. With nothing else to work on to further the investigation at the moment, he decided it was time to go home. And just the thought of what was at home waiting for him made him smile.

22

With huge tears sliding down his cheeks, the little boy's scrunched face sniffled against his mom's shoulder as he peered at her suspiciously.

"It's all over now, sweetheart, and you can get a sticker," Judith said, hoping her smile and the multicolored stickers would placate the child's utter sadness at her peering into his ears and throat. He popped his thumb into his mouth and sniffled again, his gaze now on the roll of stickers.

As he reached out to take what was in her hand, she glanced at the beleaguered young mother. "Double ear infection, but he responded really well to the antibiotic last year, and I think he'll do well again this time. I'm glad you brought him in before it became worse."

"Oh, Dr. Foster, I knew as soon as he pulled on his ears as he cried last night and then had a fever I had to get him in quickly."

"Do you still use the pharmacy in town?" Gaining the woman's nod, she continued, "I'll send the prescription electronically there now, and by the time you get there, you shouldn't have much of a wait."

"A wait won't be bad. That's why I love Stuart's Pharmacy with their diner attached. If I have to wait for a prescription, Petey can get a milkshake."

Eyes wide, Judith laughed. "You're right! My mom used to do the same when I was little!"

After checking Petey and his mom out, she stepped into the hall, immediately running into Natalie.

"Dr. Foster, patient in room two."

She nodded and opened her tablet. *Female. Twenty-nine. Headaches.* Opening the door, she greeted the young woman with a smile. "Hello, I'm Doctor Foster. And you are Tina Desmond?"

"Yes. I'm new in town and decided to take a chance that you could see me today."

"Well, I'm glad you came in. Let me take a moment and look over your information."

"Of course. I think I heard that you're new in town, also?" Tina asked.

"Sort of," Judith replied. "I was born and raised in the area but left years ago when I went to school. It was nice to come back when a position opened here."

"You must really like it here."

She looked up and smiled. "I do." Glancing back down at her tablet, she said, "Your weight is excellent, and your pulse and blood pressure are normal. Let's talk about these headaches. Can you describe them for me?"

"Oh, well, they're um... here in this area," and she waved her hand around her head.

"Can you place your hand more specifically where you feel them?"

"Here and sometimes here," Tina replied, touching her forehead.

Judith tapped notes into her tablet, then looked up as Tina continued talking.

"I understand that there was some excitement down at the harbor the other day."

Judith's head snapped up, her brow furrowed. "Excuse me?"

"I was down at the harbor the other day, you know, being new in town and all. I was just checking things out when it seemed like there was a lot of activity."

"I'm not sure what this has to do with your headaches." Doubt crept in as she offered a hard stare toward Tina.

"Well, it's just that now that I see you in person, I realize that I recognized you from the other day." She laughed, the sound grating. "I'm such a naturally curious person and just wondered what had happened."

"Since you're here for an appointment for headaches, we'll keep our comments on your medical condition."

"Sure, sure. It's just that it's important to know what's going on in your town, especially if you're new. I have to admit my headaches got much worse that night, not knowing what was happening."

Judith held Tina's gaze for a long moment, not speaking. Tina squirmed slightly in her seat, her gaze dropping to her hands before moving about the room. Looking back down at her tablet, Judith said, "I don't see anything under occupation. You must've left that off when you filled out the form in reception. What do you do for a living, Ms. Desmond?"

"Oh, lots of things," Tina replied, waving her hand. "You know what it's like when you're young, you try out all sorts of jobs."

"Actually, I don't know what that's like. But what I'm wondering is who do you work for *now*? Because I can let you know now that you and I will only be discussing your health and headaches. If you have any other reason for being here, you're wasting your time and mine."

Tina's eyes narrowed, and she leaned forward. "The rumors are that a dead man was brought in from the Bay, and you were seen there. So far, the police have been very tight lipped. But I assure you that my employer will pay very well for any information you can give me."

Standing, Judith glared. "You have wasted our time by coming in under false pretenses. You are now banned from this office and the property. If I have to take out a restraining order, I will do so. Now leave!"

"The rumor also says that there was a teenager with you. Maybe I'll just have to search them out—"

"My telling you to leave was from me, the doctor. My telling you that if you try to get near anyone you think might be involved just to get information, I'll be your worst nightmare. Do not test me on this."

Tina stood, her eyes still narrowed as her lips pinched tightly together. Slinging her purse strap up onto her shoulder, she walked to the door. "You're missing such an opportunity. The public has a right to know—"

"Goodbye." Judith followed Tina out and watched her as she passed through the reception area and out to her car. Looking at Arlene, she said, "Ban her. She's a reporter who lied to get back to see me to dig for information."

Arlene gasped and shook her head. "I can't believe she came here for that reason!"

Furious with Tina and furious that she'd lost her cool, Judith walked back into her office, plopped backward into her chair, and sighed. Calling Ryan, she told him what had happened, then held the phone away from her ear when he went ballistic. Finally cutting in, she said, "Ryan, honey, I dealt with it. She's gone, and she's banned from this clinic."

"Doesn't matter! I'm calling Mitch. He'll talk to you, and I want you to file a complaint!"

"Honey, she didn't do anything illegal—"

"I hate like hell she got close to you, Judith, but to even act like she was going to search out my daughter… fuckin' hell, no! So, I'm calling Mitch."

Knowing there was no talking him down, she simply agreed. "Call Mitch, and when he comes by, I'll talk to him. Once the case is over, we'll all go back to normal." They disconnected, and she hurried into another examination room. By the time she finished with that patient and had made her way back to her office, Mitch was waiting on her.

"Oh, Mitch, I'm so sorry Ryan bothered you.

Honestly, I got rid of the reporter, and I don't think she'll be back."

He waved his hand dismissively. "Don't worry about it. I went ahead and got her name and description from Arlene, and if she does come back, let me know. Also, you can imagine Ryan was fit to be tied that she intimated she'd look for Cindy."

"I know, and that infuriated me, as well. But since she didn't have a name, I guess that she didn't know who the teenager was. Of course, it won't take much snooping on her part to make the assumption since people know Ryan and I are dating now."

"I'm informing Colt so that he can let the middle school and high school know to not talk to anyone in the press. I have every confidence that while Cindy's at school, no one can get to her."

She sighed, nodding. "I know it's only been a couple of days, but I'll be glad when the case is over. I'm not sure Ryan's slept more than a few hours in the past forty-eight hours."

Mitch held her gaze, and then his lips quirked upward ever so slightly. "I'm really glad you're here, Judith. This area needed another doctor, and having someone who was raised here and understands the needs of a rural community is priceless. But I just gotta say, you are great for Ryan and his kids."

She smiled, his words soothing the frazzled edges left by the reporter. "I think I'm the lucky one."

"And that answer right there is why he's lucky to have you." Standing, he reached out and clasped her hand. "It's been a while since Tori and I have hosted a party at our little beach cabin but we'll have one soon. I'll let Ryan know when and will expect you to come."

"Thank you. I've been trying to slowly catch up with people I remembered from high school but haven't had a lot of free time. But I plan on making more time so that I can reconnect."

With that, he left, and she walked out of her office, just making it into the hall before Rosa called out that she had another patient. *Today, there's no rest for the weary!*

———

Ryan shoved down his anger about the reporter, glancing up at the others sitting across from him. "Sorry about that." The DEA and the local Coast Guard Chief, Jeff Monroe, had come in to discuss the latest information. Also at the table were the VMP senior officers, Callan, Beth, and Jared. He'd also asked Colt to come since there was a good chance their information might fall into the jurisdiction of the North Heron Sheriff's Department.

"Hell, if reporters were sneaking in to talk to my wife or children, I'd have handled it worse. Probably be arrested!"

Ryan nodded, knowing the DEA Chief wasn't too far off from what he'd wanted to do. "Anyway, you were telling me about Hank."

"As you know, Hank's brother, Carlton, took the news hard but drove in last night, and your ME was accommodating enough to come in on a Sunday evening to let him identify the body. And, of course, the report now shows that it was Hank Sutton that was killed… fuckin' executed." Harvey grimaced, his hands fisting on top of the desk.

Ryan gave Harvey a moment to pull himself together, understanding the man's anger, sharing a glance with Jeff.

Clearing his throat, Harvey continued, "I've spoken with Hank's DEA contact. Hank had been undercover for the past year and a half, specifically working in the Chesapeake Bay area between Virginia Beach and Baltimore. His particular interest was with the cargo ships that come through and anchor for days as they wait to continue on to Baltimore."

Jeff nodded, saying, "We're aware that there's increased drug smuggling from the ships in the Bay at night under cover of darkness, using small motorboats that are hard to trace and less likely to be caught in the act."

Nodding, Harvey agreed. "Hank had infiltrated the drug runners out of Baltimore, gathering hard evidence that would stand up in court. He'd even been on a few of the runs, gaining information from how they work." Harvey inclined his head toward Jeff and said, "That's how we were able to alert the Coast Guard stations in Norfolk and here and closer to Baltimore about the pipeline."

"Do we know where Hank was supposed to be on Saturday?" Ryan asked. "Because according to the medical examiner, he would have stayed alive less than an hour from the time he was shot to the time he was found and died."

"I hate like hell that Judith had to find him and witness that, but to be honest, we're lucky that she did," Jeff said. "Otherwise, it's not like on TV where medical examiners can pinpoint a time of death with any accuracy."

"Yeah, I agree with both statements," Ryan said. "We're lucky we have that exact time and that she is a medical doctor, but hell... I hated it. Especially with Cindy so close by."

Harvey rubbed his chin as he looked at Jeff. "I've looked at your charts and reports about the tides and currents, but you're going to have to put it in layman's terms for me."

Jeff turned in his seat, and with a few taps of his tablet, sent a map onto the screen set up in the room. "Skipping all the nautical terms, essentially, if we look at where the boat was found, which is where he died, and look at several scenarios, such as he was transported part of the way on a motorboat then put into the rowboat or was always in the rowboat from shortly after being shot, this is what we have to look at."

The three men stood and walked over to the screen, staring as Jeff moved his hand over the map. "The farthest would've been just this side of the Bay Bridge leading from Virginia Beach down over to the more southern region of the Eastern Shore."

"If he'd been killed in Baltimore and was on a fast-moving speedboat in this direction before being put into the rowboat?" Beth asked.

"The tide and currents move northeast on the side of the Bay where he was found. If he'd been killed in Baltimore or even south of Baltimore, they would've had to have gone beyond Baytown, then dumped him in a rowboat for him to have floated north where Judith found him. I'm not saying that didn't happen, but I think it was less likely."

"The only reason they'd want to do that is if they thought he'd float into the Baytown harbor or beach, but then he'd be found quickly," Ryan mused aloud. "I agree. I think it's more likely he was killed somewhere nearby, put in the boat, and then it floated to where Judith found them."

"What if he was killed out on the Bay? Somewhere on the water?" Harvey asked.

Ryan shook his head. "Remember the sand on his knees, and the medical examiner also found sand stuck to the tape that bound his wrists. It's more likely that he was kneeling in the sand somewhere, shot, loaded into a rowboat, and then pushed out into the water."

"Of course, we haven't even looked at the inlets," Jeff said.

Callan spoke up, "If he was killed near one of the small peninsulas, he could've been caught in a small current that brought in slightly south. That would only affect him if he was put into the boat near where the inlet meets the Bay."

"If we run with the possibility that he was shot nearby and put in the boat shortly after, can we start searching the beaches nearby to see if we find anything?" Jared asked, looking at Ryan.

Ryan turned his gaze toward Colt. "This is an area where we share jurisdiction."

Colt nodded, immediately agreeing. "I know I've got more manpower than you, so I'll assign some deputies to assist. You just tell us where you want us to search, and we'll comb the areas, looking for evidence."

"It's pretty amazing, you know," Harvey said.

Uncertain what he was talking about, Ryan swung his head around and stared, seeing the others in the room do the same.

Harvey continued, "A lot of times, law enforcements get tangled up and bent out of shape over who's doing what and jurisdiction. It's nice to see this kind of camaraderie and cooperation."

"It's always been that way," Ryan said.

Colt added, "Many of us have grown up out here. It's poor, rural, and there is no room for egos. Legally, we abide by jurisdictions, but where we can help, we do. It's just our way."

With that, everyone stood, shook hands, and Ryan walked Harvey out. "I'll keep you in the loop, and please let me know of anything you find out, as well."

He took a moment to stop, stretch, and let out a deep breath. Confident that Mitch was taking care of Judith and would make sure no one got near Cindy, he headed back inside. Time to divide up his resources and start looking for the execution site.

23

The next day, Judith slept late, reveling in having a rare day off in the middle of the week. One day a month, Dr. Turner had each of his employees schedule what he called their 'mental health day,' a firm believer that everyone needs a day off to do whatever they need or nothing as they saw fit. Thrilled, she skipped her alarm and, when awake, leisurely started her morning with a cup of coffee on her patio.

The day had dawned sunny and bright, with a gentle breeze. Her landlord provided basic lawn care, but looking around, she felt the desire to stay outside and trim some of the shrubs that lined the path leading to her pier. An hour later, she was almost finished and had made her way to the edge of the water. Her kayak was still in the same position as when she'd hauled it off the boat that Andy had used when he brought her home.

The urge to get out onto the water was strong, and after quickly changing, she headed back outside. Once she pushed away from her small dock, she looked to the left, but her desire to head toward the Bay waned, and she chose to paddle around the inlet instead.

The morning was quiet, and she soon relaxed in the familiar rhythm of her paddle dipping into the water. In the distance, she could hear a motorboat and wondered if it was a neighbor or a fisherman. As the sound increased, indicating they were nearing, she paddled away from the middle of the inlet, glad for her brightly colored kayak. The sound faded, and glancing over her shoulder, she watched as the boat turned and proceeded toward the Bay.

She hadn't been out long, but the idea of going into town and splurging on lunch at Jillian's Coffeehouse was a notion she couldn't pass up. Turning, she paddled back to her pier. She had just climbed onto the ladder when she heard the sound of a motorboat once again. She turned to face them but didn't recognize any of her neighbors. Granted, she hadn't met many of them, but in the month she'd been living here, she'd had the opportunity to view a number of them in their boats, friendly waves passing between them.

Standing with her hand on her forehead shielding her eyes, she waited to see who would pass, ready to wave a greeting. She instinctively took a step back as she saw how close they were to her dock. *They've got the whole inlet! Why are they passing so close to me?*

Irritated at their lack of maritime manners, she dropped her hand and started to turn away, desiring to pull her kayak up from the water before the waves from the motorboat jerked it from her hands. Kneeling, she looked up in time to see a lone man steering the motorboat heading straight toward her. Disbelief warred with panic, and she'd just jumped to her feet to race toward the shore when his boat slammed into the rickety dock, sending her flying backward into the water. It was not deep, but the shock caused her to be disoriented when her head broke the surface. *Fuckin' maniac! Oh, my God! The idiot must be drunk!*

Sputtering as she pushed past the splintered pieces of wood now floating on the water, she heard the sound of the motorboat as it turned in the water. Looking behind her, her heart nearly stopped at the sight that it was aimed toward her again. Diving deep, she forced her body to get as close to the bottom of the inlet as possible before feeling the world around her rock with the force of the boat so close as it moved past her. Swimming down through the murky water, pumping her arms and legs as hard as she could, she felt the sandy-mud bottom of the inlet. With her lungs nearly bursting, she moved toward the edge until she was sure she was out of the range of the boat's deadly motor. The sound receded again, and she crawled through the muck until she was on land, but fearful that he might have a weapon, she stumbled through the shrubs she'd just trimmed, not stopping until she was inside her house. Slamming and locking the door behind her, she stood in the kitchen, dripping muddy water onto the floor.

Chest heaving, she fought to catch her breath and

blinked water from her eyes. Her cell phone was still in the waterproof pouch around her neck, but her fingers shook, making it difficult to extract the phone and then press the numbers.

When the 9-1-1 operator answered, she blurted out her name and address and what had happened. Answering her questions, she gave assurances that she was locked inside her house, grateful that the sheriff's deputies were on their way. When the operator wanted her to stay on the line, she said, "I've got to call my boyfriend, Captain Ryan Coates of the VMP."

"Judith, I want you to stay on the line. I'm sending a message to his dispatch and will get hold of him."

"No, it should come from me," she protested. "I need to tell him I'm okay."

"We'll take care of all of that. I want them alerted in case they're able to apprehend the person in the boat from the water. I need you to stay on the line so that I can be assured of what's happening as our officers approach your house."

Already hearing the sirens, she raced to the front door but, following the operator's instructions, waited until the deputies had alighted, circling her house, several heading out for the inlet. Disconnecting her call, she opened the door, allowing two of the deputies to enter.

One escorted her back into the kitchen, where she slumped into a chair, water still dripping. "Ma'am? Dr. Foster?"

"Judith, please."

"Okay, Judith, an ambulance is on the way."

"I'm fine," she said, waving her hand. "I don't need an ambulance."

"Ma'am, your head is bleeding," he responded, grabbing several paper towels from her counter.

She took them from him and pressed them to the side of her forehead, wincing slightly.

"I hate to ask this when I know you're hurt, but I need you to describe the vessel and the driver. We've just received word that the VMP is getting on the water, headed this way. They'd like a description so they can hopefully find this person."

At the idea that Ryan was out there on the water, probably scared for her and undoubtedly furious, she sighed. Nodding, she winced again as the motion caused pain to slam into her. *I must've been hit by a piece of wood.* Realizing she was lucky not to have been injured more severely, she leaned back in the chair, her body tight with tension.

"Ma'am? Judith? The vessel and the man?"

"Shit, right, sorry. It was a white motorboat, but not huge. Single engine. Probably close to twenty feet. I didn't see any particular markings on it, but then, I wasn't looking. There was one man driving. He was wearing a white T-shirt, but I couldn't see his pants. He wore a light-colored ball cap, white or tan, pulled low, and reflector sunglasses." Looking back up at him, she shook her head slowly. "I'm sorry, that's all I remember."

"No, ma'am, that's good." He stepped to the side and radioed the information she'd just given. Turning back to her, he asked, "Race?"

"Um... white... Caucasian. He didn't have facial hair;

at least, not that I could see. I mean, he didn't have a dark beard or mustache."

Nodding, he radioed more of her reportings to the others.

Hearing another siren approaching, she pulled the now-bloody paper towel from her forehead and hoped it was the ambulance. The way the wooden dock had splintered, she was surprised she hadn't been hurt worse. *The dock!* Looking back at the deputy, she rushed, "He ran his boat into my dock. Wood flew all over the place. I know the dock isn't all that sturdy, but surely, that would have damaged part of his boat."

"Yes, ma'am. The outside deputies radioed that possibility in."

She heard her door open and looked up to see Zac and another EMT. She tried to smile, but as his gaze landed on her wet, muddy, bedraggled appearance and bloody head, the look on his and the EMT's faces gave evidence they didn't find anything to smile about.

The EMT looked at Zac and asked, "She's Ryan's?"

"Yeah," Zac replied, his one-word answer curt.

"He'll be pissed. If it was me, I'd be pissed, and I know he's going to be pissed."

"You know I can speak for myself, right?" she quipped, and while Zac threw her a narrow-eyed glare, the other EMT's lips quirked upward ever so slightly.

"I'm Luke Purdue. You must be the pretty doctor in town everyone's talking about."

"Luke," Zac growled.

"What, man? Am I lying?" He swung his gaze from

Zac to her and continued, "Dr. Foster, I meant no disrespect."

Brows lifted, it was hard to be offended when someone offered a compliment while she was fully aware she resembled a drenched cat. A chuckle slipped out as they moved in closer to assess her cut. "No offense taken."

The two men chatted amongst themselves as they assessed her injuries, and she ran down the basic list of queries for them. No, she hadn't lost consciousness. No, it didn't hurt to breathe. No, she had no joint or skeletal pains. No, she had no swelling.

"We're going to put a butterfly bandage on this cut. It's not long and it's not deep, but you know head wounds," Zac said.

Sighing heavily, she nodded. "Yeah, they bleed like motherfuckers. And speaking of motherfuckers, I hope they get this guy."

Luke chuckled, a deep laugh that was soon joined in by Zac and the deputy still in her kitchen.

"I like you, Doc," Luke said as they packed up their equipment. "You've got guts. Reminds me of some of the women I served with."

"You were in the military?"

"That's how I met Ryan. At the American Legion. While Zac and Ryan were Navy squids, I was an Army medic."

"Army medic, huh? Makes sense that you're now an EMT, or are you a paramedic?"

"My full-time job is medic at the Regional Jail and a part-time EMT with Zac."

The sound of bootsteps racing over the oyster shell pathway from the inlet met their ears, and she barely had time to stand before Ryan threw open the kitchen door with a bang, his chest heaving as his gaze landed on her.

Her hand flew up as she rushed, "I'm okay, honey. I'm o—umph!" The air was forced out of her lungs as he took one large step and pulled her against his body. She wanted to convince him that she was fine, but with his arms encircled around her, holding her tight, she let him take what he needed while drawing strength from the sound of his heartbeat underneath her cheek.

"Report," he growled.

"It's just a—"

His hand rubbed over her back. "Not you, babe."

"You do know I'm a doctor, right?"

His arms tightened slightly, and she sighed. It was evident he just needed to assure himself that she was fine.

"As Judith can no doubt tell you," Zac said, offering his nod toward her knowledge as a physician while giving Ryan what he needed, "contusion on her forehead. Small cut although quite a bit of blood. Bruising has already started to occur at the sight of the cut, and I'm sure more bruising will occur over other parts of her body soon. She didn't lose consciousness. She has no swelling or appearance of broken bones or internal injuries. She denies the need to go to the hospital—" Another growl erupted from Ryan, but Zac pressed on. "At this time, I concur that there's no reason for her to go to the hospital. If at any time her condition changes or worsens, she should go to the ER."

Ryan's arms didn't loosen as he kept his lips pressed against the top of her head. Hearing shuffling behind her, she twisted around to see Zac and Luke starting to leave. Leaning her head back, she said, "Ryan, honey, I need to thank them."

He capitulated only by shifting their bodies slightly so that their arms were still around each other and her front was still pressed to his, but their faces were turned toward the front door.

"Guys, thank you!" she called out.

"You've got my thanks," Ryan said, the words so rough she felt them rumble from his chest.

Zac offered a chin lift, then his gaze dropped to Judith's forehead and a scowl settled on his features.

Luke stared hard at both her and Ryan, then shook his head. "Gotta be something in the water out here besides whatever grows fuckin' good oysters." Judith blinked, then watched as Zac's lips quirked upward, but Luke wasn't finished. "All you guys fall hard."

"The best thing to do is fall hard for a good woman," Zac replied. "Now, you just gotta find someone."

Luke's face gave away nothing, but Judith noticed a gleam in his eyes. Zac must have felt something, as well, proving it when he said, "Damn, you *have* met someone."

It was Luke's turn to offer a chin lift to her and Ryan before he turned to head out the door, but Judith heard him mumble under his breath, "Found someone, but damn if I know what to do about it."

The door closed behind them, leaving just her, Ryan, the deputy, and now Colt, who'd just entered. He didn't say anything but stared, holding Ryan's gaze. She leaned her head back to look up at him.

"Nothing. He must've come out of the inlet and gone north. By the time we were out, scouring from Baytown toward here, there was no sight of a white motorboat," Ryan said. He looked down, his gaze moving over her before settling on her bandaged forehead. "Goddamn fucker got away."

"I'm okay, Ryan. No lasting damage other than my landlord will have to replace the dock."

Her attempt at humor was not met well. "There's nothing funny about this, babe. This could have been a helluva lot more serious."

"Honey, believe me, I'm aware."

"I know my deputy's been talking to you, Judith," Colt said. "I'm sorry, but we're going to need a statement from you as soon as you think you can handle it."

Looking over, she offered a little smile as she nodded. "As long as we can sit down, I can do it now."

They moved to her living room, and she went through the events of the morning. Ryan's expression darkened with each passing moment, but she couldn't figure out how to give an accurate accounting of her dive into the water and subsequent hiding under the water from the boat and then crawling up onto the bank without going into details. After what seemed like a continuous growl, she finally looked over and said, "Maybe you should go into the other room."

"I don't think so," he said. He was already sitting next

to her on the sofa, holding her hand while his other arm curled around her shoulder. Pulling her toward him, he whispered, "You've got to cut me some slack, babe. When I got the call, I nearly came out of my skin. I prayed that I was going to see that fucker out on the water, and we didn't. I knew I had to get here to you, but it killed me to not be able to tell you that I'd gotten him."

She reached up and placed her hand on his jaw, her thumb moving over the stubble. "This isn't on you. By the time I managed to get out of the water and back to the house, he would've already been into the Bay. And if he headed north, he was long gone by the time you guys got there."

Once Colt and his deputy had everything they needed, they shook her hand and walked out onto her front porch, Ryan following. While the men talked privately, she walked through her bedroom and into her bathroom, flipping on the light. She squeaked a small scream at her reflection in the mirror. Her curls were wild and tangled. Her clothes were muddy and still damp. There were bruises on her arms, and her face made her wonder how Luke could have referred to her as the *pretty* doctor. She had a knot on her forehead that was black and blue, and the butterfly bandage could not hide the bloody edges of the small cut. She'd have a little scar, but the idea of going to the ER to have someone stitch it up for vanity's sake was more than she wanted to deal with.

Turning, she flipped on the water in the shower and stepped in, fully dressed. She couldn't be sure that all the deputies had left her house, and she decided a great way to pre-rinse the mud off her clothes was to let the shower take care of it. The warm water felt good, and she dropped her chin, giggling as she watched the dirty water circle down the drain.

She heard a noise and looked up as Ryan walked in, leaned his hip against her bathroom counter, crossed his arms over his chest, and stared at her.

"You know, babe, most people take their clothes off when they take a shower."

"My adrenaline rush has crashed," she said as her explanation. "Plus, it's a way to wash my dirty clothes."

He pushed off the counter and stepped forward. His hands reached into the shower, gently dragging her shirt upward, taking great care to have the material pass over her forehead without causing her pain. A hiss left his lips, and she glanced down to see several faint bruises on her arms and upper body. She undid the ties of her bikini top and let the material fall with a splat onto the tile.

"Hold on to my shoulders."

She did as he asked, and he knelt to slide her shorts and swimsuit bottoms down her legs and off. He stripped quickly before stepping into the shower with her. He gently washed her body and then her hair. "I can do this," she said softly even though the feel of his hands gently massaging her scalp was soothing.

"I know you can. But let me do this. I need to do this."

No more words were spoken as he gently took care of her, and then they stepped out onto the bathmat.

Drying her off with the utmost care, he wrapped her in a thick towel before he dried off himself. She moved into her bedroom and pulled on clean clothes while he dressed.

"Are you going back to work, sweetheart?" she asked.

"Nope. You're coming home with me."

She stared dumbly, then shook her head. "Honey, I don't want to upset your routine. I certainly don't want to upset the kids. I'm fine. It's all good. I'll take a couple of aspirin and crawl into bed."

He stepped closer, shaking his head. "Judith, I can't let you do that."

"But why?"

He stared to the side for a moment, his hands on his hips, then dropped his chin to his chest, and his gaze now appeared to be on his boots. She remained quiet, not understanding what was going through his mind but knowing he'd speak when he was ready. Finally, he lifted his head as he stepped closer, his hands on her shoulders. Bending low so that their faces were close, he said, "This person was waiting on you."

She blinked, her head jerking slightly.

"This person must have found out that you were the one who discovered the body. The fuckin' reporters have been around, and we already know that your name has slipped out. This person knows who you are, and they know where you live. They were on that boat, hoping to get a glimpse of you."

"That makes no sense, Ryan. They hang out in a boat just *hoping* I was going to be out on the dock?"

"My guess, babe, is that they got lucky that you came out. Maybe they were just casing the place. Maybe they were going to stop at the dock and come to the house. Maybe if this had been a workday for you, someone would be waiting here when you got home. And if you think that doesn't make my blood run cold, well, it does!"

"Holy shit," she breathed. "I hadn't thought of that. I just figured it was some idiotic maniac out on the water who didn't know how to drive the boat!"

"I need you to come home with me. It's not safe for you right now."

Her gaze darted around the room as though she expected someone to pop out from behind her bed. Sucking in deeply through her nose, she let out a cleansing breath and tried to center her focus. "Okay, then I need to pack a bag for tonight."

"Judith, I need you to pack a bag for several nights."

She opened her mouth then snapped it shut, hating that he was right but knowing he was. Nodding, she spent the next several minutes filling a small suitcase with some clothes, jammies, toiletries, and makeup, making sure she had her purse and laptop before following him outside after they locked her door.

Standing on the porch, she asked, "Is this what you and Colt were talking about earlier?"

He nodded. "We both agreed that this would be the best way to keep you safe right now."

As much as she hated feeling kicked out of her house, she reached out and took his hand, linking fingers with him. "Okay, big guy. Let's get to your place, and I'll cook dinner for you guys."

"Fuck that, babe. We're ordering Chinese."

Her lips curved, and a laugh burst forth, which felt so good. "You know the way to my heart!"

As they walked toward her car, she heard him whisper, "And you're already in mine."

24

Ryan pulled into his driveway, glancing at Judith sitting next to him, a clean bandage on her forehead covering several neat stitches.

Her arms were crossed as she grumbled, "I can't believe you were so sneaky. Calling poor William while I packed."

"First of all, I'll be sneaky or whatever else I need to be to make sure you're taken care of. Secondly, I hardly think that Dr. Turner minded checking you out since you wouldn't go to the ER."

Her shoulders slumped, and she nodded. "You're right. He didn't mind. But now, he says I can't go into the office tomorrow."

"You're the only person I know who'd grumble about being given another day off. Anyway, when he heard the whole story, he understood you need time to heal. And I'm not just talking about physically. You're going to crash in a little bit from all the adrenaline, and you might find that you sleep most of tomorrow. The kids will be in school anyway, so it'll be perfect for you to sleep in."

Before she had a chance to say anything else, their attention was drawn to the front porch as Trevor and Cindy came out the front door, staring at the SUV. Ryan had called them to let them know what had happened. The tight, angry expression on Trevor's face matched Ryan's own. Cindy's expression was worried, and Trevor wrapped his arm around his sister as they waited. "The kids are worried, so let's get in and get you settled and let them see how you're doing."

"I feel so bad, Ryan," she said, worry lines creasing her brow. "I feel like I'm crashing your family time."

He caught Trevor's eyes through the windshield and offered a chin lift, glad when his son nodded and whispered to Cindy. Now, twisting in his seat toward Judith, he reached over and took her hand. "Are we a couple?"

She blinked, her head jerking slightly. "Um… yes."

He cocked his head to the side. "You sound a little uncertain."

"No, I'm not. Your question caught me off guard, that's all. Yes, we're a couple."

"Okay. You're in my life, and I'm in yours. We're sharing good times, and we're sharing bad times. And we're sharing both of those with my kids. They're old enough that we don't have to shelter them from all the bad that happens in the world and still young enough that we do what we can to protect them. They not only are expecting you to come here, but they're also glad you're here. You're not crashing into our family time, you're part of our family time."

She smiled and squeezed his hands. "How can you take such a fucked-up day and make it so much better?"

"The same way you do that for me also." He leaned forward and touched his lips to hers. "Now, are you ready to go in so the kids can stop worrying?"

She nodded, her smile still on her face. "Absolutely."

They climbed from his SUV, and he grabbed her bag from the back. As soon as they alighted, Trevor and Cindy hurried forward. Trevor moved to her first and wrapped his arms around her in a hug, and it didn't pass Ryan's notice that his son was taller than Judith. As soon as Trevor stepped back, he moved to take the bag from Ryan's hand, and Cindy rushed forward. She halted just before she got to Judith, her gaze roving over Judith's face, halting on her bandage, then flung forward, both women wrapping their arms around each other.

Judith rubbed Cindy's back, murmuring calming words.

Cindy loosened her hold just enough to say, "You were hurt. You could have been hurt so much worse. You could have been killed!"

Judith shushed her again with soothing sounds, one arm around her shoulders, and steered Cindy toward the front door. Once inside, Zuzu danced around all of them until Ryan herded the group deeper into the house. Knowing that, like Cindy, Trevor wanted to assure himself that Judith was okay, Ryan scooped up the dog so that she wouldn't get stepped on.

"I made dinner," Cindy said. "Think you can eat?"

He wanted to chuckle considering that Cindy's gaze was on Judith and not him. It seemed his daughter and his girlfriend had bonded tighter than he'd realized, but that fact only warmed his heart. Uncertain how hungry Judith might be, he opened his mouth to speak, but she jumped in quickly.

"Cindy, honey, if you fixed dinner, I can absolutely eat!"

"Well, you know I can," Trevor quipped.

Cindy rolled her eyes as she looked at her brother. "You're always hungry." Glancing back at Judith, she added, "Make sure you get to the food first, or Trevor might have it all gone."

Trevor walked over and threw his arm around Judith's shoulders. "I wouldn't eat your food."

Trevor's voice was light, but Ryan watched his son's body language, knowing it was anything but jovial. Trevor's gaze landed on her bruises several times, the muscles in his jaw tightening.

"Trev?"

"Yeah, Dad?"

"Take Judith's bags into my bedroom. I'm going to sleep on the pullout in the office—"

"No," Trevor protested. "I've already thought about it. Judith can have my room, and I'll sleep on the pullout."

Cindy, who'd just pulled the casserole dish out of the oven and set it on the counter, looked over, her nose scrunched. "Trevor, Judith can't sleep in your room. I mean, it's a boy's room... a stinky, teenage boy's room."

"It's not stinky. I cleaned it. I even washed the sheets," he protested again, this time with more vehemence, glaring at his sister.

"Well, I've also thought of it," Cindy said, her hands plopping onto her hips. "I have a double bed in my room. Judith can share with me if she doesn't mind."

Judith shook her head. "Please, just let me sleep in the study—"

Ryan glanced at her, seeing fatigue wash over her features even though her sweet smile was directed at his kids. "I appreciate everyone's offered a sacrifice, but it's unnecessary. I'm asserting my authority. Trevor, I'm glad your room and the sheets are clean. You get to enjoy them. Cindy, you're sweet to offer to share your bed, but Judith is going to need quiet and rest, and you and Trevor will be getting up tomorrow for school. Since there's no way I'm letting her sleep on the pullout while I sleep in the master bedroom, the discussion is over. So, take her things into the master bedroom, and I'll sleep on the pullout."

Trevor nodded and turned toward the stairs. "Dad's law."

Cindy also nodded as she moved to the cabinets and began pulling down plates. "Yep, Dad's law."

As Judith turned around and speared him with a stare, he chuckled. She moved toward him and cocked her head to the side, keeping her voice low. "Dad's law?"

"As the kids get older, they have more and more of a say about what we do as a family and how things are going to go. Sometimes, I have to step in and make the hard decision, and sometimes, it simply has to be my way."

Her lips curved upward as she moved into his arms.

"Ryan's law. I've heard that before. Sounds kinda bossy to me."

He maneuvered her into the living room and kissed her lightly. Keeping his voice low, he said, "I think you like my kind of bossy."

Laughter slipped out. "You've got that right."

Keeping his voice low, he added, "I have a feeling that Cindy's going to want to mother you. That's fine. My advice is to let her do what she needs." Seeing her nod, he continued, "I need to spend some time talking to Trevor tonight. He's pissed about what happened to you, and he's his father's son. He wants to protect, and I think he's struggling with how to do that."

"You're just the dad to guide him into being the kind of man he's going to be," she said. Lifting on her toes, she pressed her lips to his. "So, you do what you gotta do. And I'll let Cindy do what she needs to do."

The ease in which she understood the dynamics of him and his kids caused his heart to squeeze almost painfully before easing into a warm glow in his chest. He'd lost count of how many times he'd felt that way since she'd come back into his life.

"Dinner's on!" Cindy called out, and the pounding of Trevor's boots on the stairs sounded out.

Grinning, they walked arm in arm into the kitchen.

Fuck. Ryan looked out his windshield the next morning as he pulled into the VMP station parking lot and saw Leslie climbing from her car. The warm glow he'd felt from the previous evening that had continued this morning with Judith standing in his kitchen, looking adorably rumpled even with the bandage on her forehead, helping Cindy with breakfast and Trevor with his backpack, cooled at the sight walking toward him.

Climbing out, he walked the few feet toward her and waited. One thing was always for sure—whatever Leslie had on her mind, she'd be sure to let him know.

"I was leaving work yesterday when I overheard Sophie on the phone with Callan."

Before he had a chance to speak, she threw her hand up and rushed, "I wasn't trying to listen, but Sophie had both hands busy covering a piece of furniture, and she had her phone on speaker. He was talking about the doctor in town getting hurt, and I realized he was talking about Judith. Sophie asked how you were handling it, and he said you were taking her home to make sure she was safe."

Keeping his hands crossed over his chest, he leveled her with a hard stare but said nothing.

Leslie waited for a moment, but when he didn't speak, she huffed. "Your girlfriend is living in the house with the kids. Don't you think I should have a say about that?"

"No."

She blinked, her head jerking slightly. "No?"

"I've made it clear that who I'm dating is none of your business—"

"It is if it affects our kids."

He loosened his arms only to prop his fists on his hips as he continued to stare down at her. "After years of me trying to get you more involved with our kids, suddenly now, only when there's someone else in our lives, do you seem to give a shit."

Her gaze cut to the side, her lips pinched. Huffing again, she shook her head. "I just think I should be consulted. I mean, how is this to look to other people?"

"We've already established that you generally don't like to be consulted on matters that do pertain to you. So I think we can take from that there's no way I'm gonna consult you on matters that don't pertain to you. What I do find interesting is that you haven't asked how the kids are. You haven't asked if they were upset about Judith being hurt. You haven't asked how they feel about anything. All you seem to be concerned about is what other people might think."

"Once again, Ryan, you always take someone else's side."

"And once again, Leslie, this isn't about sides. Yes, the woman I'm dating and care about was injured yesterday. The kids were upset and wanted to make sure she was okay. She came home last night to stay so that they could see her and I could be certain she was safe. Now, if you think that I'm having a wild orgy in the middle of the family room with the kids around, then you truly do not know me at all, and I can't believe you think that."

"No, of course, I don't think that."

"Then there's nothing else for us to discuss. Now, I have to go to work, and I know you have to go to work, which I'll say congratulations on holding this job longer than any of the jobs you've had. That tells me that you're learning something about being an employee, and considering Sophie is a friend, I'm glad."

He started to turn when she called out. "Ryan, I really am trying. I just never had to take care of myself before. You're moving on. It's hard, and it's lonely."

"Yeah, life is hard. Lots of people go to work every day to jobs they don't like so they can take care of their families. So you experiencing something that's pretty common doesn't gain you any sympathy. And me moving on? That was always going to happen at some point after we divorced. For one or both of us. But being lonely? That's a choice you make, and I'd suggest spending more time with our kids. I know they'd like that." With his final words, he turned and kept walking, glad when she didn't follow.

Once inside, he dismissed Leslie from his thoughts. He knew they needed to get out and continue searching for a possible place of execution. He wanted this case solved for a lot of reasons, and the main one involved Judith's safety.

25

"I haven't been here in a long time. Not since I was a kid looking for treasure."

Ryan swung his gaze over to Callan. "Treasure?" He was standing next to Callan on the deck of their vessel, looking toward Milton Island, the strip of land they were heading to, when Callan's words caught his attention.

"Yeah, my grandfather used to tell me about the treasure that was buried here."

Ryan shook his head. "I used to come out all the time with my grandfather on his fishing boat, but I never heard about a treasure. Out here on Milton Island?"

Chuckling, Callan nodded. "The story is that in the early 1800s, there was a Baltimore tavern owner and merchant. Legend goes, he didn't trust banks. So, all the money that he earned from his tavern, he'd sneak offshore in a boat, and he'd bury it on the tiny, marshy island. Then, the story gets even more curious. Supposedly, he came into possession of a barrel full of gold pieces and buried that out here, as well. I guess for at least a century, people would come out here to look, but nothing was ever found. Everyone knows it as Milton Island, but my grandfather used to always call it by its old name, Hart Island, after the tavern owner, Joseph Hart."

Jared had steered them close along with the other VMP vessels, one carrying several deputies from North Heron. Walking to the surf to get onto the island, Ryan looked around, his memories moving back to the day that he and the kids were kayaking and ran into Judith. Rubbing his chin, he glanced toward Callan. "Hart Island," he mumbled, his mind traveling down the path of what Hank had whispered to Judith just before he died. "Do you think Hank meant Hart, like this place and not h-e-a-r-t?"

Callan jerked, eyes wide. "Fuckin' hell, I don't know. Was he trying to say where he'd been? Christ, I never thought about that."

With the gathering of law enforcement on the beach, Ryan shouted orders, and the group dispersed to search for evidence. As he looked, he couldn't get *Hart* and *heart* from his mind. *But if Hank did mean Hart, then what did 'mother's' mean?*

Fifteen minutes later, a call came over the radio. One of the deputies alerted everyone to a site that needed to be checked out. Jogging to the point indicated, he was pleased to see a perimeter already being set up with only the one deputy standing inside.

"I hope I didn't disturb the evidence too much, Captain Coates," he called out.

Ryan slipped on booties and carefully walked forward. While the sand near the shore had been washed clean and flat with the ebb and flow of the tides over the last couple of days, on this side of the small dune, it was evident the sand had been trampled on and disturbed—and a spot on the sand was stained a dark rusty-brown color. Looking up, he said, "Do you have any evidence bags on you?" Receiving a nod, he ordered, "I'll take them, and then you walk back, trying to stay in the same footprints that you walked over." He watched, pleased as the deputy did as he asked, disturbing the sand very little. Calling over his shoulder toward Beth and Joseph, he ordered them to begin taking photographs of the area. Squatting, he collected samples of sand, both stained and not, setting a numbered marker down for each corresponding sample. Taking several photographs, he moved back and waved Beth forward.

She approached carefully. "Yes, Captain Coates?"

"I've taken pictures of the markers, but I want backup. Get as many angles as you can."

Looking over at Callan, he said, "Keep searching the area. Once we get this evidence bagged and photographed, look for casings. Let's see if we can tie this in to the area Hank was shot."

As soon as he and Beth finished, he carefully handed the evidence bags to Andy, then turned around and walked back over to Callan. "If Hank was kneeling in this spot and the murderer was standing over him, his weapon would be pointing downward like this." Ryan held a stance that would've been similar to what would be the angle necessary. Looking over at Callan, he said, "we know the bullet went through Hank, so it would—"

"It would be in the sand."

"Exactly." Calling out, he shouted, "We're going to need a sifter."

One of the deputies nodded and said, "Got one. We have to keep them in case we're sifting through sand for evidence."

"Thanks," he said as he took it from the deputy. Looking toward Callan, he added, "Remind me to order these so they can be stocked in all our vessels."

The two worked carefully side-by-side until Ryan noticed a glint as he shook the sieve. Shaking more sand out, the spent bullet lay in the bottom of the small, wire sifter. A strange mixture of emotions hit him. Elation at having found it mixed with the bone-chilling reality that this had passed through a man's body, resulting in the death of a man giving his life to fight the overwhelming tide of drugs flooding into the country.

"Strange, isn't it?" Callan murmured. "I want to shout that we found it, and yet it makes me so fuckin' angry that we're looking at what killed him."

"I was just thinking the very same thing," Ryan said, nodding slowly. Sucking in a deep breath, he let it out before bagging the evidence while Callan marked the spot it had been found and took more photographs.

As they finished, he took a last look around, knowing there was no way they could keep visitors from trampling the area once they left. Satisfied that they'd legally and thoroughly collected everything they could, they climbed back into their boats to head to the station.

Once there, he arranged to have the evidence sent off to the state crime lab, the closest one being in Norfolk. Placing a call to Harvey, he filled in the DEA agent with their morning's findings.

"That's amazing," Harvey said. "I know you have a lot of ground to cover, and this brings us much closer to being able to find out who did this. Plus, I got news for you that might pertain to the boat that went after Dr. Foster yesterday."

"What have you got?" Ryan growled, his body tense as a rush of anger hit him.

"I know you'd sent out requests for any information about the white boat, but I also put out a backup request. Just got off the phone with one of our DEA agents outside of Baltimore that had been called to investigate a boat that was moored illegally, possibly abandoned at a private dock. The local police had been called and then called him in when their drug dogs indicated there had been drugs on the boat. It was a white, older model, deep V-Hull with a single motor. There was some serious damage on the front and side. Not enough to make it completely un-seaworthy, but it couldn't have kept going without some repairs. It hadn't been wiped down, which leads us to believe it was abandoned in haste. A shit ton of prints, but because of Hank, the agency jumped all over collecting what they could and running them through. Believe it or not, they got a hit with Hank's prints."

"So, he'd been in that boat," Ryan said, leaning back

in his chair. "That could have been the boat he was in heading to Milton Island, never knowing he was heading to his execution."

"I had the same thought," Harvey agreed.

"And probably abandoned because it had been damaged." Ryan rubbed his chin. "What did the dogs find?"

"Cocaine residue."

"I know you said there were a lot of prints, anything we can run with?"

"It's gonna take a while to go through them all, and that's only if we get a hit for someone in the database. But, at least with Hank's prints, it ties this into the fucking motherships, therefore what got him killed."

Ryan felt the air rush from his lungs, causing his chest to seize. "What did you say?"

"Um… what part? Hank's prints?"

"No, you said mothership," he growled.

"It's the term we use for the cargo and transport ships that dock in the Bay. They drop drugs and other items to smuggle to the waiting motorboats, taking the shit to the next station in their pipeline. They call them the motherships. Why? Is this significant to you?"

"The last words Hank said were to Judith Foster. He was barely able to speak, but he said 'mother's heart,' or that's what she heard, admitting his voice was breaking up at the time. It's in the report, but I know you wouldn't have paid much attention to it because, on the surface, it just sounds like the lament of the dying man thinking of his mother or calling upon his religion. But I found out something today that I can't believe I didn't think about. The small island where we found the blood is officially known as Milton Island. But to some local old-timers, it's also known as Hart Island. That's Hart as in h-a-r-t, a man's name. There's a legend that he was a tavern owner in Baltimore in the 1800s who stored his money down on the island. I was already wondering if the word that he said to Judith was for this place, and if the blood turns out to be his, then I think we can assume he was trying to tell us about it. But as soon as you said motherships, I think it's safe to say that's what he was referring to."

Finishing their call, Ryan disconnected and glanced at the clock. He had just enough time to brief his officers before their shift ended. Calling everyone into the conference room, he gave them the information from Harvey and updated them on what they now believed Hank was trying to tell them. "It looks like he was telling us where he was shot but was unable to get the words out completely."

His officers were shocked, shaking their heads, expressions hard and tension running throughout all of them.

"What about the labs?" Joseph asked

"The most important thing will be the blood samples that we found. If they can match those to Hank, then we'll at least know where he was shot for sure. And while I'm glad that the boat was found, there is such a backlog at some of the labs that it'll take a while, if ever, to find out if there were wood splinters in the boat and if they matched to Judith's pier. About the most we can hope for is that whoever thought she might be a threat has gone." Even as he said those words, he hated them, wishing he'd be able to get his hands on them.

Posting the next day's duties, he said goodbye and headed to his vehicle. Climbing inside, he thought about Leslie's ambush this morning, now seeming like days ago instead of just hours. Pushing thoughts of her to the side, he pulled out onto the road, looking forward to having everyone he loved under the same roof.

Soon, he was spending the evening in a way that he'd always hoped family life would be. They'd worked together to fix dinner while Trevor was animated as he talked about the day's practice and Cindy talked about school while sharing secret smiles with Judith. Their conversations continued as they ate and cleaned the kitchen together without the kids fussing, and he finally snuck in kisses while the kids were in another room, finishing their homework.

With his arms wrapped around Judith, he gently placed a kiss on her forehead near the bandage, then moved down to lightly kiss her lips, the soft feel of her skin like a balm at the end of a difficult day.

"How are you doing?" she asked, her eyes searching his face.

"It's a shit case, and I'll tell you more about it after the kids go to bed. But mostly, sweetheart, I can't tell you how nice it is to have a night like this, and I owe it all to you."

Her brow furrowed slightly, and she tilted her head

toward one shoulder. "I want to say thanks for the compliment, but I'm not sure what you mean."

He cocked his head in the direction of the kitchen where they were standing and then toward the living room where the kids were working. "This. Tonight. Everything. Coming home and knowing that everyone was safe. And the kids were happy. They've always been good kids, but you give them another adult that lets them just be them without expectations. They talk freely and laugh a lot. This is what I remember from my childhood, and I was around your family enough to know you and Brad had this, too. But, until the divorce, they didn't have this from Leslie."

"And being a single dad meant that you had to work twice as hard to give them the kind of life they deserve. And I'm not talking about money although that's part of it. Honey, you've always given them a safe place to be. I'm just glad that now I can share in that."

"Is it bad that I really want to make love to you right now?" he asked, nuzzling her neck.

Her arms tightened around him, and a small giggle slipped out. "No more than I want to make love to you, too."

"Dad! I'm finished!" Trevor called out.

Lifting his head, Ryan grinned. "Looks like our mini-didn't-even-get-to-first-base make-out session is over."

"Well, I did promise to look over his algebra."

With that, they walked with their arms around each other in the living room. And it didn't miss his attention that both kids looked up, noted their embrace, and grinned.

"Are you friggin' kidding me? Motherships? Hart Island?" Judith planted her forehead on his chest as they lay facing each other in his bed.

The kids were asleep, and Ryan wanted her in his bed, at least for them to talk quietly while wrapped up together.

Before he had a chance to say anything, she jerked her head up quickly, her eyes wide. "Oh, honey, did I screw everything up?"

His brows jerked down into a V. "Screw up what, babe?"

"Screw up the investigation. I mean, I just assumed when he said mother and then sort of made a hissing 's' sound and then said heart, I told you that he said mother's heart. It never dawned on me that he might have meant something else."

"Hey, don't take that on. You reported exactly what he said, and we all took it at face value. We interpreted it literally. With all the new information, it seems he was trying to indicate that his killer was someone dealing with the motherships and the location. But we had no way of knowing that. Hell, I was raised here and didn't remember that Milton Island was sometimes referred to as Hart Island. Even when Callan first mentioned it, I thought he was nuts. Once he explained the legend, I vaguely remember hearing about someone burying a treasure."

His gaze landed on her bandage as his fingers gently moved to the curls around her face. Her gaze seemed cloudy, and he could almost see the wheels turning in her head. "What are you thinking?"

Her nose crinkled, and she sighed. "What I'm thinking is terribly selfish."

"You may be a lot of things, but selfish isn't one of them," he insisted. "But where did your thoughts go?"

"I was thinking how that was the place where you and the kids met me that day when we were kayaking. After you and I had had several not-so-great inter-actions—"

"You mean when I'd been a dick to you several times," he interjected.

Her lips curved slightly. "Anyway, I always thought fondly of that little beach. It seemed like it was the beginning of us."

"I like that, babe, but why does that make you selfish?"

"Because I'm lamenting the loss of *our* place when it should be remembered as the place Hank was shot."

"That doesn't make you selfish, sweetheart. It makes you human. And we humans need to remember our connections and love so that we can deal with the parts of life that are painful. So, to us, that can still be a place of good memories."

Her eyes had widened as he spoke, and she whispered, "Love."

Grinning, he swept his thumb over her petal-soft cheek. Leaning forward, he kissed her softly. "Yeah, love."

"You love me," she repeated softly.

"I can prove it by saying that you're in my bed, and while the door is locked, we're across the hall from my kids. And the truth is, while we're not shoving too much in front of the kids' faces, they know we're together, and they're smart kids, so they know we're intimate. So, Judith, if I didn't love you, you wouldn't be here."

She lifted her hand and cupped his jaw, her gaze not wavering from his. "Can I make a confession?" He nodded, and she continued. "I fell in love with you when I was twelve years old. The first time I saw you in our kitchen with Brad. I knew beyond a shadow of a doubt at that moment you were my soulmate. I held onto that dream for six years, then set it to the side, figuring that it was nothing more than a teenage whimsy. And now, twenty-one years after I first laid eyes on you, I'm now lying in your arms. And I still love you."

His chest ached warmth, and he knew the blaze in his eyes matched the one he saw in hers. "Any chance we can do it and you can stay quiet?"

Her lips twitched and then curved, her beautiful smile piercing the left side of his chest.

"Baby, I can do anything as long as I'm with you. Even make love quietly."

He kissed her deeply and, quickly discarding their clothes, rolled on top of her, loving the feel of her luscious body underneath him. With her legs wrapped around his waist, their tongues tangling, and his cock sliding into her core, he discovered it was possible to make love with his woman and do it quietly... and love every second.

26

Judith walked into her laundry room and set the vacuum cleaner back into the corner. It had been her Saturday morning to work at the clinic, and with the VMP turning much of their case over to the DEA, FBI, and Coast Guard, Ryan was spending his Saturday at the office in briefings. From what he'd divulged, the Coast Guard had increased their patrols around the cargo and transport ships anchored in the Bay, hoping to thwart the smugglers coming in motorboats for their illegal pickups. And since the police were also patrolling more often down her street, she felt safe again.

Trevor and Cindy were out on the water with friends, an activity that Ryan allowed only because an adult was going to be present. One of Trevor's friend's family had a houseboat that was normally docked at the Baytown Harbor, and they'd decided to take it out for the day, letting several teens come along, as well. Since Cindy knew the daughter of the houseboat owner, she'd also been invited.

So, with the afternoon her own, Judith cleaned her cottage, which never took long, then stood in her kitchen, trying to decide what to do. *Sit in the sun? Read a book? Bake cookies?*

Her phone vibrated, interrupting her decision-making. Grinning as she saw Trevor's number, she answered, "How's houseboat life on the Bay?" His voice was soft as he replied, and her brow furrowed. "I can't hear you very well, Trevor."

"Cindy and I don't know what to do, Judith. She's getting upset, so I decided to call you because I know Dad is in important meetings."

Her heart immediately began to pound harder. "What's wrong?"

"David's uncle brought us out on the water, then Cindy's friend, David's sister, got seasick. So, the uncle left in the small, attached motorboat with her and headed back to their house, saying he'd come back in a couple of hours. But he left a bunch of alcohol. There are seven teenagers here, including Cindy and me. And all the guys are drinking."

"Drinking? You're kidding me?"

"I wish I was. The uncle left all the alcohol here. The only ones who aren't drinking are Cindy and me."

Jerking as another thought hit her, she asked, "Cindy is the only female there with a bunch of teenage boys?" Her voice raised in alarm with each word.

"Yeah, but so far, nobody's paying her any attention. I'll take care of her."

"I'm coming. Tell me where you are, and I'll find a way to get there."

"Are you sure, Judith? Honest to God, I hope you will come and get us, but I'm trying to do the right thing here."

"Trevor, you're doing the exact right thing. Tell me where the key is to the motorboat you guys have docked at your house."

"Dad's got it hanging on that hook by the wall near the back door. It's on a keychain with a big blue pendant."

"Okay, it'll take me about five minutes to drive to your house and get in. Give me another five minutes after that, and I'll be in the boat coming. What's your location?" As she talked, she pressed the phone between her ear and shoulder, using her hands to shove what she needed into her bag, and slid her feet into sneakers.

"Do you remember that beach where we happened to run into you when we were all out kayaking?"

A little gasp left her lips at the thought of the place she and Ryan had just been talking about. "Milton Island?"

"Yeah, that's it. David's uncle kept talking about there being some kind of treasure buried on it. I think they were going to go there until David's sister got sick. Now, David's at the wheel, being stupid while drinking, and we're moving south away from the island, but going real slow."

"I'm out the door right now. And I'm coming. As soon as you see me, you tell David to stop, and you guys are getting off. Keep your phone on, and I'll let you know if I need you."

"Thanks, Judith. I'm so sorry to have to involve you—"

"Don't apologize. You're not the one doing anything wrong! I'll call the station to leave a message for your dad so he'll know what's going on. You hang tight, keep Cindy safe, and I'll come to pick you guys up."

Disconnecting, she locked her door before racing to her car. It only took a couple of minutes to get to Ryan's house, grateful that they didn't live far from each other. Calling his phone, she left a message, giving him the essential details that Trevor had relayed to her, then let him know what she was doing. Just before disconnecting, she added, "Your kids are so great, Ryan. They did the right thing, and I promise I'm going to get them home safely. I just wanted you to know what was happening."

Pulling into his drive, she disconnected. Racing to his house, she unlocked the door and was met by Zuzu, who was thrilled someone had come to visit. She hop-danced over the dog on her way to the back door. Finding the boat key, she patted Zuzu and headed out the door, running through their backyard and out onto their pier, murmuring thanks aloud that Ryan had insisted she take the online boating safety course and had her boater education card, allowing her to legally get to the kids. Although, she knew she'd be doing this no matter what.

Also grateful that he kept his boat ready, the motor started instantly, and she pulled out away from the dock. It only took a moment to pass by her cottage since she lived closer to the Bay, and she glanced over at her dock, hoping the landlord would be able to rebuild it after the insurance claim went through.

Her phone vibrated, and she hoped it was Ryan. Seeing Trevor's number, she connected and quickly said, "I'm in the boat and on my way."

"Judith, I'm so sorry," Trevor groaned. "David got pissed that I called and ratted them out. He says he's not waiting. So, he had a kayak on board, and I've got Cindy in it, and we've headed to Milton Island since it's so close."

Her heart beat faster as her stomach plummeted. She knew there was no danger on the island, but just knowing it was where Hank had been shot made her feel sick. "He left you! That piece of shit kid kicked you off the boat?" she screeched.

"Honestly, this is better," Trevor said. "I didn't want us on the boat anymore."

"Are you there? Are you safely on land?"

"Yes, yes, we're here. In fact, we've just gotten to the spot where we met up with you that time."

"Okay, that's where I'm coming. I'll see you in a few minutes." She steered out of the inlet and into the Bay, curving north toward Milton Island. Calling Ryan, leaving another message, she had to yell over the sound of the motor. Telling him the new locality information, she added, "Just so you know, in case I get arrested, I'm going to kick some drunken, shit-for-brains, teenage boy's ass for what he did to Trevor and Cindy. Then I'm going to do the same with the uncle!"

Coming to the south tip of the island, she spied the bright yellow kayak with Trevor and Cindy not too far away, sitting on the sand. They hopped up and waved. She stopped the boat as close to the shore as she could, and they hustled toward her.

They had started into the surf when the sound of another motorboat was heard. Hoping it was Ryan, she turned but could easily see it wasn't one of the VMP vessels. With her hand held over her eyes, she observed the white, nondescript motorboat heading toward her, a single man driving and no other person on board. White T-shirt, dingy ball cap, sunglasses.

Deja vu struck as he appeared to be so similar to the man who'd rammed her dock the other day, and just as before, he was not swerving from his trajectory toward her. Trevor began shouting, and she whipped her head around to see him waving her toward the shore. She climbed over the side of the boat and began slogging her way through the surf, struggling as the water was still at her waist.

Trevor shoved Cindy back, and he ran forward, his long legs eating the distance. As soon as he could grab her, he snagged her hand and pulled her toward the beach. They'd just made it to the safety of dry land when the boat's motor was killed. Looking over her shoulder as she and Trevor ran to Cindy, she saw him climb from his boat, a gun in his hand.

"Oh, my God, keep running!" she screamed, grabbing Cindy's hand, and with Trevor's hand in her other, they raced over the dune and into the trees.

"What's happening?" Cindy cried as they crashed through the seagrass and brush.

"It's the man who tried to run me down! He's part of

what your dad is investigating," she said, her lungs aching with exertion.

"The murder?" Trevor shouted, his voice cracking.

"I think so. Just keep running!"

"Where are we going?" Cindy said, her voice much softer.

"I don't know," she confessed, still pushing through the thick underbrush and seagrass. She remembered that Milton Island during low tide was more of a peninsula, allowing waders to make it from the mainland over. "Any chance to make it to the shore on the backside of this?"

"Not at high tide," Trevor said, his voice close to her. "But maybe it's going out and we can cross."

Having no plan, she stopped and turned to them, her wild-eyed gaze holding Trevor's. "We'll split up and try to confuse him. Go, get her as far as you can. Swim across if you have to," she whispered, pushing Cindy into his side.

"No—"

"Just go!" She pushed both of them, then turned left and began running, no longer trying to stay quiet. As she heard Trevor cursing behind her, she chanced a look over her shoulder and saw him dragging Cindy in the direction they had been running. Without any plan, she prayed the kids got to safety.

Her lungs near bursting, she finally stopped and sucked in great gulps of air, barely able to hear over her heavy breaths. With her back pressed against a tree, she tried to listen but had no idea where anyone might be. *Oh, God, please let him not follow the kids!* She had made it to the edge of the woods and stared out over the water leading to the shore. She had no idea how deep the water was or if the kids had been able to cross. Torn between wanting to take a chance to escape and hating to be on an exposed beach until she could get into the water, she was afraid her choices would soon be taken away from her.

Not willing to wait any longer, she pressed her fist against her sternum in a feckless attempt to steady her heartbeat. With another prayer leaving her lips, she slipped around to the other side of the tree and started forward.

"Stop!"

Gasping, eyes wide, she halted, barely turning her head to see the man standing nearby, his gun raised toward her. Her chest depressed as her lungs seized, air rushing out.

He spoke again, but she had no idea what he said, his accent being heavily Slavic. Afraid to move, she didn't shake her head but just continued her unblinking gaze toward the barrel of the gun.

He jerked the gun to the side, but the only part of her body that moved was her head in a barely perceptible shake. As he bit out another unintelligible command, she managed to say, "I don't understand."

"Down. Knees."

Cold fear filled her veins. Hank had had sand on the knees of his pants. He'd knelt. And he'd been executed. "No," she cried, still shaking her head. She had no idea why she'd spoken, barely able to think at all. But once the denial had passed her lips, the cold fear solidified into steel, and she shook her head again and lifted her chin slightly. He was going to shoot her. And she was going to die. But while her body quaked, she wasn't going to let him kill her on her knees. For an instant, she wondered why that was important, then the faces of Trevor and Cindy came to her. The longer he stayed here with her, the more chance the kids had to get away.

Ryan's face moved through her mind. Past. Present. Future. The boy he was. The man he'd become. The partner she planned to spend the rest of her life with. She blinked, the gun still in his hands coming back into focus.

Swallowing deeply, she locked her knees into place, standing firm. "No," she repeated. "No."

He blinked, a disbelieving expression crossing his face as he waved the gun once more. "Down!"

Uncertain she could speak again as her lips quivered, she shook her head. His brow scrunched, then anger seemed to take hold as his lips pressed tightly together. He lifted the gun and pointed it toward her.

The sound of a shot firing ricocheted over the water, seeming to come from everywhere just before she was slammed to the sand, a heavy weight on her chest. The sound of screaming and yelling came from all around, but she was unable to lift her head. She struggled, uncertain what was happening, desperate to get away.

"Judith, stop, I've got you."

Gasping at the sound of Trevor's voice in her ear, she ceased fighting.

"Clear!" came a deep-voiced shout. Trevor rolled to the side, his arms still around her, and she was able to open her eyes to see the man lying in the sand, blood seeping from his arm, and Callan's weapon trained on the man as others ran forward. The shout had come from a silver-haired man approaching her, harnessing his weapon, his face an unreadable mask.

She had just managed to push up with Trevor's help when Cindy's cry rang out as she rushed from the cover of the trees. "Judith!" Cindy slammed into her and would have taken her down if Trevor hadn't planted his body behind her, creating a wall of support.

"Honey, are you okay?" Judith asked, running her hand over Cindy's back, looking for any sign of injury.

Her gaze lifted as Ryan made it to them, and he dropped to his knees, his face still hard, but his eyes filled with swirling emotions as he growled, "Christ, Almighty. Thank God." Sucking in another rasping breath, he continued to struggle to speak as his arms encircled all three of them still crouched on the sand, with Cindy crying and Trevor gasping with shaky breaths… and the combination was the sweetest sound she'd ever heard.

27

Ryan stood in the upstairs hallway of his house between Trevor and Cindy's bedrooms. His mind was filled with images from the day, all swirling and merging, and his emotions followed suit. He leaned heavily against the wall, needing the solid presence to help prop him up. Dropping his chin to his chest, he stared at his socked feet, too afraid to close his eyes in case the fact that his kids were tucked safely into their beds turned out to not be real.

The day's memories continued to play like a movie scene over and over.

He had just stepped out of the large briefing with the CG and DEA when he'd checked his phone. The kids had twisted his arm to go out on the houseboat with friends, and he'd agreed, knowing David's parents were supposed to go.

Fury filled him as he'd listened to Judith's first message explaining Trevor's call to her to report that David's uncle had gone instead, a man Ryan didn't know. And hearing that the uncle left with the only other girl on the boat, Ryan's blood threatened to boil. Knowing Judith was heading out in his boat to bring Trevor and Cindy home, he was furious that she had to do that but grateful that she could.

He'd called to Callan and Jared to load up because they were going out to officially bust an underage drinking houseboat party where no adult was in charge. Knowing there would be a group, he'd ordered Beth, Andy, and Joseph to another boat to go along. Jeff, with the CG, called into his station, and they were sending a boat, as well.

The only things that gave Ryan any pleasure were knowing David would shit bricks when he saw the law enforcement coming in numbers and when Ryan would rip into the uncle as well as the parents. As far as he was concerned, every time he'd see that houseboat on the water, he'd board it for inspection. He had no problem making them rue their day's decisions.

They'd just arrived at the houseboat, boarded, and realized Trevor and Cindy weren't there when the next call came in. Listening to the message that let him know Trevor and Cindy had been kicked off the boat and were on Milton Island, fury combined with anxiety. Shouting orders for his second vessel to stay, he'd called for Jared to take them to the island.

Arriving, he'd easily spotted the yellow kayak on the beach and his motorboat anchored just offshore but saw no one standing nearby. But off to the far side, another motorboat... white, no markings, no identification. They'd waded through the surf, and once on the sand, they saw three sets of footprints that headed over the dunes and into the trees and another set coming from the white boat, following the first sets of prints.

Heart in his throat as Callan called for backup, they'd raced over the dune, following the trail as long as it was evident. The tracks split, two moving forward toward the backside and one set moving toward the north. It was easy to discern that Trevor and Cindy had split away from Judith. *Why? Why the fuck would they do that?* As soon as the question hit him, the answer was just as prominent. *She's trying to lead the fucker away from my kids.* If he hadn't already been operating on experience and instinct, that thought would have dropped him to his knees.

His radio had crackled with the information that his backup VMP was on the island, circling toward the north. The sound of someone running had him jerk around, his eyes widening at the sight of Cindy rushing toward him through the trees. She could barely speak but through gasping breaths lifted her hand and pointed toward the north.

"Trev... Trev... after Ju... dith. Man with gun. After Judith."

With his hands on her arms, he'd set her to the side and quickly ordered his officers to continue toward the north, reporting an armed man was after Judith and Trevor was in pursuit. He'd looked down at his daughter and ordered, "Stay. Stay here!"

Not waiting for her nod, he'd raced after his officers, praying he wasn't too late. Grateful for the sand that muffled the sound of their rushed footsteps, he came upon a scene that gripped his heart in a vise, then squeezed.

A man stood fifteen feet away from Judith, a gun in his hand, and ordered her down. Ryan could see her body shaking from where he was, but Christ Almighty, she shook her head and told that fucker, "No." Her defiance seemed to surprise him, giving Ryan the chance he'd needed. Aiming, he fired. Another shot rang out, coming from another officer, and the man dropped. At the same time, a blur darted from the side, tackling Judith underneath his body. For a second, Ryan was uncertain if the man had an accomplice until he realized it was Trevor.

Callan, Jared, and Beth had immediately taken charge of the scene while another blur raced past and Cindy fell into Judith's arms. As his other officers swarmed the area, he'd stalked toward his heart's trio, dropped to his knees, and encircled his arms around them all. Other than the moments he'd held each child after they were born, it was the sweetest feeling he'd ever felt.

After he got his family home, Callan had called with the preliminary report that the man sitting under guard at the Eastern Shore Hospital was already identified as an enforcer for a Russian smuggling operation bringing drugs into the U.S., competing with the Mexican and South American cartels. Hank had closed in on their business, and by all indications, the enforcer had been sent to eliminate the threat. Once he'd been found by Judith, it appeared she'd been marked for elimination as well. Only time and more investigations by the DEA would indicate if a dent had been made in the operations. For Ryan, all he cared about was that his family was safe.

Now, still working to calm the turbulent emotions, a slight sound on the stairs caused him to lift his head and look to the side. Judith moved toward him, her intense gaze searching his face. *She's worried for me.* That realization sliced through him as her arms encircled him, and she pressed her cheek over his heart.

"Let's go to bed, honey."

Her soft voice wrapped around him as sure as her arms embraced him. They stood for another moment, then he said, "Go on, babe. I'm going to check the doors, and I'll be right up."

She lifted on her toes and gently pressed her lips to his, then smiled as she turned and walked into the master bedroom. He stood for another moment, staring after her at the realization that the woman he loved, a woman who filled him and completed him, was walking into *their* bedroom.

It didn't take long to secure the house, rub the sleepy Zuzu's ears, and then head back upstairs. Unable to stop himself, he opened Trevor's door and smiled at his son's body face-down on his bed, arms spread out the way he'd always slept, even as a child. Moving across the hall, he quietly opened Cindy's door and, still smiling, observed her sleeping, curled on her side.

Finally, he walked into his bedroom and shut the door, his smile still firmly on his face at the sight of Judith walking out of the bathroom, soothing lotion over her arms, the delicate coconut scent filling the air.

She was wearing nothing but his T-shirt. No fancy nightie, no cute pajamas. Just his T-shirt. And it was the sexiest thing he'd ever seen.

As he headed into the bathroom, they passed, stopping for another lip touch before she climbed into bed. He stood for a moment, his fists planted on the counter as he stared into the mirror. The same reflection met his gaze that he always saw. A fit body although it showed some wear and tear not evident in his youth. Steely gray hair. Scruff from the hours since he'd last shaved that morning. But something was different in his eyes. While the day had been fraught with crisis and trauma, his eyes were no longer filled with weariness. Instead, there was a life-changing force evident. The reason was under his roof. Not only were his children safe, but the woman he loved was in his bed.

Flipping off the light, he stalked into the bedroom and climbed under the covers, immediately pulling her to him as her arms encircled his body. They lay facing each other, eyes searching, letting emotions fill the air instead of words for several minutes.

"I want you here," he finally managed to say.

Her brows lowered slightly as her fingers moved to trace over his face. "I am here, honey."

"No, not just tonight. I want you here. Move in with us."

"You know I want that, too, but maybe tonight is not the time to make a big decision—"

"Do you love me?"

A soft giggle slipped out. "Yes, you know I do."

"Are you going to change your mind tomorrow?

Next week?" he pressed, his own fingertips trailing up and down her back.

"Ryan, honey, I fell in love with you a long time ago. No matter what happens, I'll always love you."

"Then there's no reason to wait. And don't worry about the kids. They love you, too. They want you to be a part of our family."

"I want that, too."

He gently pushed the curls away from her face. "So, what do you say? Move in with us? Share this bed? Wear the ring I'm going to put on your finger? Plan the wedding I want us to have? Make more babies that'll fill the house?"

She sucked in a quick breath, tears filling her eyes. "That's a lot of things to agree to all at once."

"What do you say?" he murmured against her lips.

"I say 'yes' to all of them."

Letting her words soothe him, he pressed his lips to the top of her curls and murmured, "Thank God you gave me a chance, babe. A chance to have the life I've always wanted."

They kissed long and hard, then made love soft and gentle. Finally, as they lay naked and tangled in each other's arms, his heart eased with a warm glow. Just before she fell asleep, he heard her whisper, "You were always my hero. And now, you'll always be my hero."

He pulled her close and closed his eyes, a smile on his lips.

28

THREE YEARS LATER

The sun was shining in the blue sky, and the clean, Eastern Shore air greeted the crowds. The scent of hot dogs and nachos wafted past.

The Baytown Boys were closing in on an undefeated season on the baseball field. The stands were full of supporters—parents, students, and many Baytown Boys from long ago. Ryan sat in the stands, his eyes full of pride as they focused on Trevor at bat.

He'd seen the other LEL, Mitch, Liam, Colt, Wyatt, and Dylan, all former Baytown Boys. Callan, Jared, Joseph, Zac, and Luke were there along with men and women from the American Legion.

Glancing to his side, Cindy was cheering as loudly as any, and he knew she not only shouted for her brother but for the he's-so-cute-and-sweet-and-smart junior on third base who'd been tucking his feet underneath Ryan and Judith's table for months. The thought of Cindy dating caused a sigh to leave his lips, but he couldn't deny that Johnny was a good kid who seemed to adore her. Plus, Ryan had forced Johnny to endure the "that's my daughter, and you *will* respect her or pay the consequences" speech, which Johnny appeared to have taken to heart.

On the other side of Cindy sat Leslie, her gaze on the field as well. Having her children almost killed by a gunman chasing them had shaken something maternal loose in her. While the change was difficult, she'd managed to learn that the world didn't revolve around her, and she'd worked to improve her relationship with the kids. For his part, he was just glad not to have the acrimonious conversations every time he saw her. And the biggest surprise sat on the other side of Leslie: her fiancé. A man she'd met at a furniture trade show, and while it shocked the shit out of Ryan, he actually liked Malcolm. They only socialized during events with the kids, but at least for those, everyone got along great. Judith had said that humans have an infinite amount of love to give and receive, so he welcomed Leslie and Malcolm being the kind of people who truly loved the kids.

Just in front of Cindy sat Rosanna. For the past couple of years, she and Trevor had been attached at the hip, and he could only pray that was figurative and not literal. But, just in case, he'd made sure Trevor had the respect talk also and had provided him with condoms. He had no idea how their relationship would progress, especially considering Trevor had signed with the Marines and would be leaving for boot camp after graduation in another month, but Rosanna reminded him a lot of Judith, and he wouldn't be surprised if they lasted.

Knees jabbed him in the back, and he twisted around to lift a brow at the man behind him. Brad, his wife, and their two kids. Brad lifted his brow with a "what?" look on his face before grinning. They'd stayed in touch, visiting each other several times. Next to them were his parents and Judith's parents, everyone cheering.

But of all the people in the stands, it was the woman and baby on the other side of Ryan that drew his attention. Judith's curls were held back in a ponytail. Her makeup was light. Dressed in jeans and a T-shirt, she looked casual and sexy, a look she managed to pull off every day. And snuggled in the front carrier she wore was their four-month-old son, Brandon. Judith's attention was riveted to the field, and Brandon was beginning to squirm. Reaching over, Ryan slid his son out of the carrier and cradled him, nuzzling his head.

They'd lucked out when it was time to buy a larger house. The new owners of Judith's childhood home were moving, and the house had gone up for a quick sale. He'd snapped it up, knowing it not only gave Judith and him memories but Trevor and Cindy a larger place to enjoy and would hold their expanding family.

Judith twisted to look up at him, her eyes bright and her smile even brighter. Just then, the crack of the bat sounded, and she took to her feet, screaming along with the rest of the crowd. He rose more slowly to not jostle Brandon but watched with pride as Trevor circled the bases with his home run.

As his feet stomped on home plate, Trevor looked into the stands, met his father's eyes, and grinned before looking up at the rest of his family, all screaming his name. Judith turned to Ryan and smiled widely. Lifting on her toes, she kissed the top of Brandon's head then moved to kiss Ryan.

He cast his gaze over his family once again and knew that God had blessed him. A simple man who'd been given a chance at an extraordinary life. It wasn't his job that made him a hero. It was the people that he was surrounded with every day. Wrapping his arm around her, he smiled, his heart full.

Get ready for the next Baytown Hero
Finding a Hero

And the next in the Baytown Boys
Sunset Kiss

ALSO BY THE AUTHOR

Don't miss other Maryann Jordan books!

Lots more Baytown stories to enjoy and more to come!

Baytown Boys (small town, military romantic suspense)

Coming Home

Just One More Chance

Clues of the Heart

Finding Peace

Picking Up the Pieces

Sunset Flames

Waiting for Sunrise

Hear My Heart

Guarding Your Heart

Sweet Rose

Our Time

Count On Me

Shielding You

To Love Someone

Sea Glass Hearts

Protecting Her Heart

Sunset Kiss

Baytown Heroes - A Baytown Boys subseries

A Hero's Chance

Finding a Hero

For all of Miss Ethel's boys:

Heroes at Heart (Military Romance)

Zander

Rafe

Cael

Jaxon

Jayden

Asher

Zeke

Cas

Lighthouse Security Investigations

Mace

Rank

Walker

Drew

Blake

Tate

Levi

Clay

Cobb

Bray

Josh

Knox (LSI)

Lighthouse Security Investigations West Coast

Carson (LSI West Coast)

Leo (LSI West Coast)

Rick (LSI West Coast)

Hope City (romantic suspense series co-developed

with Kris Michaels

Brock book 1

Sean book 2

Carter book 3

Brody book 4

Kyle book 5

Ryker book 6

Rory book 7

Killian book 8

Torin book 9

Blayze book 10

Griffin book 11

Saints Protection & Investigations

(an elite group, assigned to the cases no one else wants…or
can solve)

Serial Love

Healing Love

Revealing Love

Seeing Love

Honor Love

Sacrifice Love

Protecting Love

Remember Love

Discover Love

Surviving Love

Celebrating Love

Searching Love

Follow the exciting spin-off series:

Alvarez Security (military romantic suspense)

Gabe

Tony

Vinny

Jobe

SEALs

Thin Ice (Sleeper SEAL)

SEAL Together (Silver SEAL)

Undercover Groom (Hot SEAL)

Also for a Hope City Crossover Novel / Hot SEAL…

A Forever Dad

Long Road Home

Military Romantic Suspense

Home to Stay (a Lighthouse Security Investigation crossover novel)

Letters From Home (military romance)

Class of Love

Freedom of Love

Bond of Love

The Love's Series (detectives)

Love's Taming

Love's Tempting

Love's Trusting

The Fairfield Series (small town detectives)

Emma's Home

Laurie's Time

Carol's Image

Fireworks Over Fairfield

Please take the time to leave a review of this book. Feel free to contact me, especially if you enjoyed my book. I love to hear from readers!

Facebook

Email

Website

ABOUT THE AUTHOR

I am an avid reader of romance novels, often joking that I cut my teeth on the historical romances. I have been reading and reviewing for years. In 2013, I finally gave into the characters in my head, screaming for their story to be told. From these musings, my first novel, Emma's Home, The Fairfield Series was born.

I was a high school counselor having worked in education for thirty years. I live in Virginia, having also lived in four states and two foreign countries. I have been married to a wonderfully patient man for forty years. When writing, my dog or one of my four cats can generally be found in the same room if not on my lap.

Please take the time to leave a review of this book. Feel free to contact me, especially if you enjoyed my book. I love to hear from readers!

Facebook
Email
Website

Made in the USA
Columbia, SC
21 April 2022

59271561R00200